Goodnight

Susie Tate

Copyright © 2016 by Susie Tate

All rights reserved.

No part of this book may be reproduced in any form or by any electronic or mechanical means, including information storage and retrieval systems, without written permission from the author, except for the use of brief quotations in a book review.

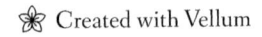

❋ Created with Vellum

Contents

Prologue — 1
1. Devoted employee — 5
2. Right up to his door — 14
3. Non-linear junction evaluator — 21
4. Who's going to look after her? — 33
5. A better solution — 45
6. Impossible to leave unsolved — 55
7. You're a right topper — 63
8. You work for me — 71
9. Camouflage — 81
10. See someone you know? — 89
11. Show weakness — 96
12. Just like she was trained to do — 104
13. Almost painful — 113
14. Ornery — 119
15. Just her and the knife — 128
16. She's worth it — 137
17. A bit squiffy — 149
18. Gogol Mogol — 156
19. Yukanol Fukov — 165
20. He's up to something — 173
21. Here with you — 182
22. Fall in soldier — 189
23. Life is pain — 196
24. They've heard her screaming — 206
25. Scared stiff — 213
26. Time and patience — 221
27. Make me better — 232
28. You promise? — 242
29. Heat from thin air — 250
30. Created from darkness — 260

31. Messy	269
32. Finished	277
Epilogue	287
Acknowledgments	301
About the Author	303

Prologue

Never been normal

THE TWO GIRLS SAT ON THE FLOOR OF THE WARDROBE waiting for the grunting to stop. For the clients, the girls could be in the living area of the flat whilst Mama went to the bedroom, but they'd learnt early on that when Mama's boss came it was better if they were truly hidden. During the day it wasn't a problem; during the day they made sure they were either at school or in the library, but when the library closed they had to come home. The smaller, blonde-haired girl closed her eyes and tried to remember one of the English stories she had read recently: visions of wardrobes leading to foreign lands, lions with magical powers and children who ruled kingdoms floated through her mind and she relaxed.

'You stupid bitch!' The gruff Russian voice shook the girl out of her mental escape and she peered through the gap in the slats, gripping her older sister's hand more tightly. 'You think you can cheat me? I know this is not full amount.'

Her mama's voice begging him to re-count it was cut off by the crack of his fist connecting with her jaw. There was silence for a moment until another crack rang out through the small room, and another. Sickening sounds of bones breaking filled the air, and the blonde girl held back a sob.

'Useless whore,' she finally heard the man mutter as he picked up the wad of notes from her mother's side table and headed to the bedroom door. After they'd heard it shut the two girls emerged from the cupboard, and on silent feet went to their mama's side; she was lying completely still on the bed, her eyes open, staring sightlessly out at nothing. The taller, dark-haired girl threw herself onto her mother's body, sobbing as she had been taught: silently. The blonde girl reached out and lifted her mother's lifeless hand, curling her small fingers around her wrist to feel a pulse. When she felt nothing she reached under her sister with her other hand to lay it on the centre of her mother's chest, and held her breath.

Minutes passed as the sisters remained like that: the brunette lying pressed into her mother's side and the blonde standing over her, feeling for a heartbeat or a pulse. As the blonde girl looked down at her mother's face she saw the Christmas lights that Mama had scrimped to buy for them reflected in her glassy eyes, and she felt the fear slowly leave her body to be replaced by white-hot anger. She withdrew her small hands from her mother's body and coiled them into fists at her sides; her fury was so overpowering it was like a physical presence in the room, and it moved her towards the bedroom door.

'*Myshka!*'* the dark-haired girl hissed from the bed, her eyes wide with fear. The blonde gestured for her sister to stay put, then pointed to the phone on the bedside table before slipping from the room.

The arrogant bastard was still there. He was sitting down on their frayed sofa, talking on the phone to one of his lackeys, telling them to come and 'clean up this shit'. She presumed the shit he was referring to was her mama. The blonde girl took a deep but silent breath and tamped down the seething fury threatening to explode so she could process the scene and decide her next move.

This particular little girl had never been normal. She could read books faster than any adult she knew, she could assess people and situations rapidly, make decisions instantly. She even paid all the bills and did all the accounts for her mother, kept a roof over their heads, bought the food, bartered for everything at the market. That's how she knew that the money her mother had given her boss was right; he was either stupid or greedy: the little girl suspected both.

After a few seconds she started inching towards the kitchen. Years of practice in having to keep quiet when her mother was with a client meant that she could move with almost eerie silence. She went to the chopping board and lifted the knife resting on top, clasped it firmly to her side, and then padded over to behind the sofa where the man was still on the phone.

Her mind flashed to the book on anatomy she had read recently; the medical section of the library was the farthest from the reception desk and the sisters found hiding there to be the most effective plan when they wanted to avoid being chucked out. She'd found the textbooks boring, but devoured them all the same, and now she was glad. Her almost perfect ability to retain anything she had seen written down meant that she could picture the anatomy of a man's neck in her mind: see where the arteries and veins ran, knew the best place to strike. She lifted the knife behind him and waited until he'd hung up the phone before lunging forward and plunging the knife into his carotid artery.

'Argh!' he shouted, dropping his phone and clutching at his neck with one hand whilst he made a grab for her with the other. He managed to drag her over the back of the sofa, and pain exploded down the side of her face when he backhanded her, one of his rings splitting the skin next to her eye. He went to hit her again but his wild eyes took in the blood that was spurting from his neck all over her face and body, and he clutched his throat desperately with both hands before losing his strength and falling forward on top of her. The little girl struggled out from underneath the huge man and rubbed the blood from her eyes. She stood next to the sofa, her face and hair soaked with red, and stared at the him before coughing up some saliva and spitting on his cheek.

'*Spokoynoy nochi zhopa,*'* she muttered under her breath as her face was lit up by the flashing lights from outside, and the sound of sirens filled the night air.

* MYSHKA – LITTLE MOUSE
 * *Spokoynoy nochi zhopa* – Goodnight, asshole

Chapter 1

Devoted employee

Smooth as silk the lift doors swept back, revealing the imposing entryway of Nick's penthouse office floor. As he did every morning, he stared straight ahead, straight at her, and just as *she* did every morning, she held his stare and smiled a smile that didn't quite reach her startlingly clear-blue eyes. They had entered into this ridiculous staring contest every day for the last three months and every day, without fail, she bloody won.

Now, Nick was not a man who took losing particularly well; in fact he was known for his stubborn tenacity. But there was something about the way she held his eyes which made him uneasy; which made him unable to stop himself from flicking his gaze away from hers by the time he had reached the front desk. Even after he had turned the corner to his office, he could *still* feel her eyes boring into his back, almost as if she was taunting him for his weakness, and it pissed him off. She was a sodding receptionist for Christ's sake, why on earth did he feel intimidated by her?

'What ho!' Bertie boomed as Nick swept past his desk.

'What ho, Bert,' Nick called back with a half-hearted grin as he slammed his door. He rolled his eyes when he was in the safety of his office; between Bertie, Ed and that bloody receptionist, he was being driven slowly insane. Snatching up the phone, he started punching in the number of the New York office, but after a couple of failed attempts to get through he realized that he was so unsettled by the receptionwitch (he'd christened her that on the first day they had locked eyes), he couldn't even dial a simple number. Everyone else seemed completely taken in by her front: blonde bimbo receptionist – happy to gossip with the girls, charm all manner of clients and business associates, babble mindlessly about nothing. But Nick was convinced there was something off about her. Her smile never met her eyes, her laugh never quite rang true, the way she flicked her hair or filed her nails looked practiced and even slightly forced.

After the first month of morning stare-downs, Nick had decided to act on his rampant curiosity. He convinced the company's industrial espionage expert to look into Miss Lucinda Quinn. The report that was produced was more than a little dull. It seemed that Lucinda had lived the most average life imaginable: growing up in Bognor Regis of all places, attending the local comprehensive school and achieving very average grades, before a string of dead-end jobs and equally dead-end boyfriends. Clearly there was nothing in the least bit interesting about Miss Quinn, and his head of security had rightly looked at Nick like he was a little unhinged before handing over the slender file.

From then on, unwilling to make any more of a fool of himself, Nick had ignored his suspicions, and attempted to ignore *her*. One slight hitch in this plan was that she stayed late in the office every night, her excuse being that she needed to study for her Open University course and shared a flat with a riotous group of girls, making that impossible for her at home. Nick had no idea what she was studying, and after the whole investigation debacle he had no intention of finding out. All he knew was that he not only had to enter into a stare-down on his way into work but also as he left, a state of affairs made worse by the fact that he had to suffer the entire ride down in the lift with her, which she invariably filled with pointless chatter about celebrities he'd never heard of, television programmes he had no intention of ever watching, and the exploits of her completely unexceptional and interminably dull family.

The weird thing was that despite her willingness to talk his ear off, and giving every appearance of a devoted employee, Nick somehow knew that she didn't like him. This was not a normal experience for Nick; from a young age he had been able to charm every female in his immediate vicinity with ease. The fact that this vacuous female seemed completely immune to it was ... odd. He also knew that she did *not* like lifts. His office was twenty floors up and he was an expert in body language. She tried to hide it, but he could feel the tension rolling off her as they descended together every day.

Determined to avoid a repeat of this torture for the fifth day in a row, Nick leaned forward and flicked through the contacts on his phone until he found Lila's number. At least Lila didn't bang on about everything under the sun or disconcert him with any penetrating stares.

She answered on the second ring (a fact that Nick barely noticed, having never had to leave a message on a woman's answerphone in his life).

'The Russians are here, boss,' Bertie's disembodied voice said through the intercom as Nick was wrapping up making plans with Lila – all of which she'd agreed to without complaint; even the weird request that she come and meet him at his office rather than the restaurant.

'Send them through to the conference room,' Nick said into the intercom, attempting to fake a level of confidence that he wasn't really feeling. This meeting was absolutely crucial: if they couldn't get these guys on board they'd lose a big part of the block of investment from Eastern Europe and might risk the site they were securing in Slovakia, setting them back by anything up to a year. The delay could come close to killing the project.

'Ed,' Nick bit out into his mobile as he dragged his jacket on from his chair, 'where are you? The meeting's scheduled for ten o'clock and it's five past, you dullard.'

'Oh, right,' Ed mumbled, sounding vague and unconcerned as usual. 'Well, you see, I had this idea and I just needed to thrash out some of the theoretical calculations before I could ...'

Nick pinched the bridge of his nose and took a deep breath. *Ed is brilliant*, he told himself. *Ed is a genius and this project needs him. You cannot kill Ed with your bare hands.* 'Just get the fuck up here, okay,' he said through gritted teeth.

'Well, you see, I'm at a bit of a tricky point in the old calculations and I –'

'Ed, there are four huge Russians here, all of whom are rumoured to have links with the mob, all of whom are scary in the extreme. You do not keep these people waiting. Even apart from the fact that they could twist you into a human pretzel as soon as look at you, there is also the small detail that if these guys say no then there is no project, right?' There was a long pause on the line; Nick rolled his eyes and clenched his jaw in frustration. 'Right, Ed?'

'The mob?' Ed whispered.

Nick sighed. 'Ed, we've been through this, the problem is that you don't listen to me. Sometimes when the lowly mortals of average intelligence but who happen to be paying your exorbitant salary speak, you need to listen.'

Goodnight

'I'm on my way.'

When Ed did finally deign to arrive Nick was seated in the conference room after some awkward greetings had been exchanged with the four large Russians, all of whom looked as though they hadn't cracked a smile their entire lives, and further that they could happily wrestle a bear to the death, bare-chested, in a Siberian wasteland and barely break a sweat. The fact that they were wearing suits contrarily made them seem even more menacing, their bulging necks barely contained within the straining shirt collars.

'Sorry, sorry,' Ed shouted as he barrelled through the conference room door; then, catching sight of the Russians, he tripped over his feet and had to grab the edge of the table to steady himself, nearly ending up head-first in a less-than-impressed-looking Russian's lap. Ed straightened up, his wide eyes taking in the wall of menace seated at the table, and he took a small step back, swallowing hard. 'Uh ... I ... well ...' He nearly fell over again as he backed into the projector stand. Nick rolled his eyes. It wouldn't be so bad if Ed was at least wearing a tailored suit like every other man in the room, but with his trademark disregard for any kind of convention he had chosen to wear an ancient ripped T-shirt with a faded poster for a lost Schrödinger's cat on the front. His black hair was sticking up in all directions and his jeans looked like they were in danger of giving up the ghost and falling down his skinny hips at any moment.

'Bertie, could you come in here for a minute,' Nick said through the intercom whilst pulling on his shirt collar to loosen it. The Russian mumbles from the other side of the table were becoming more hostile by the second.

'You called, Oh Great and Glorious Leader?' Bertie said as

he swept into the room, ignoring the atmosphere and smiling a broad, totally inappropriate smile at the Russians. 'What ho, chaps!'

All four men turned towards a red-faced Bertie. Nick rolled his eyes for what seemed like the hundredth time that morning. Bertie, in a three-piece suit, could have almost passed for normal if it wasn't for the fact that the suit was tweed, and not only tweed but *purple* tweed. Who would buy a tweed suit? Leave alone a purple one? Bertie's explanation had involved a 'terribly attractive and jolly young lady who said it was just the thing.' If 'the thing' was something to make Bertie look even more ridiculous than he already managed on his own, then Nick would have to agree. The Russians were staring at Bertie like his existence and his suit's were not only confusing but highly offensive.

'Where is the interpreter, Bertie?' Nick said through clenched teeth, trying to retain his aura of calm as he felt a trickle of sweat fall down his back.

'Ah ... well, there might be a bit of a problem there, old boy,' Bertie replied. 'The poor bloke just rang, and from what I could make out, in amongst the vomiting, he –'

'Find me another one,' Nick cut in, giving in to the urge to pinch the bridge of his nose in frustration.

'Chto yebat' zdes' proiskhodit?' the most menacing of the group barked out, lifting up from his seat to tower over Bertie.

'Sest,' a clear voice sounded from the doorway. Looking up, Nick's eyes met a pair of familiar blue ones before their owner focused on the four angry men at the table. Surprisingly the man who had stood up shifted in discomfort under her penetrating stare, then dropped back down into his chair. 'Vy sobirayetes' slushat' etikh lyudey . Vy soglasny s nimi . Vy utverdit plany.'

'Pochemu?'

Goodnight

'Moye imya "Goodnight". Vy ponimayete?'

For the first time that morning Nick saw a flicker of emotion in the Russians' expressions before their faces became carefully blank. What was she saying to them?

'What is going on?' he asked.

'Oh, I heard you boys struggling from out there and thought I'd come and help out,' Lucy said happily, her stern expression fading as she addressed him, morphing into the more familiar chirpy but vacant one Nick knew well. He frowned. 'You speak fluent Russian?'

'Of course,' she said slowly, as if explaining things to a slow child. 'That *is* why I got the job, after all.'

Nick had had very little to do with recruiting Lucinda. She'd just appeared when he arrived back from New York after a month-long waste of time trying to negotiate contracts with the Americans (he was now resigned to them being the very last people on the planet to accept Ed's breakthrough, and certainly the last to invest in it). When he'd asked who had recruited her, he had been offered some vague story about HR branching out.

Weird as this latest turn of events was, after the last uncomfortable fifteen minutes Nick was willing to do just about anything to cut through the tension and try to get the deal on the table. 'Right, fine. Are you okay to translate? Can you keep up?' he asked, and watched her cheerful expression slip. Her eyes became so cold that he actually had to suppress a shiver before she pasted a smile back on her face.

'Of course – hit me.' For a moment it sounded like she actually wanted him to physically strike her. Her head was tilted to the side and he thought he could see a challenge in her eyes; then he realized that she meant for him to start speaking.

He turned to the men opposite, who were now eyeing the new arrival warily. Bizarre.

'Gentlemen, I understand you have concerns about the

project; that there may be some conflicts of interest.' Lucinda proceeded to translate and the Russians' eyes narrowed. One of them leaned forward and spat out a tirade which Nick was quite sure featured a fair amount of swear words, and, if he wasn't mistaken, an extremely derogatory reference to his mother. He glanced at Lucinda throughout this and noticed she was staring at the Russian, her head still tilted to the side and a bored expression on her face. After a couple of minutes of the Russian's verbal attack she was clearly done.

'Stop,' she shot out (even Nick knew that 'stop' was the same in English or Russian). All eyes swung to her. With the sheer level of authority her voice carried, Nick was quite sure she could have cut off a world leader mid-tirade and the Russian man fell silent. She then leaned forward slightly and blanked her expression before she started speaking. Nick had no idea what she was saying, it was too quick to pick up anything. He even thought it might have been a subtly different dialect to the basic Russian he had attempted to learn last year. But what did strike him was her tone. She wasn't ranting like the Russian man had been; there was no anger in her voice. If anything her speech was eerily devoid of emotion, but there was no mistaking the thread of menace it carried, and the temperature of the room felt like it had dropped a good ten degrees.

When it was clear she was done, one of the other Russian men started talking to her, spreading his hands in a gesture of frustration. She replied with the same tone, and, to Nick's annoyance, they proceeded to all exchange words with each other for the next ten minutes.

When she was finally done she turned to him and smiled her fake smile.

'He said he'll listen,' she told him, and Nick's eyebrows shot up.

'That's all he said: "I'll listen"?'

She shrugged but her mouth stayed firmly shut. Nick heard a strangled noise from his side of the table and glanced at Ed to see that his face was red and he was coughing into his hand to muffle a laugh. Nick turned back to Lucinda; taking in the cold light in her eyes, he scrubbed his hand down his face and smiled a fake smile of his own.

'Fine,' he gritted out. 'Would you mind translating an actual conversation between us as a *translator*? That is, if it's not too much trouble.'

'Of course,' she said with saccharine sweetness, and Nick didn't know how she managed it but her smile dialled up a few notches whilst her eyes actually grew colder.

Chapter 2

Right up to his door

'WHAT HO, OLD CHAP.' BERTIE'S VOICE SOUNDED THROUGH the intercom and Nick sighed. 'Bit of totty waiting out here for you. Shall I send her in?' The reception area was separate to the outer office that Bertie sat in, but Nick was pretty sure you could hear most of what Bertie said from there; his voice *did* tend to carry. Nick was not entirely sure how Lila would react to being called a 'bit of totty', and seeing as her disposition was prickly at the best of times he was not eager to find out.

'One minute, Bertie,' he said into the intercom, and started tidying his papers.

'Good for you, Flopsy.' Bertie's cheerful voice sounded again and Nick gritted his teeth at Bertie's use of his old nickname (they had had words about using that name in the office, but Bertie was oblivious to how much it wound Nick up). 'Keep the fillies waiting, why not? Got to say I like your taste; good set of nashers on her, lovely rear-end, looks like a goer too.' Referring to females as 'fillies' was by no means out of the ordinary for Bertie; nor was describing their attributes much as if they were actual horses. Clearly they would have to go through the rules of the office again.

Why Nick had agreed to hire his cousin as his PA was beyond him. Bertie was a good bloke; they had grown up next door to each other and were in the same year at boarding school together. He was hilarious but totally clueless, hence his inability to get and keep a job or in fact a girlfriend for any length of time. The Family had succeeded in employing enough guilt and emotional manipulation to get Nick to agree to help train Bertie whilst Nick's real PA was off on maternity leave. So far Bertie had succeeded in pissing off the majority of Nick's suppliers and employees with his bumbling incompetence, unwitting sexism and general ridiculousness.

Nick paused in the process of tidying his papers, braced both hands on his desk in front of him and let his head fall once onto the wooden surface.

'Nick, darling, what *are* you doing?' Lila's voice caused his head to come up and he focused on her. She was, as always, immaculate. He knew that in the male-dominated world of management consultancy she used her appearance as a kind of weapon in order to get the job done with the minimum of fuss: when Lila came into a meeting she tended to command most of the attention and invariably managed to swing things her way. 'I see you're still lumbered with Tim-nice-but-dim out there,' she said, flicking her long dark hair over one shoulder and gliding elegantly down into the seat in front of his desk.

Nick sighed. 'Just ignore him, Li,' he said as he pushed up from his chair. 'Let's go.' It had been a long day and he had a sudden overwhelming desire to get out of the bloody office. Worryingly, he couldn't even remember a time when he had left before nightfall, and he needed a break. The meeting with the Russians was frustrating, to say the least. It was clear that the bulk of the conversation was not being translated, and overall he had felt out of control of the whole thing. Nick did not relish being out of control in any area of his life. In fact, he couldn't remember the last time he had been undermined to that degree. By the end of the two hours, he had been sorely tempted to chuck Lucinda out of the office window. Ed, being Ed, had been terrified in general and had not fielded the scientific questions directed at him very well, even though Nick did notice that Lucinda softened her tone when talking to him. At one point she had smiled encouragingly at him, and it was the first one Nick'd ever seen that actually reached her eyes. The fact that she'd seen fit to award Ed with this for some reason made Nick even more furious, and by the end of the meeting he'd snapped a pencil clean in half, such was his frustration.

He took Lila by the arm and gently but firmly steered her out of the office, past an open-mouthed Bertie and into the entryway, only stopping at the lift doors.

'Well,' breathed Lila through a small smile, 'I don't know what's got your knickers in such a twist but I'm going to say I like it.' Nick wasn't surprised, they'd been friends/casual lovers on and off for the last few months; he knew what she liked. He transferred his hand to the base of Lila's spine as the lift doors opened and walked them both through. As they were turning to face the doors and Nick was breathing a sigh of relief that at least he would be spared Lucinda for the rest of the day, he flinched.

'Hi,' chirped a smiling-but-not-smiling Lucinda, giving both Nick and Lila a cheery finger wave before she leaned across them and pressed the ground-floor button. Nick stared at her. He knew he was an observant man and there was nothing wrong with his hearing, so why hadn't he heard her approach or even alight into the lift? He shook his head, took his hand off Lila and shoved both of them into his pockets, determined to ignore Lucy and just bloody –

Goodnight

'I'm Lucinda,' he heard her say, and looked over to find that she had her hand out for Lila to shake. Lila flicked Nick a bemused look before taking Lucinda's hand.

'Lila,' she replied after the briefest handshake possible.

'Lucinda, why are you leaving the office now?' Nick ground out, still staring straight ahead.

'But this is when I finish,' she told him. 'It's past five after all.'

'But –'

'Here we are,' Lucinda interrupted, then strode out into the ground floor entryway with Nick and Lila in her wake. When they were all out on the street Lucinda seemed to develop the sudden need to adjust the strap on her shoe and dropped to a squat to do this. By the time she'd straightened up, Nick and Lila were beside her on the pavement. Nick always parked in his reserved space a few yards down from the office on the right; this meant he invariably had to endure Lucinda's chatter right up to the door of his car. In the process of turning to his right he stopped mid-stride.

Right up to his door.

Every day for the last month that was exactly what Lucinda had done. The question was, why?

'Let's get the tube into town, Li, and go out to eat. Traffic'll be murder now at this time,' he said, spinning on his heel and guiding Lila in the direction of the station, which was left out of his office. 'See you next week, Lucinda,' he flung at her over his shoulder, not looking back to see her expression, and for some reason feeling like he'd won a sort of small victory.

~

GOODIE SIGHED AS SHE PULLED OUT HER MOBILE. WHEN she had dialled the number she secured her hands-free earpiece and started after Nick and Lila.

'He knows,' she said into the earpiece whilst tying up her hair into a baseball cap (she couldn't wait to get rid of those fucking hair extensions – why women paid for this shit she had no idea) and tugging off her heels. 'I don't know how, but he does. I told you that this would be ridiculous.' She tossed her heels and the pink jacket she was wearing into a bin and pulled some trainers out of her bag. Without the coat, her outfit was almost completely black, and with her baseball cap pulled down over her eyes, she was pretty much unrecognizable as Chirpy Office Receptionist. Of all the roles Goodie had had to play (and some of those roles were a lot more horrifying), she thought that the last month had to have been the most taxing. Chirpy was not something that came naturally to Goodie. Her face had ached after a day of smiling – years of disuse had no doubt atrophied the facial muscles required, and if she had to make one more inane remark to one more brainless dimwit she would scream. She moved silently through the crowd, never losing sight of her target.

'Maybe we cut this fucking charade now, yes?' she bit out, her light Russian accent filtering through her words. The person on the other end of the line knew who she was: that was the main reason he had recruited her.

She shook her head as she saw Nick was going to take a shortcut. What a moron. The alleyway had no street lighting and was almost completely deserted. She rolled her eyes and turned down into it, reaching into the back of her trousers and letting her hand close around the cold steel.

~

'WHAT THE –?' NICK'S SHOULDER WAS YANKED BACKWARDS and he crashed against the wall at the side of the alleyway.

Goodnight

Before he could even register who or what was in front of him a fist slammed into his face and his head cracked back onto the brick. Reacting on instinct, he swung out and felt his fist connect with a sickening crunch of facial bones. He blinked to see the large man he'd landed a punch on stagger back, and heard a muffled scream from his other side. When he turned he saw that another man was holding Lila up against the wall. Both men were dressed in dark colours with balaclavas covering their faces; and to Nick's dismay both were holding knives.

'Do not move or I will slit her throat,' the man holding Lila against the wall said, bringing his knife up to her neck and causing her to whimper in distress. Nick froze.

'Don't hurt her,' he said, keeping his voice level and holding both hands up in surrender. 'I have cash on me, my watch, you can take whatever –'

'We're not interested in your money,' the man Nick had punched told him, reaching for his own knife and stalking forward towards Nick. Nick frowned and started running through scenarios in his mind of how this was going to go, trying to come up with a strategy, but before he could make a move the man coming at him let out a bloodcurdling scream and dropped his knife.

'What are you doing, you useless prick?' the man holding Lila shouted, obviously reluctant to take his eyes off his victim.

'Jesus Christ, Christ Jesus,' the other man swore, clutching the shoulder of the arm that had been holding the knife, with good reason: the knife he had held in his hand was nothing compared to the one now sticking out of his upper arm.

'Drop the knife.'

Nick and the wounded man turned to see a woman in a baseball cap attached to the back of Lila's assailant like a small, vicious-looking monkey. She was, Nick realized, holding her

19

own knife to the man's throat. 'Do not make me repeat myself,' the woman said as Nick watched a small trickle of blood make its way from underneath her knife down the man's neck. With no choice, the man dropped his weapon and held his hands up and away from Lila, who wasted no time scooting down the wall and falling into Nick.

'Aargh!' the man with the knife in his shoulder screamed as he pulled it out. Blood was now running freely down his arm, soaking his sleeve. He dropped onto the concrete and pressed his free hand to the wound. After taking in the scene around him with terrified eyes, he turned and ran.

'Tell your boss to back off,' the woman said into the other man's ear. 'Mr Chambers has protection, and after this little display he will have even tighter security, you understand? Next time any of you try this again it won't be shoulders I'm aiming for.' She then leapt silently from his back. The man turned to glance at her for a moment, then started reaching for something behind him. A large shape moved out of the shadows with a low growl, and the man screamed as a dog's jaws clamped down on his hand. He tried unsuccessfully to shake off the animal but was only released when the woman gave a low whistle. The hulking brown and black dog let go of the man but stayed next to him with its teeth bared and a warning growl. Taking this in, the man gave Nick one frustrated glance, then turned to run after his partner. The huge dog, a sort of Alsatian but obviously not pure bred, padded over to the woman, who bent to scratch his ears and mutter something in a foreign language.

Nick was not about to hang about with a female psychopath in a dark alley, even if she had saved his life, and began backing away with Lila in tow; but as he watched the woman straighten he registered a flicker of recognition, and when her blue eyes locked onto his own brown eyes, he froze.

Chapter 3

Non-linear junction evaluator

'LUCINDA?' NICK SAID, HIS MOUTH FALLING OPEN IN shock. 'What the fu –'

'Nick, let's *go*,' Lila's shaky voice begged as she pulled frantically on his sleeve. Lucinda simply looked past the couple in front of her and jerked her chin at someone behind them. Nick spun round just in time to see a large figure at the end of the alleyway make some sort of signal to Lucinda and jog away. 'Nick, come *on*,' Lila pleaded. Nick made a step towards Lucinda, and the dog now sitting at her side growled, its lip curling to reveal the lower half of its sharp teeth.

'Salem, enough,' murmured Lucinda, resting her hand on top of the dog's broad head. He immediately stopped growling and allowed his lip to drop over his teeth, but Nick got the impression that he wasn't happy about it. Now that he was really looking, he realized that this was the dog that had been hanging out at the ground floor reception for the last four weeks; Nick had just assumed it was a new part of the office security.

Lucinda glanced behind her, then stared straight at Nick.

'We should go,' she told him, and started walking towards them. Lila gasped and flung herself back against the wall of the alley as Lucinda went by, but this didn't seem to bother her in the slightest. She swept past them both, the dog padding silently in her wake, and it was only when she was a few feet away that Nick managed to shake off his shocked stupor and start after her, pulling Lila along behind him.

'Do you mind very much telling me what the fuck is going on?' he clipped, tucking a shaking Lila under his arm.

'We need to get back to your car,' Lucinda told him, turning onto the busy street and starting to wind her way through the crowds, back in the direction of Nick's office. 'Once we are at your apartment complex, then you'll be secure and we can debrief.'

'I am not going anywhere with you and neither is Lila,' Nick shouted after her, drawing to a halt. Lucinda and the dog stopped in their tracks and turned to him. It was almost imperceptible, but he could have sworn she rolled her goddamn eyes.

'Sir, I'm sorry but we do need to move,' a man's voice said from behind Nick, and he turned to see the man Lucinda had been signalling to standing there, his arm out to indicate that they must move forward. He was tall, even taller than Nick, who was at least six foot two, and his frame was heavy-set. He had dark hair, just a shade lighter than Nick's, and dark eyes, but the most striking thing about his appearance was the scar that ran from the corner of his eye, down his cheek and into his neck. Nick's mind flashed to the small crescent-shaped scar at the corner of Lucinda's eye, and he frowned.

'Listen, mate, unless someone starts explaining to me what the fuck is –'

'No,' Nick heard Lucinda's voice clip from his other side. 'We will explain at the flat. We need to be off the street now.'

'I –'

Goodnight

'Listen for once in your life, you arrogant son of a bitch,' Lucinda spat out at him. 'Maybe you don't give a shit about your life, or hers for that matter,' she said, indicating towards Lila, 'but it would be helpful if you let me do my fucking job, get you to a secure location, and be able to make enquires about Mr Southern's well-being, okay?'

'Ed? You think something might happen to Ed?'

Lucinda just stood her ground, glaring up at him.

'Okay, let's go,' he said, and she spun on her heel to make for his car.

∼

'OKAY, SUSAN,' NICK GRITTED OUT INTO HIS PHONE, STILL pacing the length of his bedroom, 'take me through this again. You agreed not to tell me – your employer – that one of my staff was there under false pretences. The member of staff in question is not actually a receptionist at all, she's ... well, I don't bloody know what she is, but she's certainly not a goddamn receptionist. Am I right?'

'Well, Nick,' Susan said, her nervous voice shaking down the line, 'you see, you had gotten rid of the last two sets of protection officers assigned to you. Everyone just thought that maybe if you didn't know you were being followed, you wouldn't get so annoyed by it, and then your father –'

'Dad?' Nick exploded, his temper on a knife-edge. 'Dad knew I was being followed by some crazy woman?'

'Well ... your father doesn't actually know who's providing the protection, only that it's being sorted, and those government chaps really were quite insistent that –'

'Fine, Susan.' Nick cut her off, pinching the bridge of his nose and huffing out a breath in frustration. He couldn't really blame her if his father was involved. Dad may not have worked at the company for the last ten years but he was still considered The Big Cheese, and it wasn't as though anyone would have felt able to refuse a request from him, least of all Susan. She was still bumbling on to him down the phone when he tapped it off and shoved it into his back pocket.

'Right,' he said as he pushed through the door from his bedroom out into the vast living space of his flat. His interior designer had wanted to go ultra-modern with acres of granite and hard, gleaming floor tiles, but Nick asked for something to remind him of home; hence the wide, oak floorboards, squashy, beaten-up leather sofas and Shaker-style kitchen. 'Now that I've established that you are not random deranged psychopaths, would you mind very much telling me *who* you are and what *the fuck* is going on.'

Lucinda turned to face him from her position at the floor-to-ceiling glass windows. She had totally dropped the fake smile now, and for once the rest of her face matched her eyes. Although Nick had always sensed the smile was a front, the difference in her appearance without it was quite startling. She looked hardened, cold, and had a strange air of being in total control of herself and the world around her. Nick was beginning to realize the extent of her acting skills. The dark colours she sported now were a stark contrast to her usual pinks and purples. He also remembered her voice. In her guise as Receptionist Lucinda, she had spoken with a Worsel Gummidge, country bumpkin accent. The voice she used in the alleyway and out on the street was nothing like it. If anything she sounded slightly Russian. Lying at her feet was the massive dog. Its head had been resting on its paws, but as Nick burst back into the living space it came up and both ears swivelled forward.

After agreeing to go with his newly discovered security detail, Nick and Lila had been hustled to his car, at which point it became clear Lucinda intended to travel with him, complete with the hair-shedding dog. The information that his upholstery was Italian leather and might not be the best surface for a huge and no-doubt-unwashed dog was met with stony silence from Lucinda and a brief display of sharp teeth from the dog, so he decided to grin and bear it.

Lila, having come down from her adrenaline rush of fear in the alley and realizing that her potential date with Nick was not going to go the way she had planned, asked to be dropped at her own flat. Lucinda told her that 'would not be advisable' in a tone that suggested it was *not* going to happen, and so they'd all driven straight to Nick's underground car park, trailed by the other man, who was driving Lucinda's car (yes, it turned out that Lucinda did have a car, and much to Nick's annoyance it was one he recognized from frequent sightings over the last month – she had, evidently, been following him for some time).

'My name is Goodie,' she told him. 'And this is Sam Clifton.'

'Right ...' Nick paused to take a deep breath and run his hands through his hair as he let it out. 'Okay.'

He walked across the room until he was standing in front of 'Goodie' and she was looking up at him with those cold eyes, her arms crossed over her chest. Nick could feel the animosity pouring off her but didn't back away. 'I'll start by saying thank you.'

Goodie blinked and for a nanosecond her face registered surprise before she masked it.

'Thank you for saving my life in that alleyway.'

She held his eyes for a moment, a small frown of confusion pulling her brows together; then she nodded, and after another few seconds she took a step back. Her dog followed her, and both female and canine eyes watched him with their heads cocked slightly to the side. Nick smiled at her, causing more confusion to cloud her features, but she remained silent. It would seem that this woman was a lot less chatty than his receptionist of the last month.

'Right,' he said, turning back to the rest of the room. 'Now that we've got that out of the way my next question is: who do you work for?'

'I run the security company your father hired with my partner Rob Davis. Our offices are based in Wales but take jobs all over the world,' Sam told him. 'Most of our operatives are ex-Special Forces. I believe that since MI6 took an interest in your protection they referred your father to us.'

'So you work for him?' Nick asked Goodie, who rolled her eyes but kept her mouth shut.

'Goodie's freelance,' Sam said. 'She works for herself.'

'If you were concerned: Mr Southern is secure, sir,' Lucinda a.k.a. Goodie cut in.

Nick rubbed the back of his neck mumbling, 'Right, yeah, great.' How had he forgotten about poor Ed? 'Can I ask you both to stop calling me *sir* by the way?' he asked as he crossed the room to his open-plan kitchen area. He took down a crystal glass, reached up for his brandy on the top shelf, and poured himself a healthy measure.

'No problem, Mr Chambers,' Sam said from the sofa. Nick glared over at him, then slammed back the shot before stalking over to the living area.

'It's Nick, okay; everyone calls me Nick. Mr Chambers is my father.' Sam took another sip of tea and didn't respond either way. Nick sighed. 'So can you both tell me what your roles are? Is it just the two of you or are there more?'

'I'm your close protection officer,' Goodie told him. 'Sam is the far guard. He does most of the route planning, IED checks, counter-sniping monitoring. We have another team for background checks and research.'

Goodnight

Nick sat down heavily in one of the armchairs and his mouth fell open.

'Right, Nicky darling,' Lila said, putting her cup of tea down on the coffee table and pushing up from the sofa. Nick started slightly – he'd forgotten she was even there. 'I think that talk of IED checks might be my cue to go.'

'I'll take you home,' Nick said, getting up from the chair.

'*No,*' Lila practically shouted, her eyes wide. 'I mean ...' she continued in a more measured tone, 'those nice police detectives from earlier are meeting me downstairs. They'll take me. Then I need to start booking in all the therapy I'll need to get over this.'

'Right, sorry about everything, Li.'

'Not your fault, honey,' Lila muttered, giving him a distracted kiss on the cheek. 'If you *will* go and try to save the world you've got to expect a few bumps in the road. I think us mere mortals will attempt to stay out of the firing line though.' She glanced around the room and caught Goodie's eye. 'Thank you.'

Goodie gave her another short nod and Lila turned to leave.

'Should my friends have protection?' Nick asked as he watched the door close after her.

'As far as we can ascertain, Mr Chambers, the threat is to you and Mr Southern alone. There is no advantage in the murder or kidnap of your family and friends; it's you two that are in danger.'

'How much "danger" are we talking about exactly?' Nick asked Sam; but it was Goodie who answered.

'You know how much,' she said, her voice hard. 'You were approached six months ago about this by government agents. There are multiple highly motivated, extremely well-funded organizations to whom the development of unlimited alternative power is not a popular turn of events. Those monitoring these organizations have known for a long time about the significant threat to your life and that of Mr Southern. Yet you still refused to comply with their request for a protection team to be put in place.'

Nick shrugged. 'I thought it was over the top. Made me look like a bit of a twat to be honest, having security guards trailing round after me.'

'I hope,' Goodie said, her voice now even harder, 'that today has demonstrated the need to put up with being made to look like "a bit of a twat" in order to stay alive.'

Nick leaned back in his chair and ran his hands through his hair. It seemed that Goodie might be right, and that irritated the hell out of him. He eyed the slight build and average height of the blonde standing by the window, and he felt his shoulders starting to shake. He tried to hold it in but, with the adrenaline coursing through his veins, it seemed that was impossible. Eventually the smile broke out across his face and a chuckle escaped.

'You know what I just realized,' he managed to get out through his now full-on laughter as he stared at Goodie. 'I'm Whitney Houston to your Kevin Costner. Brilliant.'

Nick wouldn't have thought Sam's face capable of it, but at this remark it broke out into a wide smile. Goodie just stared at him like he was a creature from another planet.

'I had a background check done on you,' he told her once he had managed to get a handle on his laughter. 'How –?'

'Your security staff work for you and your –'

'My fucking father.' He cut her off, frowning with annoyance.

Goodie shrugged. 'Even if you had hired an outside company they wouldn't have found anything out that I didn't want them to know. I have many backgrounds and cover stories to choose from. My past is buried deep, no amount of digging

Goodnight

will ever uncover it, no matter how much money or how many people were on the job.'

Nick cocked his head to the side. As Lucinda this woman had been annoying, a little creepy (given that he *knew* she was fake smiling, fake giggling, fake everything in fact), and definitely a whole lot less interesting. 'What's Goodie short for?' he asked.

Goodie pressed her lips together but this time Sam answered for her: 'Goodnight.'

'Is that your last name?'

'No.' This from Goodie.

'Well, what is your name?'

'Lucinda Wilson,' she replied without skipping a beat.

Nick narrowed his eyes at her. 'That is not your real name.'

Goodie raised an eyebrow and he noticed her dog push up from the floor to sit on its haunches next to her, focusing on him. 'My passport says otherwise, Mr Chambers.'

'Listen up, mate,' Sam said, and for the first time his voice was edged with annoyance. 'Her real name is not your concern. *She* is not your concern, right? All you need to know is that she's good at her job and for the moment that involves keeping you in one piece.

'If you want to know her credentials or have someone vouch for her ability, I have a list of numbers here. One of those numbers is the Assistant Director General of MI6. Happy?'

Nick noticed Goodie scowl across at Sam before she blanked her expression; having someone fight her battles for her was clearly not something she appreciated. Sam was too busy staring at Nick to notice, a muscle jumping in his scarred cheek.

'Sam,' Goodie called, and he reluctantly tore his eyes from Nick's. 'Shouldn't you be meeting the others outside?'

'Right, fine,' Sam said, slamming his cup of tea onto the

coffee table with a little too much force and getting to his feet. He jerked his chin at Nick before stalking to the door. Goodie followed him and they exchanged a few terse words; unfortunately the words were in rapid Russian and Nick couldn't understand a bloody thing. The fact that Sam's voice did not carry even a slight hint of a Russian accent confirmed to Nick that it was a deliberate attempt to shut him out of the conversation. After Sam left, Goodie walked back across the room and to her bag, from which she extracted a whole host of black electrical equipment and some earphones.

'What's that?' Nick asked, leaning forward to watch her set up whatever it was with quick efficiency, then extend a wand-like structure.

'A non-linear junction evaluator,' Goodie told him.

'A what?'

'A bug detector.'

'Oh.'

'I'm doing a sweep of your flat,' she explained, slapping some earphones over her ears. Nick huffed in frustration and pushed himself up off his chair.

'I need to get back to the office – this whole thing has made me a bit twitchy about the meetings tomorrow. I should connect with some of the key players,' he told her once he'd walked over to her and lifted up one of her earphones. She jerked her head away and pushed them down to her neck herself.

'I'm afraid that won't be possible tonight, Mr Chambers,' she told him, and was about to pull the headphones back up over her ears when his hands covered hers to stop her. Anger clouded her perfect features for a moment before she switched rapidly to a neutral expression. Her hands were small and cold under his; she felt almost fragile; yet he'd already seen that she was anything but. After a moment she jerked away from him and stepped backwards before crossing her arms over her chest and glaring up at him. 'I am sorry, Mr Chambers,' she forced out, sounding anything but. 'We cannot leave your flat today. I know this is an inconvenience, but it's not just you that would be put at risk. The people posing a threat to you are determined and they are persistent; they will not stop.'

Nick rubbed the back of his neck for a moment before pulling a hand through his hair in frustration. She was actually right, he conceded to himself. He would be a selfish bastard to put the security team at risk as well as himself; he hadn't thought about it from that perspective. He shrugged. 'You're right,' he told her. 'I'll just have to work from here.' He jerked his head towards his home office. 'Christ, I might even have to ask Bertie to *do* something for a change. Are you ... um ... do you have to stay? The night I mean.'

'I'm sorry but yes.'

'The spare room's all set up, so ...'

'Thank you,' Goodie returned, pulling the earphones back up and resuming her sweep of his flat.

∽

GOODIE STOPPED WHEN SHE HEARD THE OFFICE DOOR close, and then lowered her earphones down to her neck again. Salem, sensing her unease, as was his way, padded up to her side and nuzzled her hand. She stared at the office door for a moment as she stroked Salem's head. She could not make sense of that man, and for Goodie that was highly unusual. She'd been relying on her innate ability to accurately judge people since she was a child, when her survival depended on it. For a man of Nick's power and arrogance to make a joke about something many men before him had found emasculating was ... odd.

For once Goodie had found herself on the very edge of smiling. It wasn't as if she never smiled, but usually it was to play a role, sometimes to intimidate or sometimes to hide her anger; she hardly ever found something genuinely funny. Shaking her head to clear it and dragging her eyes away from the office door, she pulled her earphones back up and carried on with the sweep.

He's an arrogant *zhopa*,* she reminded herself. He thought he was so indestructible that he could just dismiss his security team. He'd made her job ridiculously hard over the last four weeks. Remembering all the manicures she'd had to endure, not to mention the hair extensions, the clothes, and above all the lipstick called *Fuchsia* fucking *Fusion*, she pushed any thoughts of finding him amusing out of her head.

Safer that way.

* ZHOPA — ASSHOLE

Chapter 4

Who's going to look after her?

'Jesus, mate,' Clive said as he shut the door to Nick's office. 'What's happened to your receptionist? I mean, granted, she looks a lot more fuckable now, but she's also morphed into literally the least welcoming person on the planet. You sure you want that front of house? Coming in here was like going through a checkpoint into North Korea. It was all "ID? Remove your jacket. Wait there. Sign this." No please or thank you; zero banter. Left me feeling pissed off but strangely aroused at the same time. Unsettling. And since when did people have to get sniffed by a massive dog before entering your office. Is she worried I might be smuggling drugs in to make our two o'clock more interesting?'

'I know,' returned Bertie with real feeling. He had been sitting opposite Nick and relaying the messages he'd taken that morning (those he hadn't lost or simply been too much of an idiot to write down). 'She gives me the willies.' Since Goodie's transformation from 'Lucinda', Bertie had been terrified of her. Women in general terrified Bertie, but Goodie's brand of icy control combined with her sheer beauty was enough to tip him over into a new level of stuttering incompetence; something Nick wouldn't have thought possible. 'Chap comes into work, he'd like a cheery wave from a nice dolly-bird type, not a glare from an ultra-efficient Russian ball-breaker.'

Clive laughed. 'Poor old Bert – not surprised she's put the wind up you. You remember that bird who dragged you off at the school disco? Malory Towers? After you two had gone behind the bike sheds you were so green I thought you might throw up.'

Nick flicked Clive an annoyed look. He knew for a fact that Clive had promised that girl a snog if she'd scare the crap out of Bertie for him for a laugh. Bertie had been full of sixteen-year-old bluster about how he was going to 'take a crack at some fine fillies' before the disco. Yes, that was annoying, but ultimately harmless; there was no way he possessed the balls to even talk to one of those girls, leave alone 'take a crack at them'. What Clive had done was cruel. Sometimes Nick forgot what a prick he could be. The problem with the old boys' network was when you ended up with friends doing your PR for you. Nick would have felt bloody rude had he brought in any company other than Clive's for this job. And then there was the small matter of Nick's sister and the fact Clive was currently dating her.

'Ah, yes, good one, old chap,' Bertie said through a forced chuckle.

'Give it a rest, Clive,' Nick clipped impatiently, and Clive looked at him in surprise, making Nick feel bad that he didn't stick up for Bertie more. 'Thanks for all of those figures, Bertie,' Nick said bracingly.

'Um ...' Bertie muttered, staring at him with a blank expression.

'You've really sorted a lot of the financial aspects of that deal out. I owe you one, yeah?'

'I ...'

'Would you mind checking everything for the next meeting a sec?'

'Uh ... oh right, yes, jolly good ... I'll just be ...' Bertie jumped up from his chair, his face bright red and his movements jerky.

'He doesn't change does he? Jesus, mate, you're a saint for hiring him,' Clive said through a smirk once the door had closed after Bertie.

'Don't be a prick, Clive. Bertie's actually been really useful to have around,' Nick lied. He was finding that someone else pointing out what a useless prat Bertie was pissing him off. 'Anyway, you ready to go?'

'Yup, I told them to meet us at the East India Club for one o'clock.'

Nick froze. 'Uh ... listen ... I ... I think it's better not to do business there, you know? I mean, what if one of their team is a woman?'

'Since when did you object to doing business at the East India?' Clive asked, his eyebrows practically in his hairline. 'We're meeting two other blokes, Nick; you know that as well as me. It's all set up – we go there, eat a bloody steak, choke down a few bottles of Chateau de Ciffre and the deal will be done. Simple.'

Nick sighed; unfortunately things were not quite so simple for him. 'I've got to take my receptionist with me.'

'What? Why?'

Nick readjusted his tie and shifted in his seat. 'Because she's not really a receptionist, Clive; she's a close protection officer.'

'A what?'

'A bodyguard.'

Clive burst out laughing. 'That little slip of a thing out

there is your bodyguard? You're joking. I could take her out with my little finger.'

Nick doubted that, but wasn't about to explain anything to Clive.

'Well, she is, and she won't be allowed into the club.'

'Christ, make her wait outside.'

Nick rubbed his jaw. He could predict how that would go down.

For the last two weeks Goodie had been within twenty feet of him pretty much the entire time. That first night at his flat, Nick went to bed late after working in his office, and Goodie had still been sweeping with her bug detector. Seeing as she had gone over every inch of the space with her devices, Nick knew she would be able to find her way to the spare room. With all the adrenaline he'd found it hard to sleep and at about two o'clock he went out to the kitchen to raid the biscuit tin. On his way back to his room a pile of clothes caught his eye by the front door. He stared at them for a minute until his eyes adjusted to the darkness and he realized it was in fact Goodie. She was lying on the hard wood, no mattress, fully clothed, with only a thin blanket from his sofa covering her and one of the small throw cushions under her head. Her dog, who Nick now knew was called Salem, was curled up in front of her, and her face was buried in the fur at his neck, her arm flung over his chest. Her other hand was stretched out above her, a hair's breadth from the large knife he'd seen her use in the alley.

It was such a weird sight that for a moment Nick was frozen. She looked so small huddled on the floor, and her make-up-free face relaxed in sleep was so beautiful, that he stopped breathing altogether for several seconds. He had the strongest urge to haul her up off the cold surface and forcibly put her in a bed, preferably his own. Well aware of how badly that particular manoeuvre would have gone down, and noticing the dark

Goodnight

circles under her eyes, he stopped himself, but only just. As he was about to turn away he caught movement. Salem's head had lifted from his paws and he was staring right at Nick; he flicked a quick glance back at his mistress before baring his ferocious teeth silently across the room. Nick grinned and gave Salem a one-finger salute before reluctantly turning back to his bedroom.

The next morning he had woken up at around six as normal. He used his en suite and got changed in his room before venturing out into the rest of the flat. His eyes went straight to where Goodie and Salem had been lying in front of the door, but they were nowhere to be seen and the flat was eerily quiet. He checked all the rooms. It seemed Goodie had left. On his way out to work he slammed his door shut and strode down the corridor to take the stairs (there were three other flats on his floor, all of which he owned). Movement out the corner of his eye made him jerk in surprise, dangerously close to letting out a girly squeak. He turned to see Goodie and Salem behind him. She was in the same clothes as the day before but looked totally unruffled, her now-short blonde hair tucked behind her ears.

'What the ... what on earth do you think you're doing?'

'Waiting for you, and now walking down the corridor.'

'Well, I ...' Nick was rarely lost for words and he was determined not to let this woman reduce him to silence. 'Where did you spring from?'

Goodie looked back at Nick's front door and then at Nick with a slight frown. 'I am your close protection officer. I was outside your front door, waiting for you.'

She spoke slowly, as if she were dealing with a small child, which only served to irritate Nick even more, and he threw up his hands in frustration. 'You could have bloody well said something: "Morning, Nick," "Sleep well, Nick?" "Alright loser?"

Anything rather than creeping silently after me.' Goodie's frown deepened.

'We pride ourselves on being an invisible presence, sir. Most clients *want* to forget we're there. I would have thought you were no different since you fired your last two teams.'

'*Nick*,' Nick growled out, his temper mounting.

'What?'

'Nick, my fucking name is Nick,' he said through clenched teeth. 'And I didn't fire those teams – I just didn't think they were necessary.'

Her only response was to blank her expression back to neutral, press her lips together, and cross her arms over her chest. She'd already made it obvious that she thought he was a bastard for dismissing the teams – they were probably mates of hers or something. His gaze dropped to her chest as if his eyes had a mind of their own. The pink coat of yesterday had been swapped out for a dark, close-fitting hoodie. She was slim-built, athletic, but perfectly proportioned.

When he forced his eyes back to hers he noticed irritation was now clouding her features and one of her eyebrows was raised slightly in challenge.

'What happened to your hair?' She looked so different from the receptionist Nick had employed it was a bit freaky.

'Hair extensions,' she told him.

'Why didn't you just keep them? And how did you get them out yourself?'

'They were an irritation I didn't need any more. I hacked them off late last night.'

'With what?'

'With your kitchen scissors.'

Nick tried and failed to imagine any woman of his acquaintance hacking away happily at their hair with kitchen scissors and shrugging it off dismissively the next day. They stood facing each other for a long moment, Nick shifting from foot to foot, Goodie and Salem both staying so still it was almost unnatural.

'Right,' he said, breaking the uncomfortable silence. 'I'll be going then ... I guess you'll be coming with me?' Goodie nodded. 'Does my car have to endure another doggy assault?'

'I have to come with you in your vehicle for the moment, *sir*. The far guard will follow behind but you need cover in close proximity in case you're separated from the other vehicle. Salem can go with the far guard ... if he has to.' As if understanding her words, and obviously wanting to stick close to Goodie, Salem dropped his head and looked up at Nick with wide, dejected eyes. Nick almost smiled: when it came to putting on an act, the dog was almost as good as his mistress.

Shrugging and telling himself that it was to keep on the good side of a potentially dangerous animal rather than because he was letting Salem's downtrodden expression get to him, he muttered: 'Don't worry about it. He can come with us.' Goodie signalled for Salem to follow, and the dog's head shot back up as he started wagging his tail. Nick spun on his heel and strode off down the corridor to the lift.

'You don't have to keep lurking behind me you know,' he said with irritation as he stabbed at the lift button. He was answered by silence.

One thing he did notice on that descent in the lift with Goodie and Salem was how Salem pressed himself into Goodie's leg when the doors closed and remained there until they opened again. Initially, Nick had thought it was the dog that was terrified of enclosed spaces, but after watching Goodie for the last two weeks he realized that there was more to it than that. Goodie never gave much away, she wore her neutral expression like a mask, but the enclosed space of the lift was the one place he sensed her vulnerability.

Nick was good at spotting people's weaknesses; nearly as good as he was at spotting innovative, potentially profitable ideas – he'd had to be, in order to turn the business he inherited from his father around and make it into the massive corporation it was now. He noticed how her jaw would flex as if she was gritting her teeth, how her eyes would stare straight ahead and her hand would grip Salem's fur so tightly her knuckles turned white. Goodie so rarely let anything show that he was guessing the level of fear she experienced in enclosed spaces must have been intense and he wanted to know why.

In fact, over the last two weeks, he had realized that Goodie intrigued him to an unhealthy extent. Maybe it was to do with the fact that she was always with him but somehow managed to remain separate. She no longer slept in front of the door of his flat, having been set up next door along with a boatload of surveillance equipment. The 'far guard', Sam, was installed in a flat on the ground floor. But she was there every morning waiting for him when he left, and she either followed or walked in front of him (according to how she had coordinated things with Sam) wherever he went. The few times he'd tried to extract information out of her had not been successful; if she could, she would limit her answers to one word, the fewer syllables the better. He'd even taken to calling her Kevin or Kev to see if he could get a reaction, but ... nothing.

Salem was a different matter; Nick was quite proud to have largely won the dog over. This was due in large part to the doggie biscuits he'd taken to carrying round in his trouser pockets and to which Salem was very partial. He'd slipped Salem one last week when Goodie was checking the street outside Clive's office, and since then he'd found the dog to be a lot more friendly. In fact four days ago Salem had snuck into Nick's office whilst Goodie was doing her standard interrogation routine with a couple of Nick's clients (Clive was right –

Goodnight

she was literally the least welcoming receptionist in the history of hospitality-based jobs). Nick had seized the opportunity to ply Salem with his beef sandwich, and over the last few days, the dog had taken to spending a large part of the day lying contentedly over Nick's feet.

This behaviour did afford Nick a glimpse behind Goodie's cool façade. The first time she'd found Salem in his office, she'd stormed in looking sick with worry, which in itself was a first – facial expression-wise. When Nick had pointed to his feet she'd come round behind the desk and glared down at Salem with her hands on her hips. She then proceeded to admonish him in Russian, at which point Salem had given her his Dejected Doggie routine. Instead of the anger, Nick would have expected, she'd rolled her eyes and smiled down at the dog, saying something much softer in Russian and giving him a quick rub behind the ears. Nick did not know what she'd said; all he knew was that with her guard down and real, genuine expression in voice and features she was a different person; so beautiful it almost hurt to look at her. He saw the exact moment that she realized where she was, and when the blank mask fell back into place he bizarrely felt the most acute sense of loss.

Yes, it was fair to say that for Nick, Goodie was fast becoming a very strange obsession. He shook his head as if to clear it. Clive was right: if Nick wanted to conduct his meeting in a male-only environment then that was his business – Goodie could just suck it up.

'Okay, I'll get my shit together and we'll go,' Nick told Clive whilst he started shuffling the papers he needed and disconnecting his laptop.

'No problem,' Clive said through a self-satisfied smile. 'I'll just pop out and get better acquainted with GI Jane out there.'

For some reason the idea of Clive attempting his brand of

charm on Goodie made Nick's head start pounding, and once he had everything he needed he practically ran to the door. He tried to tell himself that it was just because the bastard was supposed to be dating his sister; but he knew there was more to it than that.

∼

'Where is she?' Nick hissed at Sam. Clive and the two contractors they were meeting had given up all pretence of small talk and were instead watching the exchange with interest.

Sam folded his huge arms across his chest and stared at Nick. Thankfully, with Nick's height, they were very nearly eye-to-eye, but when it came to sheer menace there was no competing with this guy. 'She's outside the building, *sir*.'

Nick gritted his teeth; now was not the time to start up the whole name battle again. 'Why isn't she bloody well *in*side the building? I thought *you* were the far guard.'

Sam studied him for a moment. 'This is a men's club, sir. For obvious reasons she wouldn't be admitted.'

Nick threw up his hands. 'There's an area for women, for Christ's sake. Why can't she just wait in there?'

'We need eyes on you. This seemed an easy way to achieve that.'

'Well, why isn't Salem with her?'

'It appears, sir, that this establishment will admit dogs but not women to some of its areas. Salem is part of your protection team, therefore he stays as close to you as possible.'

'But what about Goodie?' Nick almost shouted, and Sam raised a thick eyebrow.

'What about her?'

'Well, who's going to look after *her*?' At that comment, *both*

Sam's eyebrows travelled up nearly into his hairline and he blinked once.

'Let me tell you a few things about Goodie,' Sam said in a low voice laced with impatience. 'She's taken care of herself her whole life, she likes it that way, and she wouldn't step inside a place like this if her life depended on it.'

Nick frowned. He didn't like the sound of 'her whole life,', it made his chest hurt for some reason; and he really didn't like the thought of Goodie out there on the streets, far away from her massive dog, watching and ready to take out any potential threat that might come into Nick's vicinity. Yes, okay, maybe he'd already seen with his own eyes that she could indeed take care of herself, but there was still only one of her; she could be ambushed easily, she wasn't exactly as intimidating as the big bastard in front of him, physically. Nick flicked a glance over to the three faces still watching him with avid curiosity and blew out a sigh.

'Well ... can you just check on her at least?' He watched as Sam pressed his lips together, looking very much like he was suppressing a laugh.

'Check on her?' he asked in a strained voice, and Nick narrowed his eyes at him.

'Yes, just fucking check on her. I do actually pay your salaries you know. I am your employer. Could you for once just show me some respect?' Nick spun on his heel and stormed back to the table as he heard Sam radioing through to Goodie and her voice replying with two terse words in Russian, which Nick thought even he could make a fair attempt at translating.

'Everything okay?' asked Terry, the head of the large construction firm they were negotiating with to build the new plant.

'Fine,' Nick bit out. *She wouldn't step inside a place like this if her life depended on it.* He frowned and scrubbed a hand down his face.

'Right, let's get the good stuff in shall we, boys?' Clive said, slapping Nick on the back. 'No reason we shouldn't be able to quaff some fortifying liquids whilst we get down to business.'

Nick forced a smile. For some reason, Clive's cut-glass accent, so similar to his own, was grating on his nerves today. He looked up at the men at the table, pushing out his worry over Goodie and his irritation with Clive to focus on the meeting.

Chapter 5

A better solution

'I don't understand why I can't take far guard tonight,' Goodie snapped at Sam, who was slouched on her sofa, smirking at her.

'No excuses, Goodie,' Sam said smugly. '*This* place will definitely be allowing birds in.'

Goodie put her hands on her hips and scowled at him. 'Will take man like you second to put monkey suit on; for me is as complicated as finding and defusing an anti-personnel mine in a hurricane.' Goodie's irritation had thickened her Russian accent, proving to Sam that she was truly rattled.

'Careful, *myshka*,* your Russian's showing. You wouldn't want me to think he was getting to you, would you?'

Goodie scowled across at him. 'I wish I could wipe your memory of everything I told you in that bunker.' Sam knew very well that if Goodie had not been convinced both of them were going to be executed when their mission failed and they were captured by a Colombian drug cartel eight years ago, that she would *never* have told him so much of her past. It was down to her that the worst long-term physical damage he'd come out of it with was his scarred cheek; she'd saved his life. He owed her; she could trust him to keep her secrets, she knew that; but that didn't mean he couldn't bait her when they were alone. 'Don't call me that again. Of course, the arrogant prick's not getting to me; I just don't want to be trussed up like a turkey. You guys never have to do this for work.'

'You sure? Seems to me like *you* might be getting to *him*: wanting me to check on you, wanting to know who was protecting you. Took all I had to keep a straight face on in there. I was tempted to tell him what you did to those Colombians in the compound after we were captured; that would have shut him up quick smart.'

'Bugger off,' Goodie told him, then muttered a few choice insults in Russian.

'Watch yourself or I'll tell Katie you threw away those chocolate brownies she sent you.'

'I was not risking another gastric assault from your wife,' Goodie said, shuddering at the reminder of the last piece of Katie's sponge cake she had shovelled unsuspectingly into her mouth and nearly choked on. It wasn't as if Goodie was even fussy; she'd happily eaten the unidentifiable, foul-smelling 're-fried beans' from the rat-infested establishments in deepest darkest Guatemala, and the raw baby octopus, *sannakji*, in Korea, which kept moving even after being chopped up. But anything produced by Sam's wife, especially in the cake line, was likely to be worse. 'Don't you tell her that, you bastard,' Goodie added quickly, and Sam smiled: there were very few people Goodie cared about but Katie was definitely one of them.

Goodie huffed and puffed but eventually, she did disappear to her room to get ready. When she came out half an hour later Sam blinked, rubbed his eyes, and blinked again.

Goodnight

'Holy Christ,' he muttered, and Goodie shot him a warning look.

'You've seen me dressed up before,' she told him, slipping on her heels and then searching around for her clutch bag. (Instead of the standard lipstick and mascara most women would carry, Goodie's bag contained a knife and pepper spray.) Yes, Sam had seen her dressed up. However, she was normally posing as something less savoury than a woman attending a posh charity ball where each ticket was worth over five thousand pounds. So Sam had never seen Goodie wearing a dress like the long, black, elegant, backless one she was wearing now; never seen her face made up with care and to perfection; never seen her short hair swept back from her face and secured stylishly at the back of her head. She handed him a familiar pot of skin-coloured cream and he stood up to take it.

'Where are your weapons?' he asked after he'd started the process of covering up the scars on Goodie's back and shoulders. She showed him the contents of her bag and then pulled the long slit at the side of her leg to the side to reveal a discreet holster on her upper thigh with a knife and a small handgun attached. Sam nodded, then watched as she stepped into four-inch heels that looked like some sort of torture device for feet. He almost felt sorry for that rich bastard now.

∼

'Ed, you look fine,' muttered Nick impatiently. 'Seriously, we've got to go.'

'Can't you just potter off to this one without me?' Ed said in a small voice. 'There's no way I'll fit in somewhere proper posh like that.'

Nick sighed, eyeing Ed's lanky form in his ill-fitting suit and his mass of uncontrollable chestnut hair. 'Of course, you'll fit in,' he lied smoothly. 'Anyway, you're a bloody genius; who cares what you wear?' Ed shifted uncomfortably whilst Nick adjusted the cufflink on his own tux; in contrast, his was perfectly fitted, as you would expect from Savile Row. On reflection he should have thought about taking Ed to a tailor himself, but how was he to know that Ed would opt for the Marks & Spencer disaster his mum had bought him a few years ago. Well, it was too late now. 'Come on, mate, you can do this, okay? There's going to be all sorts of people there interested in your advances and we need to get it out there – the time for lurking in the shadows is over, my friend.' Nick herded him out the door and to the lift. He was so focused on making sure Ed actually made it out of the flat that he didn't see her until she slipped into the lift after them, and that was when his brain shut down.

'Oh, hi, Goodie,' Ed mumbled, more intent on fiddling with his sleeves to try to get them to reach his wrists than taking in the woman standing next to them. Goodie gave him a curt nod (they were all now used to the non-verbal responses she employed wherever possible), and after a few more seconds she flicked a glance over to Nick.

Nick was frozen. He knew there was something he should be doing now but unfortunately, he could not for the life of him take his eyes off the blonde woman standing beside him, from the sweeping lines of her dress to her long lashes and smoky eye shadow highlighting the almost unnatural bright blue of her eyes. In all his years having to attend these poxy events, he'd never been more grateful for the dress code. Goodie frowned at his paralyzed state and leaned across him to press the lift button. Ah, yes, Nick thought; that was the something he was supposed to do. He shook his head to clear it and dragged his eyes away from her, only to keep glancing back. He noticed again the tension in her frame as the doors closed, and he wished for the millionth time he knew why.

'No Salem?' he asked into the suffocating silence, his voice slightly strangled for some reason.

'With Sam,' she told him as the doors swept back and she walked out into the lobby, her heels clicking on the tiles. Nick's mouth fell open; her entire back was exposed. He was suddenly torn between praising the Lord for the invention of backless dresses and wanting to rip his own jacket off to cover her. The thought of every last person in the ballroom being party to the view he had right now made a curious flash of rage shoot through him and his face flush red. Maybe he was coming down with something. After a few paces, she stopped and turned; this was the routine over the last two weeks – she would walk out, check the area, then allow Nick to walk on past her and follow behind. When he didn't move she put her hands on her hips, a slight frown marring her perfect features. Although he could feel her irritation, he knew she wouldn't say anything, what with the whole invisible-presence thing seeming to extend to any unnecessary speech on her part. Ed shuffled out of the lift still fiddling, this time with his belt, and then looked back at Nick.

'Uh ... you coming or what?' Ed asked him. 'This *was* your sodding idea.'

Nick jerked back to full consciousness. 'Right ... yes, let's ...' he looked over at Goodie for a moment and again lost his train of thought.

'You all right, mate?' Ed asked, trying to flatten his hair with little noticeable effect. 'Maybe we shouldn't go if you're not firing on all cylinders – it's not like I'll be able to handle that crowd on my own; I'd make a right pig's ear of it.'

'I'm fine, Ed,' Nick snapped, dragging his eyes from Goodie and striding forward. 'And stop bloody fidgeting.'

All the way over in the limo Ed seemed to be getting more and more worked up. He was twisting in his seat, pulling at his clothes, and chewing his lip so hard he'd nearly split it.

'Ed, calm down,' Nick told him for what felt like the hundredth time, unable to keep the frustration from his voice.

'I can't just calm down 'cause you keep growling it at me, you bastard; that's not how panic attacks work. This is ridiculous; I'm going home.'

'We're here now, you freak, no going back,' Nick told him firmly as the limo joined the queue outside the Savoy.

'Shit, shit, shit,' muttered Ed, his eyes taking on a wild look as he searched for a means of escape. Each limo in front of them was moving on smoothly and the queue was rapidly diminishing. It felt weird to actually be sitting in the back with Goodie for a change instead of driving his own car up front, even if she had separated herself as much as possible from them by perching on the backwards-facing seat opposite.

'Don't even think about it,' warned Nick as he watched Ed look longingly at the door handle nearest to him. 'The press can see us from there; you'd be eaten alive.'

'I'm going to be eaten alive anyway,' Ed replied, his voice breaking as if he were about to cry and his movements becoming more jerky and anxious as he stared out of the window at the beautiful, glamorous people disembarking from their cars. That's when Goodie moved. She had been looking out of her window doing the whole invisible-presence thing, but on hearing Ed's broken voice her head snapped around. She leaned forward into his personal space and placed her hands over his shaking ones to steady them and stop their fiddling.

Goodnight

'These people,' she told him in a low, fierce voice, 'they are *nothing*. Do you hear me?'

Ed nodded slowly, struck dumb by the unprecedented physical contact from Goodie.

'You are worth a thousand of them. You work *magic* with your science. You will *change the world*. This, this night, these people – to you they should be nothing. You use them to get what you need, and then you forget about them. They are but sand in your eye for a moment, do not let them stand in the way of what you want.'

Goodie slid back into her seat, withdrawing her hands from Ed's but keeping eye contact.

'I'm scared,' Ed whispered.

'There is no courage without fear,' Goodie told him before throwing open the door to an explosion of flashes from the waiting press. Once she was out of the car, Ed glanced at a shocked and silent Nick for a moment before squaring his shoulders and pushing out of the limo after her.

~

'Well, that's what we're hoping, Sir Talbot,' Nick said across the group he and Ed were standing in. 'Of course, driving energy prices down isn't going to be popular with everyone, but yes, that's the ultimate aim once we're up and running.' Somehow Nick had managed to manoeuvre a still-nervous-but-holding-it-together Ed into the exact group he'd wanted to discuss the project with. Sir Talbot was commissioner of the Energy Advisory Board, Ian Mowat ran a multi-billion pound Haulage Company and Irene Blake was the Minister for Energy. The more positive buzz these people heard about what they were trying to do, the better, as far as Nick was concerned.

'So, Mr Chambers.' All eyes in the circle swung to the tall, dark-haired woman who had just joined their group. Nick recognized her and wracked his brains to try to remember her name. He nudged Bertie, who was standing between him and Ed, but Bertie was staring spellbound at the woman with a vacant expression; not for the first time did Nick miss his ultra-efficient previous assistant, who would have already muttered the woman's name into his ear by now. 'It seems this idea will be making you and your company money. By all accounts, you have enough of *that* to be going on with as it is.' She had a slightly more pronounced Russian accent than Goodie and she was strikingly beautiful, her long, gold gown almost dazzling.

Nick inclined his head to agree. There was no point arguing that he had money; he'd worked hard for it. Her perfect, fire-engine-red lips smiled a smile that did not reach her eyes. 'What I would like to know is how this will benefit those who cannot afford energy? Is it only the privileged that will reap the rewards?'

'Good point, Miss ...'

'My name is Natasha Alkaev.'

'Of course, Miss Alkaev,' Nick said smoothly, causing Bertie to let out a small squeak as Nick stood on his foot. 'Forgive me, I don't know what I was thinking; of course, I recognize you.' Natasha laughed.

'Don't worry, Mr Chambers,' she said through a genuine smile now. 'I didn't peg you as the type to be perusing the pages of *Vogue* in your downtime.'

Nick smiled back; he was surprised by her; some of the supermodels he had dated would not have taken that slight so well. 'In answer to your question: yes, we hope this will benefit those most in need of electricity and power. As you may already be aware, the projects in Africa where merry-go-rounds were installed to power villages were not as successful as hoped. We think we can provide a better solution, given the access.'

Natasha's head was cocked to the side in a way that stirred something familiar in his mind, and she was listening intently. 'And underprivileged areas in other countries?'

'It is my hope, Miss Alkaev, as was my father's before me, that we can solve the energy crisis in all areas of need and do it in an environmentally sound way.'

'You talk a good game, Mr Chambers, and please call me Tasha.'

'I'm a determined man, Tasha.'

'He bally well is you know. Never known a chap work so hard,' Bertie boomed. In Nick's experience Bertie really only spoke in various different volumes of BOOM, whatever the company or situation. 'Fantastic at everything even at our old prep school, weren't you, Flopsy? Should have seen him on the rugby pitch; best damn winger Westminster ever saw.'

Nick sighed and looked down at his shoes for a moment. What possible bearing could his performance on the rugby field have to this discussion? And was it really necessary to let everyone know his prep-school nickname?

'Flopsy?' Irene Blake muttered, one eyebrow raised and a smile on her lips.

'It was because of my hair,' Nick said through a fixed smile, aiming a kick at Bertie's shin, which provoked another small squeak. 'Bert, mate, I'm not sure anyone's interested in ... ' Nick trailed off as he noticed he had lost Tasha's attention. Her gaze was fixed over Nick's shoulder, her eyes were wide and he could have sworn they were slightly glazed.

'Oh, I don't know,' Ian Mowat said from Nick's other side. 'Never does any harm to know a bloke's background.' Nick barely registered the words. He was watching as Natasha reached up with her right hand and laid it flat over the centre of her chest. Nick turned to see what she was focused on and saw Goodie standing a few feet behind him, her hand also flat over her chest and her eyes fixed on Natasha. Before he could comment, they both looked away as if they had never seen each other before, each focusing on their targets: Goodie on Nick, and Natasha on the circle of people around him.

* *MYSHKA* – LITTLE MOUSE

Chapter 6

Impossible to leave unsolved

Nick gritted his teeth. 'You told me "no problem". You said it would be *easy*. Where then is the goddamn report?' He was gripping the phone so hard his knuckles had turned white and he had the curious urge to throw it across the room.

'Well, it *was* easy – to get her cover story, that is, or should I say *stories*; because I've found no less than ten utterly convincing, completely credible backgrounds for the woman. All with the correct documentation, all with legit paper trails a mile long, all of which are complete bloody bullshit. Your girl is a ghost, mate: vapour.'

Nick rubbed his forehead. Harry Walker's firm was by far the best investigative agency in the country; they had never let him down before. Normally the backgrounds they provided for him were freakily thorough, listing friends from as far back as primary school, identifying their favourite foods, likes, dislikes, the cake their favourite Auntie makes them on Sundays: *everything*. For them to have come up with exactly *nothing* on Goodie was unbelievable. She was a human being, for Christ's sake, and they couldn't even confirm or deny that she actually purchased food on which to subsist. 'If she buys anything of importance, mate, it must be on "the dark web" or with cash,' Nick had been told. Nick did however have significant doubts that she would bother buying her biscuits on 'the dark web'; that is if she even ate biscuits. His fist thumped down on the table. Of course, she must eat biscuits; everyone eats biscuits.

'Got some info on that other bloke though; Sam Clifton, was it?' Nick's head shot up and his grip on the phone relaxed.

'Go on.'

'Ex-Special Forces: real Andy McNab type stuff. He left after being a hero in some sort of clusterfuck in Colombia. Partner in a security firm with his best mate now. Lives in south Wales, married, one kid, one on the way. Wife's a GP; and she – she can talk, believe you me.'

'Interesting,' Nick muttered.

'Oh, and your girl. She knows this couple well. Wife's face lit up when I mentioned her, described her as a "close family friend".' Nick frowned; he couldn't imagine that surly bastard with a family, and he definitely couldn't picture Goodie as a 'family friend'.

'That's great but I need more info on the girl. Keep digging.'

Walker sighed down the phone. 'Listen, Nick, you know how I love to take your money, but this is pointless; I'm getting nowhere. I'd have to actually go to Russia to even start to –'

'Go.' Nick cut him off.

'What?'

'Go to Russia.'

'I can't just swan off to Russia; I've got other cases here, I –'

'I'll double every fee in your caseload and pay it tomorrow if you concentrate on this one. I know you've got other guys who are capable of taking over whilst you go away.'

'You're a lunatic, you know that, right?' Walker chuckled.

'It's called eccentric, Walker. When you've got money it's

Goodnight

called being eccentric.' With that, Nick ended the call. At least if Walker was going to Russia it would feel like Nick was actually doing something to solve the mystery that was eating away at him. He'd told Walker that it was simply because she would have to be around his family that he wanted to know her history, but he knew that was just an excuse.

After the charity ball, he'd asked Goodie if she knew Natasha Alkaev. She'd showed absolutely no reaction to the question, merely staring at him as if weighing something up, after which she told him, 'I worked with her for a while a long time ago.' That was all she would say. And Nick noticed the significance of the word 'with'. In referring to her job as his security, she would always say she was working *for* him, not *with* him. It was a subtle difference but there was very little that got past Nick when he was paying attention, and when it came to Goodie he was definitely paying attention.

He'd told Walker about the look the two women had exchanged at the ball. Walker had paused for a moment and then asked: 'You sure you're all right, mate?' As if Nick was daft or something; and in some ways that assessment was pretty accurate. Who assumed there was a significant connection between two people who simply held each other's gaze a moment too long in a public place? And who hired private detectives to investigate their security staff? Hell, he knew that now was the absolute worst time for a distraction; until all the contracts were secured he needed to be on top of his game. But Goodie was a puzzle that for some reason he found impossible to leave unsolved. He rubbed his forehead again and then grabbed his briefcase before storming to his door and slamming it behind him.

'Where's Ed?' he blasted at Bertie, who had jumped up out of his seat at the slam of the door. This was another unwelcome change over the last few weeks: Nick was on edge. Gone was the easy-going charmer, replaced by an uptight, anally retentive pain in the arse.

'Uh ...'

'Bertie,' Nick said slowly, his patience hanging by a thread. 'You did tell Ed about the meeting? Please tell me he's out in reception.'

'Oh bollocks,' muttered Bertie, his red face turning even redder as he flailed around, going through the piles of papers on his desk.

'Bert!' Nick blasted, his patience completely gone. 'One thing ... *one thing* I expressly asked you not fuck up this week. You are the most useless –'

Nick stopped shouting as the door to the external office swung open and Goodie stepped through. She never came into the office unannounced or uninvited. Her eyes were cold and her mouth tight as she came to stand behind Bertie and crossed her arms over her chest.

'Blast,' Bertie said in a small voice. 'I really am a useless bugger, aren't I? No wonder Clive and the others think I'm just a big joke.' Goodie stared across at Nick, one eyebrow raised, her stance radiating disapproval, making Nick feel like a complete bastard without uttering a word.

'Oh buggeration,' Nick sighed, slumping down in the chair opposite his desk. 'I'm sorry, Bertie. You're not useless. You're just ... uh ...' Nick rubbed his neck, wracking his brain for a compliment. 'Look, you're a good bloke but maybe organizing and planning aren't your forte.'

'Well, what else is left, Nick? I've bally well ballsed up everything I've done so far.' His eyes dropped from Nick's and his voice got quieter. 'I know Mum begged you to give me a chance. I'm thirty-seven and my own mother had to find me a chuffing job.' Nick looked down at his shoes, lost for words and feeling increasingly guilty.

Goodnight

'Er ...' At Bertie's nervous laugh, he looked up. 'I don't mean to be rude to a lady but ... um ... what are you ...?' Goodie had moved Bertie's chair aside and was clicking on his mouse. His computer screen changed and instead of his screensaver (a picture of him and a couple of his more Bertie-like mates at a polo match, all with their collars turned up, wearing red trousers, Hunter wellies and wax jackets, and all chugging back their pints of beer), a graphic flashed up onto the screen. Nick blinked.

'Did the design guys finally come up with something decent?' he asked. For months they'd been trying to design a graphic to represent cold fusion and the energy company. The one currently moving on Bertie's screen was way better than anything Nick had seen so far.

'Oh ... um ... well, I was just messing about a bit. Thought I'd take the whole preserving-nature thing and ... well ... water and atoms and make it look somehow ...'

'It's beautiful,' Nick breathed. 'Jesus, Bertie, you didn't tell anyone you could do stuff like this.'

Bertie flushed and loosened his tie self-consciously. 'Oh ... well ... I don't know about any of that, old chap ... just ... well ... I did that graphic design course at uni.'

'You're an artist, Bertie,' Nick told him, smiling widely. 'I want this sent over to the design team immediately, we can get you working with them full time once Lisa gets back from maternity leave.'

'Gosh ... I ... golly ... are you ...?' Bertie had, Nick realized, gone into some sort of meltdown. He'd seen it before and knew that it mainly involved repeating increasingly posh words over and over and getting more and more red in the face. Nick looked up to try and catch Goodie's eye, but instead, he caught her looking down at Bertie, an almost soft expression crossing her features for a moment. When she did notice Nick looking at her, however, her face closed down again and she stepped back from Bertie's desk before turning towards the door to the reception.

'Uh, Goodie,' Nick called, standing to walk around Bertie's desk and giving him a congratulatory slap on the back on his way past, 'it's Easter this weekend.' Goodie turned to face him, re-crossing her arms over her chest and nodding. 'I've got to go home to Sussex for it.'

'Ah, yes!' Bertie exclaimed, in a much better mood now. 'Little jaunt down the old family pile, isn't it. Bit of time spent with Mater and Pater, you know. Can't wait, old boy.' Every year either Nick or Bertie's parents hosted Easter, and this year was Nick's family's turn.

'Address?' Goodie asked, not revealing whether staying in Sussex over Easter made any difference to her. As per usual not revealing anything at all.

'So ... um, you'll be coming?' Nick asked.

'You *are* still in need of a close protection officer,' Goodie told him, a hint of exasperation lacing her tone.

'I mean ... you don't have a family of your own to go to?' Nick asked, narrowing his eyes.

'I will send a team to check the location this week,' Goodie said, ignoring his question as she ignored all personal inquiries. 'I will have to be relatively close to you but I can maintain a discreet presence. Your family will barely notice I'm there.' Nick bit his lip. Goodie hadn't met his family. He thought the likelihood of her 'maintaining a discreet presence' with the bunch of nutters that would be at his mum and dad's over Easter was slim.

Just as he was about to say something to that effect, the outer door of the office flew open again and Ed's lanky frame burst through. Bizarrely he had on Bermuda shorts, a faded

Goodnight

Star Wars sweatshirt, flip-flops, and his laboratory goggles still perched on his forehead. 'Am I late?' he asked breathlessly.

Nick sighed. 'I've cancelled the meeting, Ed.' He couldn't be bothered to point out that even if Ed had been on time there was no way he could have met a potential client dressed the way he was, and Nick knew from bitter experience that any comments on Ed's outfits would fall on deaf ears.

'Is Mr Southern accompanying you for Easter, sir?' Goodie asked.

'Hurrah!' Bertie exclaimed. 'Capital idea! Eddie, old boy, you'll come on a jaunt to the country with us, won't you?'

'Uh?'

'It would make security easier, Mr Chambers,' Goodie put in. 'We work as a unit with Mr Southern's team, which is fine when you're all in London, but if you're separated by an entire county it would be more difficult.'

'Of course, you're welcome, Ed, but if you'd prefer to go back to your own family, then –'

'Mum and Dad won't mind. Doubt I'd get down to Essex anyway,' Ed said, his hand going up to his forehead, causing him to frown when he encountered the goggles as if he'd forgotten they were there. 'But a bit weird staying at your gaff, mate, no offence. And you might be a bit rammed if Goodie and the rest are going too.' Nick's mind flashed to the country estate and he suppressed a smile.

'We can fit you in, Ed; we've got plenty of spare rooms.'

'Well, I don't want your mum to have to cook for us all; bit of a cheek.'

'My mother hasn't cooked a meal for twenty years at least.'

'Uh ... crikey. You lot must be down the chippy a fair bit,' Ed said, and Nick smiled.

'Something like that, but honestly, Ed, just come back with

us. Until we get everything up and running we need to be as safe as possible.'

Ed shrugged. 'Well, if you're sure ...' He trailed off. 'Guess it's better than my bedsit.'

'Ed,' Nick said slowly, 'please tell me you've moved into the flat I got for you three months ago.'

'Um ...'

Nick rolled his eyes. Ed would live in a cardboard box and not take any notice as long as he could carry on working in the lab uninterrupted. 'I'll sort it for you.' Either Nick booked the moving company or Ed would be stuck in that dingy tower block for the rest of his life, no matter how much money was transferred into his bank account.

'Well, I must say,' Bertie boomed, 'this Easter is turning out to be a chuffing good spot of fun, isn't it? We can get a jolly game of charades going,' he went on, becoming more and more excited, 'or even twenty/ twenty-two and strip billiards if we're feeling frisky as the nights wear on.' Nick looked at Ed's blank face. Bertie may as well have been talking in a foreign language. Nick's mind flashed to his family, then added in Bertie's, in combination with a mostly-silent Goodie and a freaked-out Ed. It was going to be a long few days.

Chapter 7

You're a right topper

'WHAT HO!' BOOMED BERTIE.

'What ho!' boomed Nick's dad even louder.

Nick glanced back at Goodie whose expression remained unreadable. Ed, however, was staring up at the house, his mouth wide open.

'Guess you've likely got a spare room going then, mate,' murmured Ed by Nick's side. His eyes moved from the grand, stone, twenty-bedroom estate house to Nick's father and Bertie, who were engaged in the activity of slapping each other on the back and booming intermittently – both wearing red trousers and wax jackets. 'Jesus, you're all dead posh. I'm going to look like a right plonker staying here. What were you thinking, you daft article?'

'Ed, you knew this already,' Goodie said.

'Right, okay ... this one's got a posh accent, I'll give you that,' Ed replied, indicating Nick. 'No offence, fella,' he added for his benefit, and Nick gave him an amused nod. 'And Bertie ... well, I just thought he was ... well, he's inexplicable. To be honest I assumed he was barmy, not bloody aristocracy. Tell me the rest of your family aren't as bad as Bertie?'

'No,' Nick told him, and he relaxed for a moment before Nick added, 'they're worse.'

'What ho!' Nick's father interrupted, giving his son a hug and a few hearty slaps on the back, which no doubt would leave bruises. 'Damn good to see you, Flopsy. It's been too long since you've been out to the sticks. Your mother worries, you know.'

'Hello, old man.' Nick smiled as he hugged him back with a few back slaps of his own. "Your mother worries" was his father's repressed way of saying "I've missed you". 'Dad, this is Ed Southern; Ed, this is my dad: Monty. And this is ...' Nick looked around for Goodie but she was nowhere to be seen. He frowned.

'Great stuff!' boomed Monty, grabbing hold of Ed's hand and nearly lifting him off his feet with the violence of his shakes. 'Always good to add in some fresh blood to a family do. And I hear you're a frightfully clever chap too; you'll be keeping the old duffers like me on my toes.'

'Uh ...' Ed looked at a complete loss.

'Jolly good, jolly good,' boomed Nick's dad.

'Goodness, *the* Ed at last,' Nick's sister, who had just come bounding out of the house to stand next to her father, put in. Her long legs were clad a pair of jodhpurs with riding boots, and her dark hair and her wool jumper were lightly dusted with straw. A miniature version of her, in a nearly identical outfit, was clinging onto her hand and hiding under her jumper. 'I must say I've been terribly impressed by all this science stuff; total dunce with that sort of thing, aren't I, Flopsy?'

'Hi, Tils,' Nick said as he almost went back onto one foot with the force of her hug.

'Uncle Nicky!' The straw-covered, dark-haired little girl

Goodnight

emerged from out of her mother's jumper and wriggled in between them, giving Nick's legs a crushing squeeze.

'Hey, hedgehog,' Nick said, reaching down for her and settling her on his hip.

'You can't call me hedgehog,' she told him, snuggling into his neck. 'I'm *nine*, Uncle Nicky. You called me that when I was a curled-up baby.'

'You'll always be my hedgehog,' he said blowing a raspberry into her neck and causing her to squirm her way down. Introductions were made, involving fierce hugs and cheek kisses from Tils, and shy smiles from her daughter Arabella. Ed was looking at Tils with such an awestruck expression that Nick almost laughed out loud. She was like a force of nature.

'By Jove,' Monty said as he looked over Nick's shoulder. 'Who is that?'

Nick turned to see Goodie pulling some equipment out of the car.

'Ah, yes, now listen, Dad, Tils – it might be an idea if –'

'What ho there!' Monty boomed, and Nick sighed in defeat, his dad having already pushed him aside to stride up to Goodie, curiosity written all over his features. 'Now, you must be the lady who's been keeping my Flopsy safe for the last few weeks. I simply must tell you that I think you're a ... well, that's to say ...' To Nick's shock, Monty's eyes glazed over for a minute and when he spoke again his voice was suspiciously gruff. '... you're a right topper. Can't thank you enough. Really, really great work and all that. Big weight off my mind, if I'm honest.'

And just like that, all Nick's irritation with his father for going behind his back to organize the security team vanished. His dad had been worried; fear and worry were still written all over his features. Monty then proceeded to actually hug

Goodie, and was joined a moment later by a tearful Tils and an excited Arabella. Goodie allowed this but remained frozen in place until they released her, all except Arabella, who stayed attached to her legs like a limpet.

'You saved my Uncle Nicky,' Arabella whispered, tilting her head back to look up at her.

Just how much was reported back to his family? Nick wondered in annoyance; the last thing he'd wanted was for them to know about the alley incident.

Goodie looked down at Arabella and her face softened as she tentatively stroked her head.

'Your uncle can look after himself,' she said, and Arabella frowned.

'But you're like a superhero,' she breathed. 'Mummy told me.'

'Yes, sugarplum, she is,' Tils said in a shaky voice, and Goodie's head came up to look at her. Tils gave her a silent nod of thanks, which Goodie returned.

'Oh my goodness!' Arabella shouted suddenly. 'Is that your dog?' Goodie turned as Salem bounded up to her side and then immediately sat next to her, ears pricked, eyes forward, not moving a muscle. 'Can I pet him?' Goodie nodded again and gave Arabella a small smile before Arabella embarked on her version of 'petting', which involved throwing oneself bodily onto the dog, hugging him around his middle and shoving your face into its hair. Salem allowed this but looked to Goodie for permission. Goodie made a hand gesture and Salem licked the length of Arabella's face, causing her to giggle and give the dog another squeeze.

'Xavier!' Arabella shouted, and Nick watched the fat, snorting pug waddle around his car and right up to Salem before head-butting him in the chest, this being Xavier's form

Goodnight

of affection. Salem nosed the squirming little body and in return his muzzle got covered in a layer of Xavier's copious drool; he then cast a long-suffering look up to his mistress, whose eyes were dancing with amusement at the sight of the ridiculous-looking dog.

'Where's Mum?' Nick asked, tearing his gaze away from the new version of Goodie with some effort.

'Blasted nuisance but your mother and your Aunt have been roped into this dashed flower-arranging for the Easter service,' Monty told him. 'Left us to scramble about for some provisions afternoon-tea-wise, but I expect we'll get by with the help of the indomitable Mrs B. Come on everybody, chop-chop.'

Monty turned and started walking up to the house. Afternoon tea was enough of a draw that Arabella and Bertie went bounding after him. Nick grabbed his bag from the front seat and started walking up behind Ed. He thought Goodie would follow behind him, but when he turned to check, the driveway was empty other than the still snorting and drooling Xavier. He sighed and continued on to the house.

Goodie watched from the shadows as Nick's body turned and his eyes swept the area. She'd noticed how much more relaxed he became even on approaching the house. Of course he was still wearing his sharply cut suit as one last meeting had been squeezed into the morning before they left, but for once his face was not totally clean-shaven. His strong jaw was shadowed with stubble that usually didn't appear until early evening, and he'd loosened his tie: not big changes, you might think, but Goodie, whose very survival often relied on her ability to observe others, knew that they were significant. And quite possibly she had never observed anyone as closely as she did Nick.

She didn't understand him at all. He was beautiful, in fact he may well have been the most beautiful man she'd ever laid eyes on; he was intelligent, sharp-witted and a skilled negotiator; his appearance was immaculate, his tall, lean but well-muscled body (yes, she'd sneaked peeks at him topless on his treadmill at his massive flat) was always clad in perfectly cut, exquisite suits as he was always having meetings, making deals, accumulating more wealth and power; but despite these high standards for himself he was remarkably tolerant. In Goodie's experience, powerful men did not employ incompetent people, even if they were family; they didn't put up with them full stop. But Nick was patient with Bertie. Other than that outburst in the office, Goodie hadn't heard him shout at Bertie once before. Goodie, who had spent much of her life protecting the vulnerable, had expected to have to step in; but all it took was a small nudge for Nick to see Bertie's potential and change his demeanour completely.

Then there was Ed. How many multi-millionaires would have the patience and the belief in a man as eccentrically brilliant as Ed to take his crazy ideas and turn them into real possibilities? It wasn't even just Ed and Bertie; Nick's workforce simply loved him. He was not a dictator from on high with them, they didn't call him Sir or Mr Chambers; they *joked* with him, they *teased* him, with no detectable fear of retribution. And Nick was funny. He laughed easily and his dry, often self-deprecating sense of humour had almost on many occasions made Goodie herself lose her composure; something that never happened to her.

Not ever.

She set off into the woods on the outskirts of the property to find the far guards.

'Nice try,' Sam muttered as he turned around on hearing Goodie and Salem's approach. 'You're never going to be able to sneak up on me with that big beast in tow.' Salem trotted up to his side and bumped his hand to get a head scratch.

'Perimeter secure?'

'Yeah, well, it's a pretty isolated location. House is elevated on a hill. We've laid out a wire – should know if anything bigger than Flopsy or Cottontail crosses it.'

Goodie's mind flashed to Monty affectionately calling Nick Flopsy, and then to the look in his eyes when he thanked her for saving Nick's life.

'I need to swap with Ed's close protection officer. I'd be better out here as one of the far guards.'

Sam frowned. 'What are you on about? We agreed: Geoff should join Mike and me at the perimeter. You're better to stay close.' Goodie clenched her fists by her sides.

'This ... this is bullshit plan,' she told him, her Russian accent thickening.

'Goodie,' Sam said slowly. 'You know that the best operative should stay as the close protection officer, and I know you know who that is. Don't *you* bullshit *me*.'

Goodie looked away from him for a moment and Salem, sensing her distress, came and leaned against her leg.

Sam watched the dog and then looked at Goodie's clenched fists before he spoke again, this time in a softer tone. 'What's this about, *myshka?*'

'Urgh! Don't call me that, you prick. All I'm thinking about is strategy.'

'Is something –' he frowned again and scratched his head '– are you ...? I mean, I may never have thought I would ask you this particular question, but is something ... *upsetting* you?' Goodie's eyes flashed with annoyance.

'Fuck off,' she spat at him before stalking back towards the house.

Sam watched her stiff, retreating back, a frown still marring his features. Something was wrong with Goodie. They'd experienced some extreme situations together in the past and he'd never seen her this rattled. Even after that bloodbath in Colombia, she'd shrugged and downed a few shots of vodka once they got back to base camp. Nothing affected her. Until now.

Chapter 8

You work for me

Nick stalked down the stairs and into the dining room.

'What ho, Flopsy,' Uncle Giles boomed, the volume only slightly reduced by the copious amounts of eggs and bacon stuffed into his mouth. 'Mrs B. outdid herself again this morning. Nothing like a full English to cure a squiffy head and dicky tummy. Afraid we were all a trifle blotto last night, reunion and all that.' Nick gave his uncle a reluctant smile before surveying the table. Everyone was tucking into breakfast, including Ed, who had settled in remarkably quickly. But, then again, his family was like that: they pulled people in, made them feel welcome, put them at ease. Nick had yet to meet anyone resistant to it ... well, that was if you didn't count Goodie. Goodie was the reason behind his stalking down the stairs rather than the usual saunter. He hadn't laid eyes on her since she met his family in the drive yesterday afternoon. For a close protection officer she was decidedly distant, and it was pissing him off. He didn't quite realize how much he had come to like her being in his line of sight most of the time over the last month.

'You look cross, Uncle Nicky,' Arabella informed him around a mouthful of pancakes. She already had straw in her hair; it wouldn't have surprised Nick if she had slept in the bloody stable.

'I'm not cross, hedgehog,' he told her, and she shook her head, causing straw to fall into Bertie's tea.

'Oh, sorry, Bertie,' Arabella said quickly, and to Nick's surprise she actually looked like she was braced for his reaction.

'Don't worry, Bels,' Bertie said, smiling, and ruffling her hair so that more straw fell into his tea. 'Straw laced with manure,' he took a long sip, 'adds to the flavour, don't you know.' She giggled and her shoulders relaxed. Bertie caught Nick's eye for a moment, frowned up at him, and gave a quick flick of his eyes in Arabella's direction as if to say, 'What was that?' Nick shrugged, deciding to keep a close eye on her over the next few days. But for now he needed to get back to his mission.

'Good morning, darling,' he heard from behind him, and turned to see his mum walk in holding a bowl of muesli and a cup of tea, closely followed by his Auntie Rose.

'Hi, Mum, Rose,' he muttered distractedly before giving them both a swift kiss on the cheek and moving towards the door. Unlike the rest of the family, his mother was not widely considered to be 'obnoxiously posh', in fact she had a very light West Country accent, was quiet and very maternal (which was reflected in the way she dressed: standard Mum uniform of matching jumper and cardy, and hair in a short style that rarely moved even in extreme weather conditions). His Dad had met her at one of the village fêtes and he'd said it was love at first sight. Claire March had not been quite so sure of her feelings for him (the obnoxiously posh bit took some getting used to), but he was nothing if not persistent. A year after they met she became Claire Chambers and that was that. Her family may

Goodnight

have been apprehensive at first but Nick's grandparents were soon all sucked into the Chambers family craziness, adding some much needed sanity to the mix.

'Are you looking for someone, darling?' she asked, and he paused at the door, turning to his mum and raising his eyebrows. She smiled at him, and then sat down next to her husband.

'It's just that if you were looking for someone my advice would be to start in the kitchen,' she said, her back turned to Nick, although he could still hear the smile in her voice.

∼

'WILL HE BE ALRIGHT WITH XAVIER'S FOOD, DEAR?' Mrs Beckett asked as she bustled around the kitchen getting a bowl and food for Salem. 'Spect he'll need a mite bit more though, given the size difference.' Goodie followed the direction of Mrs Beckett's gaze to see the pug's fat little body dancing around a long-suffering Salem and alternating between head-butting his undercarriage and drooling on his paws. But Salem didn't fool her; she'd seen him lick Xavier's head before they both fell asleep next to her last night; he was a sucker for this ridiculous snub-nosed ball of energy.

Goodie started to push up to standing. 'I will do it. Please don't go to any trouble over ...' She trailed off, then stilled as she felt Mrs Beckett's hand on her shoulder.

'I'm happy to do it, love,' Mrs Beckett said gently. 'Reckon you could do with some time in that chair and some caffeine before you start your day.'

Goodie was not used to other people taking care of Salem for her. She looked after him just like she looked after herself.

Just like she had done since she was nine.

The idea of someone else shouldering some of her responsibilities, in however small a way, was ... unsettling. To Goodie this house and the people in it were *all* unsettling, and she couldn't quite put her finger on why. She'd woken up this morning to the sounds and smells Mrs Beckett was creating, and to the low voices accompanying them. When she emerged into the kitchen she had come face to face with two middle-aged women. Neither showed surprise at her entrance, almost as if she was expected – *almost* as if they were waiting for her.

'Hello, dear,' one of the women had said, moving towards her, her expression cautious but warm. 'I'm Claire, Nick's mother. They call you Goodie, is that right?' Goodie nodded. 'I'm grateful to you for looking after my boy.'

Goodie shrugged. 'I didn't do –'

'I know what you did, love.' Claire cut her off, then Goodie stiffened as she moved further into her personal space as if to hug her. Taking in Goodie's defensive stance, Claire slowed her approach and reached for Goodie's hand instead, giving it a quick squeeze before releasing it. 'So, do you eat breakfast?' she had asked, breaking the tense atmosphere. Goodie nodded slowly. 'Great, because Mrs Beckett here makes a mean bacon and eggs. Word of warning though – don't try to call her by her first name; the most informal she'll tolerate is Mrs B.'

'If you had a first name like mine you wouldn't want to be called it either,' Mrs Beckett put in, glaring at Claire. 'Anyway Beckett reminds me of my husband George, God rest his soul.'

Goodie looked over at the other woman's kind face; she was a little heavier and taller than Nick's mother and was wearing an apron with the message 'Hot stuff coming through!' on the front.

'Master Nicky got this for me,' Mrs Beckett said, having noticed Goodie's gaze dropping down. 'He's a one, isn't he, Claire; got me a whole assortment of these over the years, each

Goodnight

one cheekier than the last. Now, come and sit down, let me fuss you.'

And so, for the first time in her life, Goodie was fussed over, and for some reason she allowed it. Claire had asked if she would come up to have breakfast in the dining room, which had confused Goodie; why would they want her up there? These English people were crazy. Claire just smiled at her refusal before giving Mrs Beckett a side hug as she fried bacon at the stove, and then she turned to leave.

'Where the bloody hell have you been?' Goodie stared at a bristling Nick framed by the kitchen doorway. She'd never actually seen him without a suit on and was disappointed that even wearing jeans and a jumper he was still mind-numbingly beautiful. She stared at him, keeping her expression neutral.

'Here,' she said simply, taking another sip of her coffee.

'Want some more coffee, Nick-Nack?' Mrs Beckett asked as she came in from the dog's room.

'No, don't worry, I'm ...' Nick trailed off as something behind Mrs B. caught his eye. 'What the hell?' he muttered as he strode over to the door which Mrs Beckett had just exited, and threw it open. Goodie watched as his gaze swept the room, his body locking with tension. When he turned to face her, she realized that he was stiff with rage.

'Where did you sleep?' he asked in a low, dangerous voice.

Goodie stared at him again before inclining her head towards the dog's room. From the angry vibes he was giving out and his furious scowl, Goodie was guessing he had seen the blanket she had slept on next to the dogs last night, and for some reason he was not impressed by the arrangement.

'We've got spare bedrooms coming out of our ears, Goodie. Why in the fu–?' Nick broke off, flicking an almost nervous glance to Mrs Beckett who had crossed her arms over her ample chest. Goodie stifled a laugh; she would put money on the fact that Mrs Beckett had been a fixture at this house since Nick was a child, and the fact that he was unwilling to swear in front of her was testament to that and kind of ... sweet. *Sweet?* When had Goodie thought anything was *sweet* in recent memory? She frowned; he was confusing her again. 'Why on earth did you choose to sleep on the goddamn floor?'

Goodie pushed back in her chair and stood slowly from the table, keeping her gaze focused on Nick's furious brown eyes the whole time. 'You forget,' she told him, 'I am here to do a job.'

Nick threw up his arms in frustration and let out an angry breath. 'You can do your job and sleep in a *bed* for Christ's sake.'

'Nick-Nack!'

'Sorry, Mrs B.,' he muttered, and Goodie had that ridiculous urge to laugh again.

'I assessed the perimeter of the grounds yesterday, and then I assessed the security around the house. This back entrance to the kitchen is the weakest point. If I were looking for a way to get in, that is where I would start. With me sleeping at the entrance it is secure. This is *me* doing *my job*. You will note that I do not tell you how to do yours. I would appreciate the same courtesy.'

Both Nick's hands went to his hips. 'I'll not have you sleeping on the floor with the bloody dogs.'

'That is not your decision to make.'

'Urgh!' Nick huffed. 'You are literally the most stubborn woman I have ever met.'

'I'm not surprised,' Goodie returned, her lip curling.

'What do you mean by that?'

'Nothing,' she said, forcing her expression back to neutral; she didn't know why she was letting him affect her like this.

Goodnight

She didn't *do* angry exchanges with clients. In general she didn't reveal any emotion at all if she could help it.

'Bullshit.'

'Nick!'

'Sorry, Mrs B.'

She shrugged and turned away from him.

'You're scared to tell me what you meant, aren't you?' he said, skirting the table to approach her. Her eyes snapped back to his and she felt her temper rise.

'If you must know, I am not surprised you find me more difficult than the other women of your acquaintance. I'm quite sure that when it comes to you they are *very* accommodating. But you're not dealing with one of your simpering little idiots now, you arrogant *zhopa*;* I have a job to do and I am going to do it in the way *I* choose.'

Nick stared at her and narrowed his eyes. He was so close she could feel his breath on her face and smell his clean, masculine scent. For a moment her mind went blank.

∽

NICK WATCHED AS GOODIE'S PUPILS DILATED AND HER breathing grew shallow. It was subtle, but he knew he was affecting her. For a brief second she looked a little lost, as if she couldn't understand what was happening.

'Goodie,' he called softly, and she nodded without breaking eye contact. He took a risk and brought his hand up to the side of her face to cup her jaw, his thumb going to the small crescent scar next to her eye and his fingers sliding into her silky hair. 'I don't want you to sleep on the floor.' She frowned slightly, as if she wasn't following the thread of the conversation. 'What will it take for you to sleep in one of the bedrooms?'

'An alarm system that covers the perimeter of the entire

house, with motion sensors at every door and window, a direct line to me, the far guards and the central office.' Her eyes were still locked with his, and she spoke automatically, as if she wasn't even really aware of what she was saying.

'Right,' he muttered, his face descending even closer to hers.

'Ahem.' He heard Mrs Beckett clear her throat when his mouth was literally a hair's breadth from Goodie's, and he closed his eyes in frustration. He loved Mrs B.; she was a most excellent woman, but her timing was atrocious. Goodie blinked and took a frenzied step back, smacking straight into one of the chairs. Her face was clouded with anger and maybe even fear until she reined it in. Nick had never seen her in the least bit clumsy before; she was always so composed, her movements always controlled. But yes, he affected her, that much she couldn't hide. One side of his mouth hitched up in a lopsided grin and the fear in Goodie's expression was replaced entirely with anger. Mrs B. turned back to the stove, but not before she gave Nick a disapproving look. He winked at her and reached into his back pocket to pull out his phone.

'Conner? ... Right, need you to set up an alarm system at the country house ... High spec, best you can get ... no, no that's not good enough; it's got to be today. I don't care if it's Easter weekend.' Nick frowned as his head of security in London banged on about all the reasons they couldn't do any installation today: things like delivery times, workforce, transport. Nick rolled his eyes; if he still had his old, eminently competent assistant and not Bertie, *she* would be dealing with this crap right now.

'Conner,' Nick said again, his tone now a good deal firmer, 'I want this done *today*. I don't care how much it costs; keep throwing numbers around until you get results ... whatever, okay? Right, good. I'll expect someone here by lunchtime.'

Goodnight

He disconnected the call and searched the kitchen for Goodie. She was standing next to Salem at the door to the dog's room, as far from him as she could get without actually leaving the room. For the first time since Nick had managed to tempt Salem with a biscuit he was baring his teeth at him, his ears flattened against his head. Nick knew it wasn't just Goodie's anger Salem was reacting to: the dog could smell the fear in the air. Nick slowly returned his phone to his pocket and took a step towards her. Salem gave a low growl and he stopped in his tracks, lifting both his hands palm up.

'You are crazy man,' Goodie said, her Russian accent stronger now. 'You already have an alarm system. The only weak point is here. I can easily sleep here. You think I haven't slept in worst places?' Her voice lowered almost to a whisper. 'You have no idea the places I've slept in before, the conditions I've survived. Don't patronize me. This –' she threw her hand out to the dog's room '– this is nothing to me.'

'I don't care what conditions you slept in before,' Nick said slowly, holding her gaze and crossing his arms over his chest. 'You'll not sleep on the goddamn floor in *my* house. It's time you realized that *you* work for *me*.' Goodie's eyebrows went up at that. 'And you will do as I say.' Her mouth opened to speak but he cut her off. 'Now, I was led to believe that you are my *close* protection officer. Since I've not laid eyes on you for the last –' he checked his watch '– sixteen hours, I'd say that was a very loose interpretation of that job title.' By this stage Goodie's slight frame was literally vibrating with anger, her face flushed red. Nick was so enthralled by the absence of her emotionless mask that he decided to push his luck. 'You will be joining my family today. You will be having meals with us and you will be spending time with us. This invisible presence bullshit ends right now.'

'I will do my job as I see fit.'

79

'You'll do as I say ... that is unless you're *scared* to spend time with my family.' Her sharply indrawn breath of outrage almost made him smile. 'After all, I do realize that we can be a little intimidating en masse; but I wouldn't have pegged you as the type to worry about –'

'Fine,' Goodie snapped. 'Whatever you say, *sir*.'

Nick clenched his jaw. He'd let that go.

For now.

Chapter 9

Camouflage

'AH! TILS, DARLING. YOU LOOK RAVISHING AS ALWAYS,' Clive said through a smile that was just that little bit too wide.

They were in the drawing room and it was four o'clock, which in the Chambers household meant afternoon tea. Mrs Beckett and Nick's mum had brought out all manner of food so far, and Nick knew this would only be the first wave. His dad and uncle were sitting together in their favourite armchairs, which were very conveniently placed for the coffee table piled high with food. Nick, Bertie and Clive were standing by the massive fireplace sipping their tea. Nick hadn't realized that Clive's relationship with his sister had progressed to the level where she would ask him for the Easter weekend, so his unexpected arrival that afternoon had been a surprise, and not an altogether good one.

'Oh gosh, Clive, don't be an idiot,' Tilly said as she breezed into the room, closely followed by a dishevelled, red-eyed but smiling Ed and a laughing Arabella. 'I still haven't changed since doing the horses.' She gave Clive a kiss on the cheek through a mouthful of sandwich and Clive smiled at her, but

Nick could see his jaw was tight for some reason and his eyes had flashed at the 'idiot' comment. Clive could dish it out, but he had always had a problem taking it when it came to being teased.

'I took Eddie to see the horses, Uncle Nicky,' Arabella said proudly, skirting Clive to get to the sandwiches. 'He said he'd never even patted a horse before in his *entire life*. Can you imagine?' Arabella's face was totally aghast, as if a life without horses was a fate worse than death.

'I think we've remedied that one now, kid,' Ed said, ruffling Arabella's hair and giving her a wink.

'But Ed, I thought you said you were allergic to horses and more than a little scared of them,' Nick said, his lips twitching.

'Arabella has her own special brand of flooding therapy,' Ed told him. 'I've brushed a horse …'

'Groomed.'

'Sorry, Bels, I mean I've *groomed* a horse, I've fed a horse, I've shovelled a horse's crap, I've even sat on a horse.'

'He's cured!' Arabella shouted, smiling and throwing her hands in the air. Nick took in Ed's red-rimmed eyes and slightly swollen, mottled face, and pressed his lips together.

'Yes, well,' Tils said, her voice shaking with suppressed laughter. 'He was only bitten *once* I suppose, and Merlin didn't *quite* manage to throw him off, so I'm sure he's much more keen on horses now, darling.'

Ed was smiling at Tils. It was obvious to Nick why he had endured his equine torture session. He'd been in Tils and Arabella's company for only twenty-four hours now, but it appeared that he was firmly under their spell. Clive must have also noticed the way Ed was looking at Tils, and he wasted no time in reaching out and pulling her into him to plant a possessive kiss on the side of her head. Ed looked away quickly from this display and hurried over to the coffee table to grab a cake.

Goodnight

'Alright, squirt?' Clive said to Arabella, giving her a forced smile.

'Fine thanks,' Bels returned in a small voice, retreating from him and her mother to the other side of the room to stand next to her grandfather and her great-uncle. Nick frowned. The way Bels shrank away from Clive seemed odd; she was a very outgoing child. He glanced at Goodie and noticed that she was staring at Clive; then her gaze dropped to Clive's hand on Tils's shoulder, where Nick could see he had Tils in an almost white-knuckle grip. She eventually caught Clive's eye but he looked away from her cold, unblinking expression quickly.

'So, Goodie, how does a girl like you get involved in the security gig?' Clive asked, his grip on Tils's shoulder easing. 'Seems an odd choice for someone of your build.'

'Odd in what way?' she asked, her expression neutral.

'Well, don't you need to have a bit of muscle behind you in your business?'

'Yes.'

'Well ... well, I mean ...' Clive waved a hand in Goodie's direction to illustrate his point. 'You're not exactly Goliath.'

'Correct me if I'm wrong but didn't David win?' Goodie asked, her head cocked to the side. Clive huffed out an annoyed breath.

'You know what I'm getting at. Surely you'd be at a disadvantage in hand-to-hand combat.'

'You think that because I am smaller than you I am weaker?' Goodie asked, her tone sounding curious rather than confrontational.

'It's just a matter of simple physics,' Clive told her. 'I can't think what would possess a woman to go into your field to be honest.'

Goodie smiled at him, but it was so cold that Nick actually had to hold back a shiver. 'No, I imagine you can't,' she said, taking a step back and then skirting around the group to walk over to Arabella.

'You're crazy if you ask me, mate,' Clive said under his breath to Nick, who was staring across the room watching Goodie squat down in front of Arabella. She had pulled a silver coin out of her pocket and was making it flip over and over on top of her fingers before making it disappear and reappear behind Arabella's ear. 'Wouldn't want a dolly-bird managing my security if I was being threatened left, right and centre.' Arabella was giggling now as she attempted the same trick under Goodie's guidance.

'From what I've seen she can handle herself, Clive,' Nick said levelly. He wondered how he had missed the low-level misogyny Clive tended to spout.

'Alright, Whitney,' Clive sneered, annoyed that his friend wasn't instantly agreeing with him.

'Careful, mate,' Nick said, turning away with reluctance from Goodie and Arabella and fixing Clive with a stare.

'God!' Clive huffed, lifting his hands up in surrender. 'What's happened to you? Can't take a bit of ribbing all of a sudden? You make that joke yourself all the bloody time. I don't care what you say; she wouldn't stand a chance against any decent-sized man. You're nuts if you think she's your best option.'

∼

'I. WILL. NOT,' ARABELLA BIT OUT, HER FACE FLUSHED with anger.

'Oh come on, darling,' Tils said, making another grab for her hand. 'You just can't stay in your jodhpurs for tonight. You promised. Please. Just this once,' she cajoled. Clive was shifting impatiently next to them, rubbing the back of his neck and staring up at the ceiling. The three of them were at the bottom of the stairs that Goodie and Salem were coming down. They hadn't heard her approach – even in heels Goodie could be silent when she wanted to. Tils was wearing a fairly functional black dress which looked like it had been chosen in a hurry. Her eye make-up was smudged and her dark hair was haphazardly pinned on top of her head but she was still stunningly beautiful – like a feminine version of Nick: tall, long limbs, elegant.

'Stop pandering to the little brat,' Clive bit out, and Tils gave him a sharp look. 'Drag her upstairs and force her to get changed. This is a pointless waste of time.' What Goodie saw next stopped her in her tracks. Clive reached down and closed his large hand around Tils's slim forearm, dragging her upright from her squat in front of Arabella forcibly. Goodie caught a wince of pain in Tils's expression, and when she looked at a wide-eyed Arabella she knew she wasn't the only one who saw it. Tils yanked her arm out of Clive's grip.

'Just go in without us, Clive,' she hissed at him. Clive threw his hands up the air in exasperation and Goodie saw Tils flinch.

'Arabella,' Goodie called from her position halfway up the stairs, and three sets of surprised eyes turned to look up at her. 'Why don't you come with me? You can show me your room. Maybe there's something you wouldn't mind wearing? You would make your babushka happy.'

Arabella started climbing the stairs towards Goodie, who stretched out a hand.

'What's babushka?' she asked.

'It is how we say grandma in Russia,' Goodie told her as Arabella's small hand slipped into hers. Goodie turned to look at Tilly, who mouthed 'Thank you' as she backed away down the corridor. Clive paused for a minute at the bottom of the stairs. Goodie thought he was going to say something until she heard Salem vibrate with a low growl. Clive's gaze snapped to the dog, whose teeth were bared, and backed away to follow Tils.

'What's wrong with Salem?' Arabella asked as they walked up the stairs.

'Salem is picky,' Goodie explained. 'He doesn't like some people.'

'Me too,' Arabella muttered darkly.

When they reached her room, Arabella stopped in the doorway and pointed an accusing finger at the offending items of clothing she had been so adamant not to wear: a sailor dress and white tights. She was eyeing it like it was a MRSA-covered sackcloth. 'I am not wearing that.'

Goodie shrugged.

'Find something you will wear that your babushka would like for the party.'

'She only likes skirts and dresses on little girls. It's not fair. I don't want to wear stuff like that.'

Goodie gently pulled her into the room and sat on the bed next to the dress, facing away from the doorway and patted the space next to her. Arabella jumped up onto the bed, tilted her jaw at a stubborn angle and crossed her arms over her chest.

'I do not like these things either,' Goodie told her. Arabella let her arms drop and looked up at Goodie with a confused expression.

'But you're wearing a dress,' Arabella informed her. 'A really pretty dress.' Goodie nodded; her midnight-blue dress had a high neck, long sleeves and was close fitting to just above her knees where it flared out subtly. She knew it was beautiful; she knew her hair and make-up were perfect.

'I hate *this*,' she said, grabbing a handful of blue material, 'and this,' she indicated her face and hair, which was swept up

Goodnight

off her neck in an elegant style, 'with such intensity that sometimes I feel like they're actually burning my skin.'

Arabella's mouth dropped open and her eyes widened. 'But why do you wear them then?'

'In my job I have often had to wear clothes I dislike. I have been in outfits far, far worse than this. And I have had to also be ... nice to people I hate whilst wearing clothes I detest in places that made my skin crawl.'

'Why?' Arabella asked, her hand moving to stroke Salem's head as it rested on Goodie's knee.

'Sometimes I needed information from them. Sometimes it was to get closer to someone I needed to ... talk to. There are some reasons I cannot tell you, not just because you are a child, but because they are secret and, the type of secret they are means that if they were known it could hurt people.'

'Wow,' Arabella breathed. 'Really *secret*, secret then. But how can you stand to wear this stupid stuff if you hate it so much?'

'There are times where I have had to wear camouflage to blend into the natural environment. In a jungle this would be greens and browns, in the snow it was white. I wore that to get the job done, because it gave me an advantage, made me more powerful than my target; this is how I look at these clothes and this make-up: it is my camouflage, it gives me power.'

Arabella nodded. 'I like the idea of camouflage; that's cool.'

Goodie smiled and stood up from the bed. 'You'll change then?' Arabella nodded and jumped up to start toward her wardrobe, but stopped when Goodie laid a hand lightly on her arm. 'You know that nobody has the right to hurt you or your mother, don't you?'

'Yes,' Arabella said, turning to Goodie and tilting her curious face to the side.

'If that happens you tell *me*; understand? I saw you with a phone earlier. Have you got it with you?'

Arabella nodded, grabbing a stuffed polar bear off her bed and unzipping the back. 'Mummy got me this for when I use the bus from school. It's dead boring though; can't even get onto the internet or anything, just make calls.'

Goodie reached for the phone and Arabella handed it over.

'I am going to put my number into this. Do not use it unless you need to.' Goodie slipped it into the back of the polar bear and zipped it up.

'Okay,' Arabella agreed easily, her face lighting up at a new contact going into her phone.

Goodie smiled at her excited face, her heart clutching when she thought of Clive's fingers digging into Arabella's mother's arm. 'Now get dressed or we'll be late and disappoint your babushka.'

∽

NICK LEANT HIS HEAD BACK AGAINST THE WALL OUTSIDE Bella's room and closed his eyes. He had the almost overwhelming urge to punch something, but stifled this with the knowledge that Goodie would not have wanted him to overhear that particular conversation. He had insisted Goodie come to the party tonight just like he'd made her have her meals with his family and spend time with them over the last two days. He wasn't stupid; he could read between the lines of what Goodie was saying, and he was beginning to realize that her past might be a good deal darker than he had predicted.

Chapter 10

See someone you know?

NICK SAW HER FROM ACROSS THE ROOM AND MADE A beeline for her immediately. He could not believe she was here at his family's annual Easter party, of all places. For a moment he had a wild thought that she was here for Goodie, but then he noticed the man with his arm around the brunette's shoulders. A Russian oligarch had bought one of the estates nearby in recent months, and Nick's family had invited him as a welcome to the area.

Monty had visited the Russian's home last week and described it as: 'Bit more swish than when old Isaac Winthrope was living there, all very modern, acres and acres of marble. No clutter; not much *stuff* though.' Seeing as the entire interior of the Chambers' vast house was crammed with various *stuff* – from the overstocked library, to the ram-jam motley collection of paintings on the walls accumulated after decades of very ill-advised commissioned portraits – Nick wasn't surprised that a bit of minimalism would have struck his dad as alien. Luckily for Nick, this minimalist, super-rich Russian had accepted the invite to Nick's family's Easter party that they held every year, and he'd brought along Natasha Alkaev, of all people.

'Hello, Natasha,' Nick said smoothly, holding out his hand and smiling wide enough for his dimple to make an appearance – he knew from years of experience, starting at a surprisingly young age, that his smile and his dimple could invariably get him what he wanted. He noticed Dmitry Alexandrov tighten his grip around her waist and fix Nick with an assessing look; he was almost as tall as Nick and his hair was as dark as Natasha's but liberally sprinkled with grey.

'Mr Chambers,' Natasha said through her own wide smile, shaking his hand before her eyes darted over his shoulder to scan the room.

'Nick, please,' Nick told her, disconcerted when she just nodded distractedly, glancing behind herself with a slight frown on her face. 'And you must be Mr Alexandrov; my family and I are so glad you could make it tonight.'

'I'm so sorry,' Natasha put in, focusing back on Nick, 'I was miles away. Dmi you remember? I told you I met Mr Chambers at Clarence House last month.'

'Nick,' Nick said through gritted teeth, extending his hand to shake the Russian's.

'Dmitry.' Alexandrov's handshake was just that bit too firm, but as far as Nick could see there wasn't any reason for the Russian to be jealous: Natasha was ignoring them both very effectively.

'Okay, Tasha?' Dmitry asked as she glanced over her shoulder again.

'I'm fine, Dmi, I just –' She broke off as her gaze, which had been darting around the large ballroom, came to rest on whatever she'd been looking for. Her lips tilted almost imperceptibly into a smile, which ironically seemed a lot more genuine than the one she had bestowed on Nick earlier. Nick had a fair idea of whom she'd been searching for, and he waited. 'I just might have had a little too much champagne on an empty stomach. Sorry, darling, I was miles away.' She lifted her free hand across her body to pat Dmitry's chest, then moved it to her own, resting it in the centre for a moment, her eyes fixed past Nick's shoulder. He glanced behind him and he saw her. As always she was on the outskirts of the room, slightly set apart from other people. She looked almost painfully beautiful, her dark dress skimming the curves of her slim body, her smoky eyes contrasting with her pale lips, and her hair swept away from her face. Everything about her was perfect; her dress blended in with the others – in fact she was indistinguishable from the other guests. Nobody would realize from looking at her that she was part of his protection team, and he suspected that was her intention; she was the ultimate chameleon.

'See someone you know?' Nick asked as he turned back to Natasha. Dmitry had been approached by another of their neighbours and was being quizzed on whether they would be allowed to hold the village fête in the grounds of his estate; something which Old Man Winthrope had always allowed, and, by the look on his face, something that Dmitry would equate to being boiled in oil.

Natasha focused back on Nick; her eyes widened for a moment before she masked it and gave him a cool smile. 'I thought I saw someone I knew but ... but I was mistaken.'

'Really?' Nick asked, his eyes narrowing, 'because I could have sworn you were looking at one of my protection team.'

'I –'

'What does this mean?' Nick asked, dropping his voice to an almost whisper and laying his hand flat over his heart.

'I don't know what you're talking about,' Natasha said, frowning at him like he was nuts. 'Quite eccentric, aren't you, you English aristocracy? I thought that was a myth.'

'What ho!' boomed Bertie, slapping Nick on the back and holding his hand out to Natasha. Nick closed his eyes slowly and gritted his teeth; Bertie's timing, as always, was atrocious. 'Dashed good to see you again,' Bertie boomed on, shaking Natasha's hand so vigorously that her whole body was jolted. 'Natasha, isn't it? Ah! And you must be the Russian chappy we've all been dying to meet. How's Old Man Isaac's place working out for you? Gotten rid of the fungal infection in the orchard yet? Monty Harris has a great spray which does the trick; splendid fellow, absolute bloody genius with fungal wood rot.' Dmitry opened his mouth and closed it again as his body was also jolted with the force of Bertie's handshake. Nick could imagine that in the world of Russian oligarchs conversations about fungal tree rot were few and far between.

'I'll ...' Dmitry gave a firm tug on his hand and Bertie released him, 'I'll bear that in mind.' Nick sighed and noticed Natasha's lips were pressed together, her eyes dancing.

'Hello!' Tils cried, pushing Nick to the side as she inserted herself into the group. 'You must be the Russian fellow I've heard so much about, I'm Tilly.'

'Dmitry,' Alexandrov ground out whilst enduring an equally vigorous handshake from Tilly. 'And this is Natasha.'

'Gosh,' Tils breathed, dropping Dmitry's hand as she moved to shake Natasha's. 'You're frightfully pretty, aren't you?' At this point Natasha lost her battle to keep her amusement under control and let out a chuckle.

'So are you,' she told Tils, who just waved her hand in the air dismissively.

'Pah! That's a good one. Now, Dmitry, I was wondering if you might be interested in my manure. Terribly good fertilizer you know, and we've so much we don't know what to do with it.' Nick shuffled Natasha back slightly whilst Dmitry was distracted by making excuses as to why he was not in the market for horse shit; but as Nick went to speak, Tasha laid her finger on his mouth for a moment, silencing him.

'I don't know why you're interested, but I can't tell you what you want to know.' She flicked her eyes nervously across to Dmitry who was still trying to extricate himself from an increasingly bizarre conversation with Tils and Bertie, then fixed Nick with a stare, 'I'm sorry you need protection,' she told him. 'But you're lucky. I *know* you'll be safe.' She held his eyes for a moment longer before turning back to the group. 'Tilly, I wonder if you could help me find your parents? We wanted to thank them for inviting us along today.' As the women moved away Nick felt a tingling at the back of his neck, but when he looked behind him the space where Goodie had been standing was empty.

∾

He was waiting. He was going to nip this shit in the bud. He didn't know where she was but he knew her eyes were on him. The last of the guests were staggering out towards the taxis waiting in the drive, with Bertie's repeated, over exuberant farewells somewhat hampering their departures – as if the people currently leaving were about to embark on a trek into the unknown Amazon never to be seen again, rather than the rather short taxi ride back to Little Truddlington, which was where most of them were staying.

Once he'd finally given Nick one last drunken side hug and stumbled up the stairs, Nick turned on his heel and walked slowly to the library.

'You can come out,' he said slowly, focusing on pouring the brandy from the decanter into one of the crystal glasses they kept on the oak desk in the centre of the room. 'I know you're there. I can feel you watching me.' He turned and rested back against the solid wood, crossing his legs in front of him and taking a sip from his glass. Goodie stepped forward out of the shadows at the far end of the room. In stark contrast to the guests who had just stumbled their way out of his house, Goodie's appearance was still unnaturally perfect. She took a few more steps towards him, then paused a good ten feet away, crossing her arms over her chest and tilting her head to the side.

Nick took a deep breath. 'I'm sorry if you didn't want to come to the party tonight. I didn't ... most women don't mind ... I mean, I didn't think dressing up would be a chore. I –'

'I know you overheard me with your niece,' she told him.

'Uh ... right, well ...' Nick was at a loss for words, he didn't know whether to apologize for being a nosy bastard as well. All he knew was that the thought of Goodie forcing herself to wear what she was wearing, to go to a party he and his family had insisted she attend, made him feel slightly ill; as did the reasons he suspected she didn't enjoy doing it.

'I know what you're thinking; I don't need your pity, Nick,' she said, allowing her arms to uncross and fall to her sides, then clenching them into fists.

'Okay, fine,' Nick snapped, deciding to move on to the next item on his agenda. 'I don't want you sleeping in the boot room again,' he told her, trying to inject his voice with the kind of steely authority that always worked in the boardroom. He would *not* spend another night thinking about her lying on the cold fucking floor with the fucking dogs; for some reason the thought of it made him want to scream.

She nodded and remained silent for a moment before asking: 'How do you know Dmitry Alexandrov?'

He frowned. 'I don't know him. I just met him tonight.' She turned her head away from him to look out of the large windows into the gardens, lit only by the small lamps they had set up to line the drive for the party. Nick clenched his jaw in frustration; without exception all the females of his acquaintance were quite happy to let him know even the most trivial of their thoughts. The one woman whose head he actually wanted to get inside used silence as some sort of weapon.

'Why?' he asked. 'How do *you* know him?'

'I don't know him; I know *of* him,' she said to the window, the small tic in her jaw the only sign of her anger. 'In future I would like to have a *complete* guest list for my team to go over before events like this.' Her eyes shot to his and there was no mistaking it now: she was furious.

Nick shrugged. 'Mum and Dad asked him at the last minute. They must have forgotten to –'

'If you and your parents want me to do my job effectively then I would appreciate it if you would follow the few simple rules I have laid out.' She turned to go and Nick pushed off from the desk.

'Wait a minute.' When she didn't look back or even pause he huffed in frustration, slammed his drink down on the table and strode over to her, catching hold of her arm before she disappeared through the door. 'Wait, I have some questions I'd like to –'

'Is that an order?' Goodie asked in a low, dangerous voice, her cold gaze fixing on his, then dropping to his hand on her arm as if it was diseased. He released her and stepped back, showing her his palms in a gesture of surrender. She shot him one last filthy look before turning on her heel and exiting the room on silent feet – something that Nick was surprised she could achieve, given the height of her stilettos.

Chapter 11

Show weakness

Nick padded through the dark kitchen to the fridge, pulled out the large jug of milk and moved over to where he knew Mrs B. kept the biscuits. He smiled as he opened the jar and grabbed the oat and raisin one that she knew were his favourite. He was a spoilt son of a bitch. As he was filling his glass and loading up his plate with his spoils, he noticed the door to the boot room was ajar. As silently as he could, obviously nowhere near Goodie's level but he thought he was doing pretty well, he walked over to the door and pushed it open. He blinked down at the blanket laid out next to Salem, who was curled up in the centre of the tiled floor with Xavier. No Goodie. Maybe she'd decided to listen to him. He backed up a step, preparing to leave, then felt cold steel on his neck and froze.

'Don't ever try to sneak up on me again,' she whispered in his ear and he let out a slow breath as the knife pressed in for a moment before falling away.

'Jesus Christ,' he swore, spinning on his heel to see Goodie crouched on top of the utility sideboard, her arms resting on her

Goodnight

bent legs and her hands, including the one holding the knife, hanging between them. She was almost unrecognizable from earlier in the evening, now wearing dark skin-tight trousers with a black hoody. He glanced at her short hair and saw that it was mussed on one side; the only sign that she had been asleep. For some reason that uncharacteristic sign of humanity made his chest feel tight and he had the inexplicable, given that she had just been holding a knife to his throat, urge to hug her. 'You're a bloody lunatic.' He gestured towards her, causing some of his milk to spill onto his hand and a biscuit to fall to the floor. 'Shit.'

Goodie was staring at the milk before her eyes dropped to the biscuit. Nick could just about make out the corners of her mouth turning up very slightly, her cold expression banished briefly as her eyes danced. She slid forward and off the counter, bending down to stroke a now awake Salem's head (the pug was still snoring at his side), tuck the knife into an ankle strap under her trousers, and finally retrieve the lone biscuit. As she straightened to standing, she held the biscuit out to him, placing it on top of the stack on his plate.

'You're eating? Now?' she asked, her eyes still focused on the plate and her almost imperceptible smile still in place. Nick shrugged.

'Couldn't sleep.'

'So you ... eat?'

'Ugh, it's comfort food ... stuff I used to have as a child. Didn't your mum ever give you milk and biscuits when you couldn't sleep?'

Goodie's gaze shot from the plate to his, and her amused expression blanked back to her natural cold one. 'No.'

Nick waited a beat, hoping that maybe she would give something away, but when he saw a muscle tic in her jaw he knew it was futile. 'Well, you've been missing out. Come on.'

He backed out through the door, the memory of cold steel on his neck making him reluctant to turn his back on her. When she didn't follow he stopped and waited at the doorway to the kitchen. 'I'm not leaving until I've seen you eat some milk and biscuits.'

'I am not a milk and biscuits type of woman.'

'You are tonight.' They went into stare-down, and to Nick's surprise, after a robust shove from Salem into the backs of her legs in the direction of the biscuits, she sighed and gave in. Nick smiled, backing further into the kitchen so he could put his glass and plate down on the table and pull out a chair for Goodie. She looked from him to the chair, gave a slight headshake and let her eyes close for a second whilst running one hand over the mussed side of her hair. She must be tired, thought Nick, her movements were somehow more ... human. As she went to sit in the chair he pushed back to retrieve the milk, another glass and the biscuit tin, setting them on the table in front of Goodie before delving into the tin and throwing one of them to a waiting Salem. He sat down opposite Goodie, took a bite of his own biscuit, and waited. Goodie rolled her eyes, another rare sign of humanity, then extracted a biscuit from the jar and bit into it.

'There,' she said after swallowing her first bite, 'happy now? May I sleep?'

'You can do whatever you like, Goodie,' Nick said softly, noticing that now she'd started the biscuit, she was devouring it at a fairly rapid rate. She took a sip of milk and threw Salem another one. 'Okay, you and your mother may be onto something,' she conceded, as she was halfway through her second. Nick sat back in his chair and smiled at her, watching in fascination as one side of her mouth actually curled all the way up for a moment. It might have been a half smile, and it might have only been for a second, but it was something.

Goodnight

'You told me you weren't going to sleep in the boot room again, Goodie. The alarm is up and running now.'

Goodie shrugged. 'I lied,' she said simply.

'I realize that,' he huffed. 'What I want to know is why; when I expressly asked you not to and when there is no bloody need.'

'It is still the weakest point of the house. It's where I would choose to come in if my target was inside. Alarm system or not.'

'Is that something you've done often then?' he asked. Goodie stared at him and lowered her half-eaten biscuit back onto her plate.

'I think I've had enough,' she said. Nick didn't know if she was talking about the biscuits or the questions, but the return of her cold expression had him gritting his teeth. She pushed back her chair and gestured for Salem to follow; the dog sent the biscuit tin a longing look before reluctantly traipsing after her.

Nick watched the boot-room door close and ran through his options: he could attempt to throw Goodie over his shoulder and carry her to the guest room – this option had a few drawbacks, not least that he would likely end up in intensive care; he could shut off the downstairs heating, but somehow he wasn't convinced that the less-than-freezing spring temperatures would have much effect on Goodie. So what was he left with? Making his decision, he pushed away from the table.

∽

GOODIE ALLOWED HERSELF TO SMILE AS SHE CURLED around Salem under the blanket and buried her face in his thick fur. A thirty-seven-year-old man sneaking down to the kitchen for milk and biscuits in the middle of the night was one of the funniest things she had ever seen. He hadn't even been embarrassed to be caught; but then again his absolute and total confidence seemed to override embarrassment in most situations: he shrugged off Clive's obnoxious taunting about his protection being provided by a woman; tonight he might have been dragged to the dance floor by his sister but once there he had danced like a maniac (at one point Goodie'd lost him in the crowd and was about to radio Sam when she realized that the reason he wasn't in her line of sight was because he'd dropped down to the floor to perform some sort of break-dancing move for Arabella. The fact that he could not actually break-dance did not seem to hamper his enthusiasm and he'd ended up doing some sort of bizarre forward roll, much to Arabella's delight judging by her unbridled laughter); he interacted with people seamlessly, talked easily, smiled readily; he was ... charming. Yes, that was by far the best word to describe him: charming. And ... and he was kind. He gravitated to the people on the outskirts of the party, pulling them into conversations, making them feel at ease, listening earnestly to whatever they had to say. It was clear he was protective of Bertie and that he was growing tired of Clive's continued subtle digs at him; she noticed that he'd started stepping in whenever Clive tried to put Bertie down – more often than not turning things around to help Bertie come across as the eccentric but hilarious man he was, and not the fool Clive for some reason wanted to make him out to be.

Yes ... he was kind. Goodie swallowed, her throat for some reason closing over. What was the matter with her? A plate of biscuits, a glass of milk and someone giving a shit that she slept on the floor and she was turning soft. She needed to pull herself together. Her eyes flew open as she heard footsteps on the stairs in the main house. She lifted her head from Salem to listen; the tread was unmistakable. Clenching her teeth, she sat up against the cold wall and waited. After a minute or so (his progress through the corridor and kitchen was surprisingly slow and

Goodnight

peppered with low expletives and at least one chair falling to the ground), he pushed open the boot-room door.

All she could see at first was a massive duvet suspended in midair before a large hand reached up to pull the top down and Nick's smiling face appeared above it, complete with that *fucking* dimple. Goodie was rarely affected by men and the way they looked; she could usually manage to view them in a rather abstract way. She could tell if a man was attractive, she could sense that appeal; it just never affected her the same as it would other women. But with Nick ... she couldn't put her finger on it but over the last two months those smiles, those brown eyes often shining with humour, his strong jaw and that fucking dimple were working their way under her skin. They made her feel ... odd. They made her stomach hollow out and her chest feel tight.

Maybe she was ill? She could have easily picked up dengue fever on that last job she was on.

'Room for one more?' he asked, shoving the duvet and about four pillows in through the narrow doorway with some difficulty. Salem looked at Nick, then at the mass of bedding next to him, gave a loud humpf and turned away from the chaos to go back to sleep. Goodie wished she could do the same but had a feeling that was not going to happen any time soon. Nick scooted down next to her and sat up against the wall, close enough for their arms to be touching. Goodie could feel his heat, smell his masculine yet clean, citrussy scent, and was gripped by a desperate urge to move away – but that would show weakness, that would show he affected her, it would expose vulnerability; and Goodie *never* showed weakness, she *never* allowed herself to be vulnerable. So she sat perfectly still where she was, hoping he'd give up on whatever game he was playing and simply go away.

'I'm not going anywhere,' he said into the silence, as if

reading her thoughts. 'If you're going to sleep on the floor then I'll sleep here with you.'

'Have you always managed to get your own way?' Goodie asked, and Nick shrugged.

'Most of the time,' he told her unrepentantly. 'Although I find most people easier to manipulate than you.'

Goodie sighed. 'I'm tired,' she admitted before she could stop herself, and felt his body jolt in surprise. She could see out of the corner of her eye his face turning towards hers, but her gaze remained fixed straight ahead.

'Do you know,' he asked, then paused as he reached up to her chin and turned her face towards his, 'that's the first time I think I've ever heard you admit any kind of frailty.' He was staring straight into Goodie's eyes, and his breath was fanning her cheek. She stopped breathing. For some reason she felt like she was falling; she felt out of control. Then his hand left her chin and reached up to the side of her head, smoothing her matted-from-sleep hair down as his gaze roved over her face and his mouth hitched up at the side in a small smile.

'What –?' Goodie started to say but was cut off by Nick's mouth on hers. It was a light kiss, tender even, and after a moment he pulled back a small distance, searching her expression as if asking for her permission. Her chest felt tight, her heartbeat stopped altogether and then sped up uncontrollably and she experienced a flash of real fear.

'Goodie?' Nick whispered, concern now washing over his features, his brows drawing together in a frown. Goodie closed her eyes slowly, blocking his out. Her quick mind was able to step back up into gear now that she had broken the connection between them, and she went through her options at lightning speed. She had slept with targets and informants before, but rarely clients. However if she needed to manipulate someone she would do what she had to do to get the job done. Nick's concerned face flooded her mind and she knew that he must have seen the fear in her eyes. If she backed off now she would be confirming that to him; she might even garner his ... pity. The thought made her feel sick. She could treat this like any other job. All she had to do was claw back her shields and go to the place in her mind she always went whenever something intimate was on the agenda.

She would wipe that look of pity from his face.

Chapter 12

Just like she was trained to do

Nick watched as Goodie's eyes opened again, and searched for the panic he could have sworn was there before she closed them, but her ice-blue gaze was now blank, all emotion wiped from her expression. She moved quickly, her mouth crashing down on his and her hands going up into his T-shirt.

'I want you,' she told him, her voice husky and unbearably sexy as her hands traced over his abs and the muscles of his chest. He sucked in a sharp breath – he could tell something was off, there was an unnatural desperation about her; but with the woman he had been obsessing over finally touching him, he became incapable of rational thought.

'Christ,' he rasped as one of her hands moved down to his crotch and all his ability to think was obliterated. He drove both his hands into her soft hair and took control of the kiss, pushing her back to lie on the duvet he had dumped on the floor. He pulled her hands from him and unzipped her hoody, revealing the black bra beneath. Her body was more amazing than he had imagined (and he had a good imagination and had invested a fair amount of time on this endeavour when it came to her, so that was saying something): she was all defined, toned muscle, combined with softer curves. She was magnificent. She rocked against him and her hands went to his belt, frantically pulling at the buckle. Something about her movements jolted Nick out of his lust-induced haze. He dragged his eyes from her breasts and stomach to her face and he almost flinched. Her expression was blank and her jaw was clenched.

'Goodie?' he whispered, and her gaze flew from his belt to his face briefly before focusing just over his shoulder. 'Hey ... hey,' he muttered, grabbing her hands to still them in her frantic attempts to undo his belt.

'What is problem?' she asked sharply, her Russian accent thicker than normal and a frown marring her beautiful face.

'Where did you go?' Nick asked, his eyes roving her face. He gathered both her small hands in one of his and reached up to cup her cheek, stroking across her cheekbone and up to her crescent scar with his thumb.

'I am here,' she said, jerking her head to the side, away from his touch.

'No,' Nick told her, 'no you're not here. Where have you gone? Why are you so scared?'

'*Scared?*' Goodie spat, wrenching away from him, and then scuttling back against the units next to Salem, who raised his head in surprise.

∼

GOODIE WAS BREATHING HARD, HER EXPOSED CHEST RISING and falling. She desperately wanted to zip her top, but knew that would show yet more weakness. She had perfected the type of meditation that took her out of her own body many years ago. The fact was that there were times in her life that she needed to be able to separate from herself; torture situations being one example, any form of intimacy being another. But nobody, *nobody* had ever called her on it. Nick made a move forward and she flinched – fucking *flinched*. What was wrong with her? Salem could feel her tension and flattened his ears against his head, letting out a low growl. She stroked his head and muttered to him that everything was okay in Russian – Salem could smell fear and the only other times Goodie had been as tense as this was when they had been in mortal danger, so she didn't exactly blame him for his reaction. Nick continued to move towards her, his palms up like he was approaching a terrified wild animal. When he was inches away he reached down to her zipper and surprised her by hooking it together and pulling it up, covering her to just under her chin.

'Are ... are you okay?' he asked softly, and for the first time since Goodie was eight years old she felt her eyes sting with tears. She blinked rapidly and gritted her teeth. What the fuck was going on? Nick turned and sat next to her on the floor up against the units leaving just a little more space than before, which she was grateful for. They sat in silence for a few minutes.

'Um, Goodie?' he asked.

'Yes?'

'Look, I don't want to pry or anything –' Goodie sucked in a breath preparing to have to explain her reaction to him '– but ... well, you don't seem to have the full complement of toes.'

Goodie blinked, letting out a short bark of laughter in her relief (but unusually for her not noticing Nick's body jolt at that rarity) and staring sightlessly down at her bare feet. Yes, she was two toes down – both her little toes were missing and part of her third toe on her left foot; ugly scars marked where they had once been.

'I have never noticed this before,' she deadpanned, curling

Goodnight

the few toes she did have into Salem's fur so that he would settle back down to go to sleep.

Nick sighed. 'You won't give anything away, will you. You are the most closed person I've ever met. It makes me crazy – do you know that?' Goodie shrugged. 'Can't you just tell me this one small thing? Give me that at least – you know everything about me.' Goodie rubbed her temple and closed her eyes slowly. After a few silent moments Nick puffed out a frustrated breath and she felt him start to push up to stand.

'Frostbite,' she blurted out. She had no idea why, as his questions annoyed her to death, but the idea that he would give up asking them made her stomach clench with actual pain. He eased back down and turned his body towards her. She could feel him watching her face closely.

'How did you get frostbite badly enough to lose actual bloody toes?' He sounded incredulous, and weirdly furious, about something Goodie considered relatively trivial. She had been lucky to come out of what happened that winter alive, leave alone largely intact.

'I lay in the snow for a long time,' she told him.

'Why did you do *that* for God's sake?'

'I had to be still, and I had to wait.'

'Well, that's just goddamn ridiculous. Whoever ordered you to –'

'Nobody *orders* me to do anything,' she told him. 'I had a job and I was going to complete it. I knew the risks.' And she'd finished the job too. The cold had driven her nearly insane and she'd thought she would go blind if she had to stare down the sight of her rifle any longer. Even now she could still feel the surge of excitement as her target finally came into view after so many hours waiting, and the internal battle she had to fight to remain in control of her heartbeat and breathing. She'd resisted the urge to just fire immediately, taken three deep breaths, and on the respiratory pause at the end of the last breath she'd taken her shot. Adrenaline had been pumping through her system but she still had to make sure that even after the shot had broken she maintained a slow steady squeeze on the trigger; follow through is everything. So despite the cold and the pain, when she did get her shot she took it; she finished it.

Just like she always did.

Just like she was trained to do.

'Do you still take jobs like that?' Nick asked, his big body tensing next to her. She turned to look at him and saw he was scowling down at her toes.

'I no longer take jobs in the cold.' She told him the truth. Didn't matter what the money was, there was no way she'd get that cold again. Anyway there were plenty of jobs to do in the blistering dry heat of the desert or the suffocating humidity of the jungle. Maybe after enough of those she'd be happy to go back to Siberia or Alaska, but she felt it best not to tell him that.

'What ... what exactly do your jobs involve?'

Goodie looked up at the ceiling and took a deep breath. For some reason she didn't want him to see her true nature, to know what she was. But that was stupid. Why should she care what he thought? She balled her hands into fists and made a decision.

'Sometimes I am asked to acquire information, sometimes I am providing protection or performing an extraction, and sometimes ... ' She trailed off, losing her resolve for him to know what she was capable of. She felt an almost disabling wave of tiredness come over her, and her eyes closed again in a long blink.

'I'm sorry, honey,' she heard Nick say softly, his voice sounding far away as she slipped further into unconsciousness. 'You sleep. I won't ask anything else. I'm sorry you had to wear those clothes tonight. If I'd known ... well, I know I can be a

Goodnight

selfish prick and my family can be pushy. You can wear whatever you want from now on. And I'll call Mum and my sister off, give you some space.' His voice had the strangest soothing effect on her; it made her feel safe.

I'm losing my mind, she thought as she finally let herself drift. But she wasn't fully asleep when she slumped onto Nick's shoulder, or when he gently lifted her like she was made of bone china to lay her on the duvet. She felt his breath on her cheek as Salem snuggled in next to her on the other side, and then she felt his feather-like kiss on her temple. Finally, before everything went black, she felt her head lifted and rested on his chest, his heavy arms wrapping around her. She didn't know why she was allowing it. Nothing about the situation made any sense, but for the first time in twenty years she felt a tear slide down her face as she drifted off.

∽

Nick woke to the feeling of cold at his side and sat up. The first light of dawn was trickling through the windows of the boot room and he was lying alone – no Goodie, no Salem, not even the pug was still with him. He lifted his hands to scrub them down his face, an overwhelming sense of disappointment flooding him. He'd taken his life in his hands (he was still a bit leery from the whole knife-to-the-throat experience) when he decided to lift her up and move her onto the duvet next to Salem. Luckily for him she didn't stir, didn't even protest when he shifted her so that she was lying tucked into his side. His gut clenched as he remembered watching the lone tear fall from the corner of her eye, over her scar and into her hair. He'd take her assaulting him with a deadly weapon any day over seeing her shed actual tears.

He pushed up to standing and winced as he stretched his

back and neck. Lying on the floor of a cramped boot room was not what he was used to. Beds were very important to Nick; one of the only instructions he'd bothered his interior designer with about any of his properties (including his yacht) was: 'No pink and a fucking good mattress.' He'd been camping once in his life (for his Duke of Edinburgh Award) and had decided that was quite enough.

He thought about Goodie sleeping on the wood floor in his flat by the door, on the tiled floor of the boot room, and then remembered her missing toes. Unlike him, it would appear that home comforts were not high on her list of priorities. On that thought he stepped over the mass of duvets and pillows (not pausing to think that maybe they needed to be tidied away – another thing that Nick was not that big on) and pushed open the back door.

She was standing in her bare fucking feet in the middle of the lawn leading down to the rose garden. The grass was stiff with frost and the temperature was below freezing. Her piercing whistle cut through the air and he saw Salem bounding towards her from the treeline, followed by a far slower and, by the sounds of the snorts and pants he was giving off, struggling Xavier. Nick's hands bunched into fists at his sides. He was about to storm over to her and physically remove her bare feet from the bloody freezing grass before she lost yet more toes, but the sight in front of him stopped him in his tracks.

As Salem ran headlong towards his mistress, Nick realized that the dog was not going to stop. He came barrelling straight at her, reared up so that his large paws fell onto her chest and took her back a step with the force of the impact. Christ, he thought, the dog's turned savage.

Just as he was about to run over to intervene he saw Goodie push back against the large animal and both fell to the floor, rolling over and over until Goodie had Salem on his back and was tickling his stomach. Salem managed to flip her over again, pin her to the frost-covered ground, and started licking her face. Xavier had at this point made it to them, drooling, panting, snorting and very much the worse for wear, but still able to get a few licks in himself. Then a sound that Nick would remember to his dying day drifted across the lawn to where he was standing.

Giggling.

Goodie was giggling. He blinked: if he'd ever imagined Goodie giggle (which he hadn't – as far as he had known the woman barely knew how to *smile*), it would never have been in the carefree way she was now, and when he caught sight of her face in between the licks from the dogs he was even more shocked: she wasn't just smiling, she was fucking beaming. The joy in her expression transformed her features, her face so beautiful it almost hurt to look at her. He could have watched it all day, it was only the nip in the air and his own breath steaming in front of him which brought him back to himself and out of his spellbound trance.

He cleared his throat and started stalking across the lawn. Of course, she heard him; her head shot up from her dog-tickling endeavours (she now had one hand scratching pug's tummy as well – much to his snorting, grunting, wriggly delight) and she focused on Nick, the light in her eyes and her face dimming until she had pulled back the mask of indifference she was so adept at wearing.

She wasn't the only one to notice his approach; Salem flipped up from his back quickly as Goodie pushed up from the ground. By the time she was standing he was sitting next to her, ears forward and the picture of obedience, none of the playfulness from moments ago in evidence. Nick was guessing that was the way Salem was trained: never to let his guard down when other people were on the scene, always to maintain a controlled, guarded façade – much like his mistress. Nick focused on her feet, then back up at her face, and tried to tamp down his anger, unfortunately without much success.

'What in the fuck are you doing out here?' he asked, coming right up into her personal space and standing toe to toe with her.

Chapter 13

Almost painful

GOODIE FROWNED UP AT HIM, DESPERATE YET AGAIN TO move away but frozen in place by her pride. However, she did allow herself to rest her hand on Salem's head to combat her stress at having Nick this close again, but removed it quickly when she saw Nick glance at what she was doing; judging by his expression he knew exactly what it meant – what it revealed.

'I had to take the dogs out,' she told him, annoyed that she had to tilt her head back to look straight into his eyes. Goodie was not tall but normally a man's height did not intimidate her, she could easily best those twice her size; but there was something about the physical differences between her and Nick which made her feel out of control.

Deciding that she didn't care anymore what kind of weakness it revealed, and that she could not be this close to him for a second longer, she took a step to the side. To her annoyance he mirrored her movements, continuing to block her path to the back door.

'Then you open the goddamn back door,' he told her

slowly, as if she were a wilful and stupid child, 'you let the dogs out and you find some goddamn shoes, preferably a coat, and *then* you go outside.' Goodie dropped her eyes to Nick's torso, which was clad in only a T-shirt, and then down to his sock-covered feet. When she looked back up at him her eyebrows were raised and her mouth was hitched up at the side in a half smile.

Nick was distracted by her mouth for a moment, then shook his head to clear it as she took another step to the side, which he mirrored again. He glanced down at her bare feet one last time, noting their bluish tinge, and decided to risk life and limb by reaching out and putting his hands on her hips to lift her straight up in the air and walk her back to the house.

~

GOODIE'S BREATH CAUGHT IN HER THROAT AT THE FEEL OF his large hands on her hips, and then she stopped breathing altogether as he lifted her and carried her inside. Her normal reaction to anyone moving her somewhere she did not want to go would have been to take them down, and to make it so they stayed the fuck down in a way that would ensure they never even considered laying hands on her again.

But with Nick ... she couldn't explain it but the concern on his face as she stared at her feet, combined with how glorious he looked with slightly mussed hair from sleep, thick stubble on his jaw and his T-shirt stretched tightly across his chest, had scrambled her brain. So instead of causing bodily harm she allowed him to carry her right into the house, through the boot room and into the kitchen. He placed her gently back on her feet by the kitchen table and started rummaging in the cupboards until he found a large washing-up bowl and began filling it up with water.

Goodnight

She watched him, too curious to see what he was going to do next to say anything. He walked back to her, put the bowl down on the kitchen table, and then got in her space again, this time with his hands to her shoulders to shuffle her back to the nearest chair and push her down to sit. For some reason she allowed this as well. He took the bowl, placed it on the floor in front of her, methodically folded up her trousers, lifted her feet, and put them in the water. Goodie hadn't actually noticed how cold her feet were until the warm water sent sharp tingles of feeling back into them.

She opened her mouth to speak but snapped her lips shut when Nick came into the kitchen grappling the ridiculously huge duvet through from the boot-room door, and then wrapping it around Goodie and the chair she was sitting in so it was pulled right up to her chin. Goodie blinked up at him, now looming over her with his hands on his hips and a face like thunder.

She felt it building and pressed her lips together to try to suppress it, but the sheer insanity of the situation meant she couldn't physically hold it in. Her face broke into a smile and she started laughing. The fact that this beautiful man should be so concerned about her being out in her bare feet on frost-covered ground for less than twenty minutes, when she had regularly endured sub-zero temperatures since childhood, often with no food in her stomach, and certainly with nobody who gave enough of a shit about her to help her warm up when she came in from the cold, was bizarre.

'I think,' she managed to get out through her laughter, 'I think my toes were safe this time. This level of re-warming might be overkill.' He was staring down at her still, but instead of the scowl he had been directing at her, his features had softened and the edges of his lips tipped up in a small smile.

'Christ,' he breathed, dropping down to his knees in front

of her and then shocking her out of her hilarity when he cupped her face in his hands. His eyes were searching hers and the look in his was almost reverent when he said: 'You are so goddamn beautiful it's almost painful to be near you.'

Goodie's stomach hollowed out and her breathing sped up. Memories of milk and biscuits, him pulling back last night, him sleeping on the floor with her and holding her, his expression when he saw her bare feet on the frost, all of it flooded her mind and she lost it. Pushing the duvet away, she surged forward to dig both her hands into his hair and she kissed him. Really kissed him. No meditation, no pretence; just her and him. After a moment he pulled away. She gave a small moan of protest and tried to tug him back to her, but he took some time to scan her face.

'You're with me this time, aren't you?' he whispered. She closed her eyes slowly and summoned all the courage she could to let her armour crack and to allow him in.

'Yes,' she whispered back, opening her eyes to meet his. 'I'm here, I'm with you.' And his mouth crashed back down on hers, pushing her back into the chair.

'What th –' The spell was broken as Bertie's voice cut through the silence and they pulled apart. '... Oh. Ah ... right. Gosh ... terribly sorry, folks. Didn't think to knock on the kitchen door, to be honest. No, no please ... you carry on with whatever ... well, I'll just jog on down to the ... um ...'

'Bertie, is fine,' Goodie managed to get out, pushing the duvet off her shoulders and lifting her feet from the water. Nick moved back reluctantly as she stood up. He was scowling fiercely at Bertie and then at Goodie as she nipped around him, whistled for Salem to follow her, and left the kitchen with her dog padding silently after her.

'Bert, mate,' Nick said through gritted teeth, 'You know I

Goodnight

love you but sometimes ... sometimes I could happily strangle you to death.'

'Ha-ha!' Bertie laughed, striding over to Nick and giving him an extremely ill advised, given his mood, pat on the back. 'Always the joker.'

'Bert –'

'I don't want to assume anything, old boy,' Bertie carried on, his tone now less jovial, 'but from what I saw I'm guessing there may be some shenanigans afoot between you and Miss Goodie, of possibly ... well –' Bertie's face was bright red now as he fumbled with the kettle in an attempt to get the lid off to fill it up '– of the bedroom variety,' he continued in a whisper, and Nick looked up at the ceiling in despair at the situation he had found himself in. 'I just ... well, I ...' Bertie had now abandoned his kettle-filling attempts to puff up his chest as best he could and cross his arms over it, his face burning red again. 'Well, she seems a damn decent sort ... bit on the quiet and ... well, slightly violent side, but I'd hate to think that she ... that you ...' Bertie trailed off, his chest deflating and his brows drawing together. Nick's furious expression softened and he smiled at the thought of Goodie's reaction to Bertie defending her honour.

'She can look after herself, mate, I promise you,' Nick said with conviction, the memory of last night's knife incident coming to mind. Bertie uncrossed his arms and walked over to the kitchen table where Nick was still standing until he was directly in front of him and staring straight into his eyes.

'I know it looks that way, old chap,' Bertie said softly. 'But I get the feeling that she's a damn sight more fragile than you think. All I'm asking is that you're careful. She saved your life; don't bugger hers up.'

Nick stared at him a beat, thinking that underneath all that bluster and ridiculousness Bertie might actually be one of the wisest men he knew. He reached up and gave Bertie's shoulder a squeeze. 'You're a good bloke, do you know that, Bertie?' Bertie smiled and clapped Nick on the shoulder again before he turned to resume his attempts at opening up the kettle – an activity that made Nick immediately question the whole wise thing.

'Now, now, Bertie,' Mrs B. said as she bustled into the kitchen and rounded the counter to gently extract the still-closed kettle from his hands. 'You know better than to go fiddling with the kitchen appliances – always gets you in a right muddle. Sit yourself down and I'll bring you your tea.

'Mrs B., you are a most excellent woman,' Bertie boomed, kissing her on the cheek and backing off from the kettle to take a seat at the breakfast bar. He winked at Nick, who thought of all the times Bertie had managed to weasel out of making his own tea, and just like that Nick was back to thinking Bertie a genius.

Chapter 14

Ornery

NICK GROWLED WITH IRRITATION AS THE DOORBELL sounded again. Whoever was out there was an impatient bastard. He was not in the best of moods as it was. Goodie had taken him at his word when he said she wouldn't have to socialize with his family if she didn't want to. Everyone had asked after her (other than Clive, that is), but when Tilly and his mum had been about to literally search the house, he'd had to have a word. He told them she had a job to do and that she needed space to do it. He thought a strategic retreat was the best way to go, but now, after not laying eyes on her for the last ten hours, he wasn't so sure. Nick had a sneaking suspicion that he wasn't going to see her at all until they went back to London. So as he approached the front entrance he was already pissed off, and the fact that the doorbell sounded twice more as he crossed the large hall didn't help.

'How about for once you follow protocol?' he heard Goodie's voice say just before he was about to wrench open the front door. He stopped in his tracks and turned towards the sound, seeing her emerge from the shadows under the stairs. Instead of her usual black, she was wearing a soft cream jumper, which hung off her shoulder on one side to reveal a white vest, with a pair of faded and slightly frayed jeans. He did a double take when he looked at her feet, clad in the most incongruous items of clothing he had ever seen her wear. She had slippers on. *Slippers.* They were bright purple and they were fluffy. His previous annoyance was forgotten as he pressed his lips together to suppress a smile, his eyes dancing.

'You find something to amuse you?' Goodie asked, her arms folding over her chest. Nick shook his head but couldn't hold back his smile any longer.

'I –' The doorbell pealed again, cutting him off. He sighed, back to feeling annoyed, and strode to the entrance. Glancing back at Goodie who had both eyebrows raised expectantly, he rolled his eyes and checked through the customized peephole that had been installed along with the alarm system.

'There's nobody there,' he muttered, and heard Goodie start to move behind him. She might be his protection officer but there was no bloody way that she was answering this door instead of him if there was a question as to what was behind it and whether it was safe. He didn't care what training she had, what she could do or how deadly she was; he was not letting her put herself in harm's way for him. He wrenched open the door and stared straight forward, still seeing nothing.

'Oi!' Nick looked down. There was a boy standing on the stone steps. He had scruffy blonde hair and looked about nine or ten years old. 'Took you long enough, didn't it?' Nick frowned down at the defiant little snot. 'I'm Benji,' the boy said, putting his hands on his hips and standing as straight as he could in order to gain some much needed height.

'Right,' Nick said slowly, crossing his own arms over his chest and assuming the most intimidating scowl he could muster (one that usually worked at board meetings or

Goodnight

international negotiations, but which this kid was wholly unaffected by), 'okay. I'm Mr Chambers and I'd like to know what you're doing on my property.'

'I know who you are, *Nick*,' the child said, his confident stance not wavering for a moment. 'Big shot, change the face of the energy industry, yada yada yada ... who cares. I'm here to see Goodie.' Nick felt the door being pulled from his grip as Goodie widened it and then ducked under his arm to squat in front of the blond kid.

'There is a difference, Benji, between confidence and insolence,' he heard her say; but the kid just smiled, shocking Nick by leaning forward and giving her a hug around her neck. She smoothed his hair as he pulled back, and then very briefly laid her hand over the centre of his chest and encircled his wrist with her other hand.

Nick's mouth dropped open in shock.

'Where are your parents?' Goodie asked whilst she straightened to stand.

'In the Maldives.'

'Then who ... oh, *derr-mo*.'*

'I know that means shit in Russian,' the Benji kid said through a wide grin. 'You were the one who taught it to me that time you showed me how to throw a kni –'

Benji was cut off by Goodie's hand over his mouth, and then she started pushing him down the steps and away from the doorway. She was focused on something out of Nick's eye line, further up the drive. Nick of course followed her. She shot him an irritated glance and said in the most urgent tone he had ever heard from her: 'This is none of your concern. Go back inside.'

Nick smiled at her.

'She's bossy,' Benji put in helpfully. 'But you get used to it.' Nick then heard the crunching of the gravel and saw a small woman wearing a bright purple coat with matching stripy

121

earmuffs and scarf making her way down the drive. She had on her hip an equally purple-clad and wrapped-up little girl. Both had dark curls in various states of disarray and both were almost startlingly pretty.

'Benji for goodness sake, *cariad*,'* the woman scolded in a thick Welsh accent. 'I cannot run all the way up the sodding drive, not with Anya on my hip, you lunatic.' When she'd finished scowling at the child her attention was transferred to Goodie. She gave a squeal of delight on seeing her, stepping up her pace until she was toe to toe with her and could engulf her in a tight hug, toddler and all. For her part the toddler latched onto Goodie's neck so that she was forced to take her from the smaller woman. Now that she was closer Nick could see the open buttons of her purple coat around her midsection; he was guessing she was at least five months pregnant.

'*Preeveet*,* Anya,' Goodie said through a smile.

'Good Good Good!' shouted the excited toddler.

Benji laughed and said something in Russian to Goodie.

'Benji!' the purple-clad woman said sharply, 'I've told you it's rude to speak in a language other people can't understand. How you managed to pick up Russian at Llandough Primary and not the Welsh you're actually taught I'll never understand.'

'Goodie's teaching me.'

'How can she teach you? You barely see her.'

'We skype.'

'I'm not sure you two skyping is a good idea.' The woman narrowed her eyes at Goodie, who just shrugged.

'I don't encourage the boy and I haven't taught him anything dangerous since Sarah got a little excited.'

'Goodie, you taught a seven-year-old how to take apart and reassemble a semi-automatic weapon; you have to see why that might not have gone down well.'

'Came in useful in the end though,' Benji said, then

Goodnight

muttered something under his breath in Russian to Goodie, who laughed again.

'Good, Good!' the little girl called Anya cried again at Goodie's laughter.

'*Preveet,*' Goodie said again to her.

'I told you she's a lost cause, she can barely speak English,' Benji said, shaking his head.

'You little bugger,' the Welsh woman said, punching Benji on the arm. 'That's why I don't want you talking in Russian. She is *not* a lost cause.'

'Ben, Ben, Ben!' Anya shouted at Benji, and he looked at the woman, raising his eyebrows, his point apparently made. Nick's feet crunching on the gravel of the drive as he came to stand next to Goodie alerted the woman to his presence, and she stopped scowling at Benji to openly gape at Nick.

'Uh ... hello,' she managed to say, tipping her head back to look up at him (she couldn't have been much more than five feet tall). She looked at Goodie, who simply pressed her lips together and ignored him.

'Hello,' Nick returned, smiling down at the small woman and extending his hand. 'I'm Nick.'

'Of course you are.' The woman smiled, reaching for his hand and shaking it vigorously. 'I know about you,' she continued, still shaking his hand and showing no sign of releasing it any time soon. 'I read them all, see: *Heat, Hello, Now,* all of them. Sam thinks I'm a *twp** bugger for poring over them, but what would he know ... he doesn't even really watch *Gogglebox.*' She'd widened her eyes at the last sentence as if the disregard for the brilliance of whatever *Gogglebox* was were as good as being declared criminally insane, and would therefore negate all other opinions about other media outlets. 'I'm Katie by the way.'

Nick concluded that even though this woman was a little

123

nuts, very difficult to understand (her thick accent was tricky enough to decipher without her throwing in words he had never heard of), and slightly over familiar, he liked her. It was as if the universe had conjured up Goodie's complete opposite and dropped her at his doorstep.

'Now, I know you've probably got a lot to be getting on with seeing as you're an important businessman and you've probably got all sorts of ... um ... businessing and such like to be doing, so we'll just get out of your hair. Come along, Goodie, honey.' Katie bustled over to Goodie and extracted Anya before walking around her to give her a little push from behind. To Nick's satisfaction Goodie held her ground.

'Katie, I cannot go with you,' she said, stepping away from the gentle shoving. 'I am the close protection, remember?' For some reason Katie's face went soft at this statement and she circled around Goodie to stand in front of her again. To Nick's surprise Katie's eyes then filled with tears and she moved forward to give Goodie yet another hug.

'I know you are,' she said in a choked voice, and followed up with a loud sniff. 'I'm so grateful.' Goodie rolled her eyes and tolerated the hug briefly before pulling away.

'We've been through this. You have nothing to be grateful for.'

'Oh!' Katie shouted as Goodie moved back. 'You wear them! I knew you would wear them. Sam thought I was crazy but I *knew* you would. Everyone needs warm feet.'

Goodie rolled her eyes. 'I'm wearing them because I was *hoping* not to have contact with any actual human beings today, Katie. *Not* because I need warm feet.'

Katie just looked at her through her tear-filled eyes and gave Goodie's arm a squeeze. 'Whatever you say, *cariad*,'* she told her in an indulgent tone that you might use with a lying child. The fact that she would take that tone with Goodie, of all

Goodnight

people, was so comical that Nick had to stifle a laugh. 'But look, see, you don't have to worry about that close-protection business; Geoff's back from Somalia and he's going to take over for a couple of days. You can come and stay at The Coach House.'

Nick stiffened. He knew one thing that would not be happening and that was Goodie leaving, even if it was just to The Coach House at the end of the drive. 'Do you mind me asking exactly what's going on here?' he asked, crossing his arms over his chest and straightening to his full height.

Katie flashed him a nervous smile as she took in his combative stance with a look of some confusion. 'Well, we're just switching up your close protection officer for a couple of days so that Goodie can spend Easter with us; it's kind of become a family tradition to dig her out of the woodwork at this time of year. She absolutely refuses to be found at Christmas, you see. We've had to get quite sneaky with it, haven't we, Goodie; what was the excuse we used to get you down to Wales last year?'

'I believe you told me that Sam wanted to debrief me on a *very* lucrative private contract but the only time he could see me was on Easter Sunday.'

'Ah yes! That was funny, wasn't it?'

'Hilarious,' Goodie deadpanned, her hands going to her hips.

'Well, you shouldn't be so stubborn, should you? You little tinker.' Katie risked life and limb to chuck Goodie playfully under the chin. Nick had the feeling that if Goodie hadn't held herself back she would be reaching for her knife again. 'Anyhoo, Geoff's ... ah, here he is!' A Land Rover pulled up next to them on the drive and a giant of a man unfolded himself from it. 'Great,' Katie said brightly as the large man approached the group.

'Jif, Jif, Jif!' shouted Anya, squirming in Katie's arms and practically leaping into Geoff's massive arms. Nick heard Benji mutter 'lost cause' under his breath, earning him another scowl from Katie.

'Right – Geoff, Nick; Nick, Geoff Rodgers. He'll be replacing Goodie,' Katie flashed Nick a smile, took Anya back from Geoff, and made a grab for Goodie's hand.

'Whoa, whoa, whoa,' Nick said, stepping in between Katie and Goodie. 'Goodie's not going anywhere.' He crossed his arms over his chest and scowled down at Katie.

Katie frowned. 'If you're worried about Geoff's credentials I can assure you that he –'

'I don't care if he's protected *the Queen* for the last decade. Goodie's staying here. Who are you to her, anyway?'

'Well, I'm your far guard Sam's wife, and we're Goodie's … well, we're her friends.'

'You didn't say you wanted to spend Easter with your friends,' Nick said, turning to Goodie. 'What about your family?'

'I have no family,' Goodie told him in that emotionless voice that she did so well, 'and I didn't tell you about spending Easter with my friends because I had no idea Katie was coming here.' She turned to Katie. 'You know I do not celebrate holidays, Katie. It does not matter where I am.' She turned back to Geoff. 'Go back to Swansea and spend Easter with your wife, for God's sake.' With that she turned and walked away from them all, slamming the front door behind her as she stalked into the house.

'Well, that went well,' Katie muttered, frowning after Goodie and shifting Anya onto her other hip.

'What did you expect Katie,' Benji said, 'she's ornery.'

'What's ornery mean?' Katie asked. 'Don't tell me you're speaking Russian again; it really annoys me when you slip into other languages.

Goodnight

'It's not Russian, it's Texan; it means "stubborn and difficult to deal with". I learnt it off that American bloke who helped Dad out with the film-set security.'

'Wow, that's perfect for her,' Katie said, 'and for you in fact,' she carried on, nodding towards Benji. She sighed and looked over at Nick. 'You weren't much help. Thanks for nothing, Mr Important Business Man. Now she can hide out and brood to her heart's content in your vast mansion. Come on, Geoff, this has been a waste of time.'

'Wait,' Nick said as she started to walk away. If there was a chance that even a small chink of light could be shed on Goodie's background he was going to be grabbing onto it. 'Where are you staying?'

'We're all in The Coach House,' Katie told him. 'Sam had to stay so we decided to invade.' She looked panicked for a moment and rushed on. 'He did check that it was okay, and The Coach House is bloody huge and so far away you'll barely know we're even here.'

Nick smiled slowly and shook his head. 'I think you'll find we can do better than that.'

---

* DERR-MO – SHIT
    * *cariad* – sweetheart
    * *twp* – stupid, simple-minded
    * *preeveet* – hello, hi

Chapter 15

Just her and the knife

'THERE IS NO NEED FOR THIS,' GOODIE SAID TO NICK after she'd practically dragged him away from everyone in the living room. It had taken surprisingly little time to convince Katie that he could accommodate her family plus Benji for the weekend. Various excuses had come into play: his mother loves children (this one was true); it would be too complicated for him to alter the security arrangements at this stage what with MI6 being involved (this was stretching the truth – MI6 may have been keen that he was protected but he was sure they didn't give a monkey's about the logistics); his family would be offended (this was an outright lie – the Chamberses were thick-skinned in the extreme).

Fortunately, with the mention of MI6, Katie's eyes had widened almost comically before she had leaned in and asked: 'Do you think they could be watching us right now? From satellites?' She sounded both terrified and hopeful. 'It's like that film the *51st State*, isn't it? You're like Will Smith.' Nick had fought his smile down with ruthless efficiency, widened his own eyes

Goodnight

and blinked slowly. 'Oh my God; you can't even speak about it, can you?' Katie whispered. 'Say no more; I'll go back to The Coach House and talk to Sam.'

'I'll come with you,' Nick told her, and she'd nodded distractedly, not for one second questioning the fact that he wasn't taking his close protection officer with him, which had been one of the main points of his argument. 'You do know that that little boy has slipped away again.' Stealth-wise, Nick would have to put Benji right up there with Goodie: he'd only just noticed the little shit was gone.

'Bloody hell,' Katie said, scanning the house and gardens. 'He's a slippery bugger that one.'

'Is he yours?' Nick asked. There was no resemblance and he'd noticed Benji calling her Katie.

'Oh *no*,' Katie said as she started walking down the drive, Nick easily keeping pace with her short strides – her voice was so full of relief that he almost laughed. 'His mum, Sarah, is my best friend and his dad, Rob, is Sam's partner in the security company. Sarah and Rob have gone away for their first child-free week in ten years and all the kids –they've got five in total by the way – apart from Benji have gone to their grandparents'.

'Why not Benji?'

'There's no way they could handle him,' Katie muttered darkly. 'He needs a trained professional.'

'Are you a nanny then?'

'Me? I'm a GP; I meant Sam.'

'*Sam's* a trained nanny?'

Katie burst out laughing. 'No you *twp* bugger; I meant Sam's *military* training. That's what you need with Benji – tracking skills, endurance training, counter-intelligence stuff.'

Nick started laughing.

'I'm not kidding,' Katie said, now deadly serious.

When they arrived at The Coach House Nick stood with his arms crossed over his chest and an amused expression on his face as Katie told her husband how they had to stay at the main house, giving some garbled explanation about satellites and national security, even bizarrely adding in another Will Smith reference for good measure. Sam had listened patiently, sipping his tea. When her rant was over he simply looked at Nick and raised an eyebrow in the non-verbal style which seemed to be his main method of communicating, and Nick just shrugged one shoulder.

'Fine,' was Sam's one-word agreement, which earned him an excited kiss on the cheek before Katie dumped Anya into his arms and sped out of the kitchen to pack up their stuff.

'I don't know your game but I'm watching you, mate,' Sam said to Nick once Katie was out of hearing distance, and Nick just nodded, smiling slowly.

∼

'WHY ARE YOU HIDING IN HERE, LOSER?' BENJI SAID AS HE sauntered over to the darkest corner of the library, where Goodie was curled up in an armchair. Goodie put down the book she was reading and narrowed her eyes at Benji.

'How did you get in, kid?' she asked. 'You know you'll get in trouble if the Chamberses find out you broke into the house.'

'Broke in?' Benji scoffed. 'You must be joking. That Nick bloke practically dragged us all up here. We've all moved into the "guest wing". Ha! It's like a whole other house. Rich people are weird.'

'What are you talking a –'

'Oh, by the way he's looking for you, so are Katie and Sam. They're so dumb; I knew exactly where you were, all I had to do was ask where the library was.'

Goodnight

'What are you all doing in this house?' Goodie asked.

'We're spending the weekend.'

'No you are not,' she told him, jumping to her feet and stalking across the room. Benji caught her arm as she went past, and she paused to look down at him.

'What's with that Nick bloke anyway?'

'What do you mean?'

'He looks at you funny and he ... he pushed you behind him like he thought he was the boss of you or something.'

'He's not the boss of me, Benji,' Goodie told him, her eyes flashing with anger. 'You know that, nobody is the boss of me.'

'And you're weird too,' Benji said, regarding Goodie's stance analytically. 'You don't usually get mad like now, and outside you were ... well, you were acting all ... I dunno, twitchy.'

'I was not *twitchy*,' Goodie could feel her face heat.

'And that!' Benji said, jumping up and down and pointing to her face. 'You're all red. You never show any feelings and stuff. It's *weird*.' Goodie puffed out a breath and tried to claw back her aura of lethal calm that she was used to, but for some reason having Katie under the same roof as Nick and his family was making her feel ... well ... fuck, she *was* twitchy.

'Shut up, squirt, and tell me where they are.'

~

'Nick, for Christ's sake what's going on?' Goodie heard Clive sneer as she made her way down the corridor to the kitchen. 'Why are you letting staff invite their bloody mates and even worse their mates' kids to your gaff? You do know that there are three children in that kitchen right now. Three.' Clive grunted in disgust and Goodie heard him add under his breath: 'One was bad enough.'

From Nick's furious expression, and knowing how much he loved his niece, Goodie was pretty sure he'd heard the arsehole as well.

'Well, Clive,' he said, his voice so low and dangerous that it actually shocked Goodie – he was always so charming, so laid back. 'Why don't you get the fuck out of *my gaff* then, and stay away from my sister.'

'Calm down, mate,' Clive laughed a little nervously. 'Just kidding around; no need to get radgie. You've got to admit, it's weird enough having a little girl provide your protection without her mates and their kids getting in on the act.'

'That *little girl* could fuck you up without batting an eyelid, you prick,' Nick told him. 'Advice: don't piss her off.'

'Hello, boys,' Goodie said, deciding to make her presence known. Benji was standing next to her smirking – that was one of the things she liked about the kid: he knew when to keep his mouth shut, he hadn't said a word or moved a muscle throughout that whole exchange. It was like she always told him: knowledge is power. She moved to go past them towards the hum of noise from the kitchen, but paused inches away from Clive in order to turn to him, stare him straight in the eye, and bat one of her eyelids before moving away.

Once she made it into the kitchen Goodie sighed as she saw just how settled in Katie and the kids were.

Control was very important to Goodie. She had spent her childhood in possession of so little of it that now she found it almost essential. And in all honesty staying in control of her life was usually a piece of cake. She had nobody to answer to, no ties or responsibilities … nothing. This, she always told herself, was good; it was safe. So what if sometimes she lay awake at night staring into the dark and feeling it invade her consciousness? Darkness and emptiness had been a part of her life for so

Goodnight

long she wasn't sure she could live another way or that she would even want to try.

It was certainly safer this way. Only two people knew her background: Sam, she knew, would never tell anyone; and Natasha ... Natasha wanted the truth to stay buried as much as Goodie, maybe more. So yes, control, keeping her secrets, keeping the past buried: these were all very important to Goodie, and she did not like the feeling that it was slipping.

You wouldn't think that a small, overexcited, ridiculously friendly, touchy-feely woman like Katie would be dangerous to someone like Goodie. But in Katie's mind Goodie had saved her life three years ago and Katie was not going to forget it. She'd told Goodie: 'Our way lies together. With the speed of Allah. You have saved my life. Christian. Now I'll stay with you, until I've saved yours. That's my vow.' True, it was a direct quote from *Robin Hood Prince of Thieves* and was delivered in Katie's attempt at Morgan Freeman's Arabic accent; but she meant every word.

Not that Katie could actually stay with Goodie, but she did make sure she was in her life any way she could be in various over-familiar and invasive ways, exactly like this current episode. Compounding Katie's feeling of gratitude towards Goodie, which fuelled her crazy behaviour, Goodie had made the mistake of revealing a little too much about what went down in Colombia with Sam nine years ago. So, not only did Katie believe she owed her life to Goodie, but also that of her husband. The fact that both times Goodie was simply doing her job was totally lost on Katie.

Goodie squared her shoulders. There was little chance of removing the Katie Tornado from this situation anyway, and there was no way Goodie could remain hidden away in the library; not if she wanted to keep an eye on her.

'Unlikely mate of yours,' Ed said to Goodie. They were both sitting at the kitchen table, slightly removed from the chaos around the large island. Katie was attempting to teach Tilly and Bertie how to pronounce various Welshisms, and then demanding they teach her to 'speak like a posh bird'. Results were mixed but, even Goodie had to admit, pretty funny. Occasionally she was called upon to throw in a bit of Russian and Ed was made to add various Essexisms such as 'sharr-arrp' and 'minging', but they had not as yet been dragged away from the kitchen table.

Anya had found the most direct route to the biscuits and was being cuddled by Nick's mum who was intermittently sneaking her some from the jar next to her. Nick's charm and dimple were thoroughly winning over Katie, Benji and even Sam (who was naturally cynical and distrustful – not quite as bad as Goodie, but close) and the kitchen was full of laughter.

'She's tricky to shake,' Goodie muttered into her coffee, and Ed smiled, his eyes drifting back to Tilly, who had her head thrown back in laughter.

'Why don't you do something about that?' she asked, and Ed jerked in his seat, his eyes snapping from Tilly to Goodie.

'What you on about then?' he said sharply.

'You know what I mean.'

Ed sighed. 'She's got a bloke, Goodie.'

Goodie watched as Clive skirted Benji and Arabella as if they were contaminated with a flesh-eating virus, making his way to the kettle.

Anya wriggled her way down Nick's mum and then waddled her way over to where Clive was standing.

'Live, live, live,' she shouted, grabbing onto his legs with her

Goodnight

chocolatey fingers, proud of her ability to remember the stranger's name. Ed was focused back on Tilly again, and nobody other than Goodie could see Clive's legs or Anya, as they were on the opposite side of the kitchen island. So nobody saw Clive give his leg a rough shake so that Anya landed on her bottom next to him. Goodie's hands tightened on her cup of coffee, but she controlled her fury for now; he would keep.

'Oh, baby!' cried Katie, as Sam moved round the island to pick up his daughter.

'Live,' Anya sniffled miserably into her father's neck, and Goodie felt a fresh wave of anger that the little girl should have had her first lesson that the world was not always the rosy place her mother painted it; that some adults could not be trusted.

'For somebody who's made the most significant breakthrough in the 21st century, you're still a couple of kopeks short of a ruble,' Goodie muttered under her breath to Ed.

'Come on, Goodie,' Benji said suddenly, cutting off anything Ed might have said in reply, 'do your thing. You know Annie loves it.'

'Benji,' Katie said in a warning tone, which Goodie was sure she meant to sound dangerous but came out as more like another bad impression of Morgan Freeman, 'Goodie knows not to do that ever again in front of children. It is not appropri –'

Goodie saw an opportunity to annoy Katie, and she was just about angry enough to take it. 'Sure thing, squirt,' Goodie said, standing from the table as all eyes swung to her.

'Goodie, I don't think –'

'Mrs B., can I help with that?' Goodie asked, cutting Katie off. Mrs Beckett handed Goodie the knife she was using to peel and cut the vegetables for the casserole she was making. Goodie started chopping the vegetables slowly and felt Katie relax as

Bertie started talking about the back orchard and what they were going to do about the tree rot. Goodie let her mind drift; she didn't register the room gradually falling more and more silent, or the fact that Anya had stopped crying. It was just her and the knife.

Chapter 16
She's worth it

NICK SLOWLY LOWERED HIS CUP OF TEA TO THE KITCHEN counter whilst his eyes dropped to Goodie's hands.

'Holy *Long Kiss Goodnight*,' he heard Tilly mutter next to him as the knife started moving so fast it was almost a blur. The stack of onions, carrots, potatoes in front of her were nearly decimated. Despite the speed of her hands, the look on her face was that of complete calm and he had the eerie feeling that she was somewhere else.

Just as she finished the last carrot, Benji shot forward to a pile of tomatoes on his side of the kitchen island and threw one of them at Goodie. Nick opened his mouth to shout at the little shit but closed it when he saw Goodie automatically lift the knife, slice the tomato in midair into perfect halves, throw the knife up to spin in the air before catching its handle and cutting the halves into quarters, all within less than a second. This was repeated for the remaining three tomatoes, then she paused, flicked up the knife and balanced the sharp end perfectly on one of her fingers before tossing it to spin high in the air, almost to the ceiling, catching it by its handle and then throwing it with deadly accuracy the length of the room so that it ended up stuck in a large chopping board, inches from Clive's arm.

There were mixed reactions to this display. Benji, Arabella, Anya, Tilly, Bertie and Nick's aunt and uncle started applauding, shouting out, 'Jolly good show!' and, 'Bravo!' Nick himself kept his eyes on Goodie and watched as she slowly came back to herself and handed the knife to a dumbfounded Mrs B. Nick's mum had gone a little pale, as had Ed. Nick's dad was looking at Goodie with renewed curiousity. And Clive ...

'Jesus Christ,' Clive shouted, his face flushed with fear and anger. 'You psychotic bitch – you could have killed me!'

'Yes,' Goodie said slowly, 'I could have but I chose not to ... this time.'

'Pahaha!' Bertie laughed, breaking the now tense silence that had fallen over the kitchen. 'She's messing with you, old man. It's like a circus trick; no need to get shirty – you know, like the time Giles-Bullhammer-Fentywick stuffed that artichoke up his –'

'Bertie. Shut. Up,' Clive clipped, his patience completely gone. He scowled at Goodie one last time before storming out of the room.

'I only meant to say that it was a bally good trick,' Bertie said bracingly.

'Not sure the comparison quite matches up, Bert,' Nick said dryly. 'After all, there wasn't exactly much talent involved in old Bullhammer's artichoke stunt, and very little risk to life and limb for anyone but the idiot himself.'

Goodie ignored them both and moved across the kitchen to Claire. 'I am sorry,' she told her. 'I did not mean to scare you.'

'Oh ... I wasn't ... I mean ...'

'Yes you were, but I promise there was no risk.'

Claire smiled.

'Oh, I know that, dear. I was just a little ... taken aback.

Goodnight

Anyway, now you can teach me and Mrs B. how to do it, can't you?'

'Oh yes, that would be wonderful,' put in Mrs B. 'Did you train with a chef in London?' Goodie tilted her head to the side, a small smile playing on her mouth.

'Not ... exactly,' she replied.

'Splendid, we can all learn,' put in Nick's Aunt, who had rarely taken any interest in cooking but whose eyes were now bright with enthusiasm.

So the rest of that afternoon was spent in the kitchen. Even Nick's dad and uncle, who usually absented themselves from anything even vaguely related to food preparation, hung around watching Goodie as she showed the adults how to slice and dice at warp speed (the kids much to their disgust were relegated to audience status and it was made clear that in their cases knife-play of any kind was strictly forbidden – although Nick did catch Goodie's wink at Benji during one of these lectures; he had a feeling that she'd already crossed that bridge with him in the past).

Once everything that could be chopped had been, Goodie started to slope away. Nick was about to head her off when he saw that his dad had beaten him to it, steering her over to the armchairs by the huge Aga and extracting his chess set from the shelf above. Goodie hesitated before she sat down, but Monty simply carried on setting up the chess pieces. After a few moments she sank into the armchair opposite and made her first move. It reminded Nick of the times as a child that he'd watched his father with an unbroken horse: he never pushed, he waited for the horse to come to him, keeping his voice low, no sudden movements. His dad was a clever bastard.

Nick decided to take the same approach and went back to the group around the kitchen table, all of whom were now grilling Ed about cold fusion. It had not escaped Nick's notice that his sister, not known for her fascination with anything scientific (the only science GCSE she hadn't failed miserably at school had been Physics, and only then because she'd convinced some of the boys to set up her circuits for her), was hanging on Ed's every word as if he was Albert Einstein himself. Nick was hoping this would make the ejection of Clive from their lives slightly easier.

After an hour had passed, Nick quietly got up to boil the kettle. He made a pot of tea, which his mum bustled off with, but then after remembering that Goodie hated tea he went to the cupboard for the cafetiere.

When he placed the coffee-filled mug and a plate with oat and raisin biscuits next to Goodie, she looked up at him and for once the blank mask slipped. Her wide eyes flicked from him to the mug and back again and her features softened. He reached down to tuck a stray lock of blonde hair behind her ear and she blinked, staring at his hand as he withdrew it. He watched her swallow before she shook her head as if to clear it and her attention went back to the chessboard. She didn't flinch away from him, she didn't close down; he was getting somewhere, he felt. Before he moved away, his dad caught his eye and he smiled.

∼

Monty Chambers looked down at the chessboard again, his smile still in place despite the fact he was losing to this woman for the second time in a row. His son had brought a fair few women home in the past. They had all been perfectly reasonable fillies: attractive, well-bred, personable types, but what they had *not* been was a challenge.

Everything in his son's life had come easily to him; his charm, his good looks, his intelligence had meant that there had been very few bumps in the road. But Monty knew why Nick

Goodnight

had expanded the business, why he was on the brink of changing the energy industry throughout the world: he was a risk-taker, a thrill-seeker; he loved a challenge. So maybe it was a strange outlook to have, but Monty rather thought a beautiful, mysterious, knife-wielding Russian suited Nick far more than any of the lukewarm women he had presented to his dad in the past. Life was there to be lived and this woman ... this woman could help his son live it as he was meant to.

Monty jumped when he heard 'Anya!' shouted across the kitchen, then looked down to see that the two-year-old had made her way over to where he was sitting and was reaching for his tea. He tutted at her and ruffled her hair. When she stretched out her little chubby arms he pulled her up onto his lap to help him with his next chess move. She was such an enchanting child that he did not notice Goodie's head shoot up when Anya's name was shouted out. Nor did he notice his son's eyes widen as he took in her reaction.

∼

NICK WALKED DOWN THE CORRIDOR AT PACE. HIS MOBILE was already clamped to his ear and he was waiting impatiently for his call to be answered.

'Anya,' he snapped when the ringing was finally cut off.

'Hello to you too, mate,' Walker's voice said patiently. 'Bloody freezing over here by the way – thanks for that.'

'I've got a name for you: Anya.'

'You sure?'

'Ninety per cent.'

'You realize that's still fuck all to go on, don't you?'

'It's more than you had before.'

'Yeah but –'

'I'm paying you enough to be out there,' Nick clipped,

losing patience. 'You've never come up empty-handed on other jobs before.'

'This is not like your typical spot of industrial espionage, Nick. This shit is seriously scary, the people who know anything about it are like vapour and any information is buried deep. You peel back one layer and you're faced with another. I'm not sure trundling around Russia asking this stuff is even safe. So no, maybe you're not paying me enough.'

Nick rubbed his eyes and sighed. 'Sorry. I just ... I just need to know more.'

'Yeah, I think I got that.' Walker's voice was now annoyingly laced with humour, but Nick was relieved that he hadn't just jacked in the whole thing altogether. 'I'll add Anya into the mix, okay? But I'm not promising anything.'

'Thanks, mate; I owe you.'

'I hope she's worth all this,' Walker said cautiously. 'Got to say, some of the stuff we've found, well, it's a bit ... um ... fucked up.'

'She's worth it,' Nick told him firmly.

When he hung up the phone he almost dropped it in shock when Sam materialized from the shadows of the corridor.

'Christ, how do you people do that? What's wrong with just walking along like a normal person and announcing your presence with a simple "Hi there"? Jesus.'

'Sorry, Whitney,' Sam said through a smile. Nick rolled his eyes and was about to turn away to go back to the kitchen when Sam caught his arm.

'Some things are best left buried,' he told him, his smile having dropped and his eyes boring into Nick's. 'Don't poke the hornets' nest.'

'I don't know what you're talk –'

'You understand me. What you don't understand is what

you could find. You don't know what you're dealing with. You don't know who she is.'

'That's what I want to find out,' Nick told him.

'You think you do but trust me, I'm telling you the truth, you don't.'

∽

CLIVE WAS FUCKING FURIOUS. HE'D PUT MONTHS INTO winning over Matilda Chambers. Horse-obsessed single mothers were not exactly his usual type, but he'd made an exception; he needed a way into the Chambers family and he most definitely needed a way to get his hands on some cash.

His P.R. firm had been floundering for the last year, and Nick's account was about the only lucrative contract he had left. Tilly might only work off and on at the stables, but she had a huge trust fund, not to mention a massive divorce settlement, seeing as her ex-husband had been enough of an idiot to be caught cheating on her. The stupid bastard had thought he could fuck with a Chambers and get away with it. He probably should have taken into account the kind of adversary he would be taking on with Tilly's brother; poor sod didn't stand a chance, not once Nick got his army of private investigators involved.

Clive wasn't making that mistake, no way. He was marrying the horsey bitch and he'd keep his dick in his pants for as long as it took to get what he wanted. The last thing he needed was for some scrawny science dweeb sniffing around, upsetting all his plans.

And now she was going to end things?
With him?
Unbelievable.

He slammed the door to his room, pulled off the fucking

wax jacket he'd bought to fit in with these freaks, and threw it on the floor in disgust. No way was he going on some lame Chambers family fishing trip, not in this mood and not after he'd just been dumped. 'We can still have a nice evening tonight,' she'd said. 'It doesn't have to get ugly, Clive.' She could say what she liked; Clive was not giving up without a fight. He knew things about the Chamberses and he was not above blackmail. Tilly was weak; she'd soon crumble when confronted with his brand of persuasion.

He kicked the leg of the bed in frustration. Complacency – that had been his problem; he hadn't thought for a moment that Tilly would actually dump *him*. Maybe he should have made a bit more effort with the kid, but Clive hated children and that brat was a mouthy little shit that could use a good ...

Something caught his eye across the room. His head whipped round and he was staring straight at that bloody great dog. Clive did not like dogs. The pug was bad enough (although it thankfully left him alone, having learnt that any attempt to slobber on him would be met with a swift kick when Tilly and the brat's backs were turned) but this one gave him the creeps. He took a step back as the animal's upper lip curled to bare its teeth, a low growl resonating through the room. It was then that he felt something sharp pierce the skin of his neck and everything went black.

∽

'HELLO SLEEPYHEAD.' CLIVE BLINKED UNTIL THE BLURRY figure in front of him swam into focus. She was sitting cross-legged on the bed, staring at him with an eerily neutral expression.

'What the ...?' he slurred slightly, then shook his head to clear it. 'What in the fuck is going on?' As he slowly blinked awake he could tell that he was propped up against the large headboard.

'That is an interesting question, Clive,' Goodie said with apparent genuine curiosity. 'What in the fuck *is* going on with you? What exactly are you after? I, for one, do not like unanswered questions.'

Clive attempted to swing off the bed but was pulled back by strapping around his chest and abdomen, attaching him to the wide slats across the headboard. 'Jesus Christ!' he shouted, struggling against his restraints. 'What in God's name are you ...? Have you completely lost your mind?'

Goodie smiled at him, and laid her hand on Salem's head as he was sitting on the floor next to the bed, his teeth still bared at Clive.

'I would stop all that thrashing about if I were you,' Goodie advised as another low growl rumbled from the beast next to him. 'You're upsetting Salem and he's already not your biggest fan.' Clive glanced down at Salem nervously before staring at Goodie again. 'And nobody can hear you anyway; even Mrs B. went along to watch the fishing.'

'What possible reason could you have for this?' he asked. 'You do know that you're going to prison already for what you've done so far. Don't make it any worse for yourself by –'

'Research, Clive,' Goodie said, cutting him off. 'People think that protection work is all about leaping in front of bullets and swanning around after your potential targets; they forget about research.'

'What are you talking about? Let me off here. Help! Somebody –' Goodie moved so fast that she was almost a blur. Before he knew what had happened he had gaffer tape sealing his mouth shut, his cries muffled behind it.

'What does this research involve? you might ask,' she carried on conversationally, as if they were having a casual chat down in the living room rather than him tied to a bed after being knocked out by God only knows what. 'Well, it involves looking into every business associate, every neighbour, every friend. Turning up all their skeletons. Assessing any potential threat there might be. You were an interesting one, Clive. You're not *actually* a threat to my client; so why, may you ask, do I give a shit? That's where things get interesting.

'You see I've always known that your P.R. firm is in trouble financially, that the contract you have with Nick is the only real one you have left, and even that's on dodgy ground. I know why you're with Tilly; I know exactly how much money she won from her divorce settlement with that cheating arsehole and how much her trust fund is. What was it you said in the latest meeting with your accountant? She lowered her voice and put on Clive's posh accent: "'Give me a year, mate. Once everything's squared away legally, good old Tils won't want her husband's company to go down the swanny. She's got enough cash for anyone to get over the smell of manure after a while."

'Now, at this juncture, Clive, I will say that I still didn't really give much of a shit. Nick is my client; Matilda is not. But –' Goodie drew the last word out as her eyes flashed with anger '– then I saw you put your hands on a nine-year-old little girl, and unfortunately for you that *did* spark my interest. Still, you may have been able to slope away quietly; Ed is unwittingly doing all the hard work for me in that direction anyway. But Clive, I'm afraid you hurt the wrong two-year-old in the kitchen earlier.' Goodie moved to within reaching distance and he made a grab for her. She caught his hand and pulled it back viciously, almost breaking his fingers. Then leaned right in to whisper in his ear.

'In your wildest dreams you have no idea what I am capable of. There is nothing I don't know about pain – how to endure it and how to inflict it. If I were you I would do as I say.'

Goodnight

She pulled the tape from his mouth and leaned back to resume her cross-legged position.

'Listen,' he said, his voice now trembling. 'I don't know where you come from, but this is illegal. You can't threaten me. You can't do any of this.'

'Ah!' Goodie said, smiling again, and Clive felt a shiver of fear down his spine. 'That is where the research comes in again; so important. Knowledge is power.' Clive blinked and began to look uncertain in the face of Goodie's confidence.

'What –?'

'Lisa Summers,' Goodie said, and Clive felt all the blood run from his face. 'I think the police report described how she "fell down the stairs", but in the medical reports her injuries weren't really consistent with –'

'What do you want?' Clive knew when he was beaten. He wasn't going to risk his reputation. He'd given that grasping slut a pay-off five years ago, but there was no telling what would happen if all that crap was dredged up again. Clive lived and died by his reputation and the psychotic bitch sitting in front of him knew it.

'I want you to leave and I want you to never look back.' Clive stared at her for a long moment weighing his options, until he came to the depressing conclusion that he didn't really have any.

'Fine,' he spat out, and Goodie smiled, reaching into her boot and pulling out a much scarier knife than the one she had been using in the kitchen. Clive flinched away from her as she cut through the strapping holding him on the bed, and scrambled off the other side once he was free. He went for his suitcase and started throwing clothes and belongings in at random.

'You,' he said, pointing at Goodie with a trembling finger, 'you stay away from me.'

Goodie cocked her head to the side and her hands went to

her hips. 'You must be very angry though, Clive. Don't you want to show what a *big man* you are, like you did with Lisa Summers? Teach me a lesson; I dare you. You can even have this.' She threw the knife within reaching distance and Clive stared at it for a moment before resuming his frantic packing.

'Just ... just bugger off,' he said, his hands still shaking.

Goodie sighed. 'You're no fun.'

He looked up a moment later but she, the dog and the knife were gone.

Chapter 17

A bit squiffy

GOODIE LOOKED DOWN AT SALEM'S PLEADING FACE AND stroked the top of his head.

'Not much longer, my little mouse,' she murmured to him in Russian, her hoarse voice rasping over her sore throat.

They had arrived back in London yesterday, and today was catch-up time. Nick and Ed had meetings all over the place; the latest was in the room Goodie and Salem were standing outside. No reception desk and no security guards meant that Goodie had to guard the door. She blinked her sore eyes and sniffed to try and clear her blocked nose. The last week with Nick's family had turned her soft, and that bloody two-year-old had infected her with the toddler equivalent of the viral plague.

One week of eating regular meals (even eating biscuits, and not just once) now meant she couldn't stomach a simple ten-hour fast. Goodie had eaten breakfast that morning, but nothing since. There was food provided in the conference rooms but nobody had thought to bring any out to her. In the normal way of things this was not unusual, and she had a technique of pushing away the gnawing hunger pangs and focusing on what was important. In the endurance training she underwent in Russia she was hands down the best they'd ever seen, better than hardened operatives male or female, and Goodie had only been twelve the first time she went through it. Hunger, pain, exhaustion were normally things she was able to push away in order to get the job done.

She straightened her shoulders and flashed Salem's pleading face an annoyed look; somehow he'd gone soft as well. Nick emerged from the conference room deep in conversation with two men and one woman in suits, heading towards the lift at power-walking speed. Ed, looking a little bewildered, was trailing behind at his usual pace, which seemed firmly set to amble, with Bertie bringing up the rear holding a tray laden with cups and a teapot and saying to the flustered catering staff, 'No, not a bit of it. Can't have you ladies carting all this heavy stuff around when there's chaps aplenty to do it. Not when you've rustled up some most excellent pastries.' Goodie rolled her eyes: the catering ladies looked quite well-built enough to shift a few bits of crockery.

'Bertie,' Nick snapped from the lift, his foul mood showing itself yet again today. Bertie jumped and a cup toppled off the edge of the tray, which was caught midair thanks to Goodie's lightning-quick reflexes. 'Come *on*.' Nick was holding open the lift door and scowling across at them. He didn't say anything to Goodie and she couldn't really blame him. He was furious with her; that was probably why he was happy for her to starve. So much for him giving a shit. Since they'd arrived back in London she had gone back to absolute professionalism. To Goodie that meant invisible presence, and after three days of attempting to engage her in conversation or even coax a smile out of her, Nick had given up.

She didn't hold it against him. Not really.

Well ... maybe a bit.

Goodnight

Goodie shoved the cup onto the tray and put the tray up on the reception desk, then gave Bertie a gentle shove in the direction of the lifts. He gave the reception and catering staff a cheery wave and a couple of 'What ho!'s, then trotted off towards the open lift doors and an impatient Nick. Goodie slipped in next to him and the doors swiftly closed. She felt the familiar panic claw at her throat, and fought it down. But with the way she was feeling, and the fact she hadn't eaten in ten hours, this proved harder than normal. She felt for Salem, leant into him, and he licked her hand.

'You okay, old girl?' Bertie asked her, and she stiffened.

'I'm fine,' she rasped out, feeling a trickle of sweat run from her forehead down to her cheek.

'If you don't mind me saying, you look a bit squiffy.'

Goodie wasn't sure what 'a bit squiffy' meant; she felt like shit but there was no way she was admitting that in the confines of this lift with Nick listening. Luckily she was saved by the doors opening, and was the first to step out so she could check the foyer. She was about to move to the side and let the suits pass when she felt her upper arm enclosed by a large, warm hand. She looked up at Nick and blinked to try and clear the aching feeling behind her eyes so she could focus.

∼

'BLOODY HELL,' NICK SWORE AS HE STARED DOWN AT HER flushed face and bloodshot eyes. 'What's the matter with you?'

'Nothing,' she croaked out with visible effort, before swallowing and trying to jerk her arm away from him. The halfhearted attempt made him frown. He had no doubt that if she was operating at full par he would have been shoved halfway across the building by now.

'You're sick,' he said in amazement. In truth it was difficult to comprehend any illness having the guts to brave this woman's immune system, but as he laid his hand across her forehead (much to her visible horror) and felt the burning skin beneath, he had to conclude that she *was* actually ill. She dropped her eyes from his and shoved her free hand into Salem's fur, something he noticed she did whenever she felt uncomfortable or stressed. He had long since stopped insisting that Salem stay in the car on these trips, for that very reason. Every lift they went in he could feel the tension radiating off her; it would only ease if Salem was next to her and she could lean against him in some way.

Little did Goodie know, but Nick had actually wasted a fair amount of time and even made a few threats in order to have advance permission to allow that mongrel into buildings which were otherwise always dog-free zones. But there was something almost obscene about seeing someone as powerful and in control as Goodie tense up with real fear. For some reason he couldn't abide it and would do anything to stop it. Even if that meant he was now labelled 'that eccentric billionaire with the dog obsession'.

'I think,' she rasped out, then cleared her throat, 'I think I need to talk to Sam.' Nick barely heard her; he was mentally going through the day and trying to remember if he'd seen Goodie eat or drink anything at all.

'Goddamn it,' he muttered as he dropped her arm and turned on his heel to walk back to the group of investors, who were staring at him like he was a few sandwiches short of a picnic. After a couple of curt explanations and a bit of manoeuvring on his part, he turned back to Goodie.

'Ed, Bertie,' Nick snapped. 'Let's go.' Goodie was on her phone. He resisted the urge to touch her again, knowing how much it might annoy her and not wanting her to build up any sort of defence against what he was planning, and instead

Goodnight

simply nodded towards the exit. She shoved her phone back in her pocket and followed them. But before they could leave the building, Sam and that Geoff bloke Katie had brought up to the house strode through the double doors and blocked their exit. Sam's eyes zeroed in on Goodie and he frowned.

'Geoff'll take over now,' he said to her, and the big man next to him stepped forward towards Nick. 'Go home, get some rest.'

As always Sam's tone was brusque, and his words to the point, but those last were much softer than was his norm. Nick flicked the enormous Geoff an annoyed look and stepped around him to get to Sam.

'She's not going anywh –'

'She's sick, mate,' Sam snapped, stepping between Nick and Goodie. 'Geoff's going to take over. She needs to go home; she can't work like this.'

Nick glanced over Sam's shoulder at Goodie; she was looking worse by the minute, and arguing in the middle of a busy foyer probably wasn't helping matters. He looked back at the three key investors he had almost convinced to come on board, and rubbed his jaw.

'Okay, fine,' he bit out. 'But someone should go with her, she's –'

'I can look after myself,' Goodie rasped, her eyes flashing with anger. 'I have a fucking cold. Go to your meeting.' With that she spun on her heel and left the building, Salem trotting along behind her.

'Well?' Nick asked Sam.

'What?'

'Well, aren't you going to go with her, you prick?'

'She'll be fine, Nick,' Sam said, his eyes losing some of their former annoyance and looking suspiciously bright with humour. 'I promise; she can look after herself.'

'I don't think –'

'Listen, big man,' Sam cut him off, 'we have to stay with *you*. Understand? That's the deal with this gig. We're not here for shits and giggles, okay? Goodie can look after herself; she's been doing it her whole life.'

Nick clenched his jaw and his hands balled into fists by his sides.

'Um ... listen, Nick, mate,' Ed mumbled, rubbing his unshaven face and shifting uncomfortably on his ratty old Converse. (Nick's attempts to coax Ed out of his ironic science-geek T-shirts, ill-fitting jeans and falling-apart trainers had not been successful. To be honest as soon as he started describing the science behind the idea, his stutter dissolved, genius shone through, and nobody in the room gave a fuck what he was wearing anyway.) 'Maybe we should get going.'

'Um ... ' Bertie put in. 'Think old Ed might have a point, Flopsy; the natives are getting a bit restless.'

'Right,' Nick clipped, shooting Sam one last frustrated look before he strode back towards the waiting executives.

~

NICK STARED AT THE CUP OF TEA IN FRONT OF HIM, taking a deep breath in through his nose and letting it out in a huff from his mouth. Goodie's beautiful but bloodshot eyes, flushed cheeks and the bead of sweat on her forehead flitted through his mind as he tried to focus on Ed's excited voice. Everyone else around the conference table was absolutely transfixed by Ed's enthusiasm and the revolutionary ideas he had developed.

Unlike in other meetings of this kind, Nick had barely said a word. Surprisingly Bertie had stepped into the breach rather well: introducing Ed and discussing some of the financial details of the project. Nick tried to focus back onto what was

Goodnight

being said but all he seemed to be capable of hearing was Goodie's hoarse voice and seeing the wince on her face when she swallowed. Before he knew what he was going to do, he had shoved his chair back and was standing up. All eyes swung to him. He scanned the surprised faces, mumbled a few weak apologies and told Bertie and Ed, 'I'm sure you chaps can finish up without me.' With that he shoved his laptop in his briefcase, slammed it shut and strode over to the door.

Chapter 18

Gogol Mogol

Goodie tried to control the shaking that was raking her body but it was no use. Salem licked her hand as it was hanging off the edge of the bed until she shuffled back slightly and patted the space beside her so he could leap up next to her. She was so cold. She pulled the duvet up further and cuddled into Salem's large, warm body, but nothing could tamp down the shaking. Sleep, she thought, as she closed her aching eyes, I just need to sleep. In the back of her mind she knew that what she really needed was some fluids and paracetamol, but for the moment that wasn't happening. She'd survive; she always did.

'Goodie,' she heard his deep voice and felt gentle fingers shift her hair away from her forehead. 'Jesus Christ, you're boiling.' Her duvet was being pulled back and Salem's warm body was pushed from her side. To her horror a whimper of protest left her lips as she tried to snatch the covers back.

'You're too hot, honey,' his voice told her again, closer now, and she could feel his breath on her cheek. 'Have you taken anything for the fever?' She shook her head. Where was her knife? She needed to stab this sadist in the throat.

Next thing she knew she was being sat up in bed supported by a strong arm at her back. 'You've got to take these, baby.' She felt two tablets in her hand and managed to lift them to her mouth, wincing as she swallowed over her ravaged throat. 'Drink this.' A glass was brought up to her lips and she took a few sips, but the cold water hurt her throat even more than the tablets had. Thankfully the sadist didn't push it any further, and let her settle back into the bed. She pulled the duvet up to her chin again and curled into a ball, her shaking back with a vengeance. Moments later she could hear the low mumbling of his voice and blinked her eyes open to see that he was on the phone. When he caught her eye he moved to the bed and put the phone up to her ear.

'Goodie, *cariad*?'

Goodie rolled her eyes and shot Nick a filthy look.

'Katie,' she rasped.

'Oh no, you sound rough. Nick's worried, bless him.'

'He *should* be worried. When I have strength back I am going to kill him,' Goodie said, trying to make her voice menacing but in reality the croaking just made her sound pathetic.

'Tell me your symptoms.'

Goodie told her to fuck off in Russian and Katie snorted a laugh. 'I know enough to know that was a naughty word, you cheeky girl. Humour me, okay?' Even though she was laughing as she spoke, Goodie could detect a thread of unease in Katie's voice; she really was going to kill Nick when she was able, for worrying her like this.

'I have cold,' Goodie told Katie, letting her Russian accent thicken in her exhaustion. 'Tell me, can you section people under Mental Health Act.'

'Um ... Goodie, I'm not sure ...'

'Can you do this or not?'

'I ... uh ... I can but I need a social worker and a –'

'Call these people. Get them here. This man has lost his mind. I have cold; tell him to leave me alone.' Nick scowled at Goodie and snatched back the phone, stalking out of the room. She was just thinking that maybe he had taken her at her word and left her alone (why that made her chest constrict and her nausea worsen she had no idea) when he pushed open the door to her bedroom again.

'Right,' he said, using the no-nonsense voice she had often heard him employ in meetings. 'Katie thinks you have flu. I spoke to Mum because I couldn't remember what she used to give me, and I made this.'

Goodie stared at him and blinked. 'You ... spoke to your mother?'

He didn't answer and just moved to the side of the bed to pull the duvet down from under her chin. She shivered and tried to snatch it back.

'Katie said you shouldn't overheat.'

'You are sadist,' Goodie muttered, her teeth chattering together.

'Drink this.' He shoved the cup he'd been holding under her nose and she tried to push it away, shaking more violently now. 'Fuck it.' He put the cup down, slid one arm under her knees and the other around her shoulders to scoot her down the bed, then got into the bed behind her, pulling her shaking body back against his broad torso. Not used to sharing personal space, her first reaction was to push away, but then his warmth seeped through her clothes and she almost sighed with relief as her shakes subsided. Maybe it was the fever, maybe the intoxicating feeling of having him so close, she couldn't be sure, but

Goodnight

after a moment she actually buried deeper into him, pressing her face against his neck.

She felt his chest expand as he took a deep breath, then one of his hands started stroking her hair and her back as he reached across with the other for the cup he'd brought in. 'Try it, baby,' he murmured against her hair, wafting the cup under her nose. The smell of lemon and honey drifting up to her was surprisingly soothing and she found herself reaching up and grasping it before taking a long sip.

'That smell,' Nick said, still stroking her back. 'Reminds me of my childhood, you know?' Goodie shrugged, swallowing the rest of the cup and almost moaning at how soothing it was to her throat. 'Didn't your mum ever make you honey and lemon when you were sick?'

Goodie shivered again and instinctively buried further into his chest. As a child she had had to rely on herself. She had long ago blocked the distant memory of her mama from her mind. When her thoughts strayed back there it tended to only be the image of those Christmas lights reflected in those glassy, unseeing eyes. But now something swam up from the back of her mind; she felt the soft brush of her mama's lips on her forehead again, and a warm mug placed in her hand.

'*Gogol Mogol*,' she muttered against his chest.

'What?'

'I'd forgotten ... the pain, the darkness, it pushes the other memories down.'

'I don't understand you, baby,' Nick murmured, kissing her temple and stroking her hair.

'I mustn't forget ...' she muttered, her voice growing weaker, 'must try not to forget ...' She trailed off and her body went slack as her breathing evened out.

'That looks bloody gross, mate.'

Nick scowled at Ed, then peered over his iPad again to check the recipe before stirring the thick glop in the glass a couple of times.

'Well, Russians are weird, aren't they,' Nick grumbled, 'and anyway I haven't warmed it up yet.'

Ed shook his head. 'Think Goodie is more of a straight vodka type of girl. Not an egg, milk, honey with a dash of brandy drinker.'

'I know what I'm doing,' Nick said, wishing he hadn't asked Ed and Bertie over for the strategy meeting they needed before tomorrow. 'She said Gogol Mogol, and this is what it is.'

'She said that, but did she actually request it? Maybe it was a fever-induced nightmare of some sort of torture she'd been through.'

'Looks a bit like that time we dared Dicky Vom-it-up Dickerson to drink that pint of curdled Baileys and whiskey that had been sitting on a radiator for a couple of days.'

'Fun times,' Nick deadpanned, and then rolled his eyes when he realized that yes, to Bertie it had indeed been fun times. Sometimes he thought Bertie would be happier in an alternative universe where you remained forever institutionalized in boarding school or at Oxford in the Bullingdon Club; not in the real world, where downing a pint of curdled Baileys with your trousers round your ankles and then vomiting it up over the bar wasn't considered the height of entertainment.

Nick slammed the door of the microwave shut and scowled at them both, but was distracted by the bedroom door opening. Since yesterday Goodie had done a lot of sleeping. He'd decided not to risk moving her into his apartment: she may be weak but she could still probably inflict severe bodily harm if provoked to that extent. So he'd just moved into hers. It wasn't

Goodnight

like he was invading her privacy; she had almost no personal possessions whatsoever in her flat. Nick had bought the whole floor off plan when he decided where he wanted to live, thinking it would be convenient for his family when they came down to London. The developer had fully furnished and decorated them all, but the ones Nick and his family stayed in were full of books, pictures, old umbrellas, useless nick nacks ... stuff. Goodie's apartment had never been used before and still had the picture frame complete with fake family on the mantelpiece. She'd lived there for two months now, and literally nothing had been changed or displayed; it was almost eerie.

He smiled as he saw her emerge from the bedroom in just his shirt with Salem at her side; her hair was rumpled and her eyes slightly swollen, but the feverish flush was gone from her cheeks and her hands were steady. Her eyes widened as she took in the three men standing in her kitchen, then she narrowed them to glare at Nick

'Oh hello, old girl,' Bertie said into the silence, ignoring the uncomfortable atmosphere, as was his wont. 'Heard you were feeling a bit flipperty-gibbert. Get well soon and all that.' Goodie didn't spare Bertie a glance, she was still staring at Nick.

'What are you doing in my home?' she said, her voice hoarse, but you could still hear the menace.

'Making you this,' Nick said cheerfully, turning back to the microwave as it pinged and pulling out the mug. Goodie stalked across the living area to the small kitchen. It looked as though she might physically eject them all for a moment, and then she stilled, her eyes flicking down to the mug Nick was holding out to her.

'What?' she whispered, the anger falling away from her face to be replaced by confusion.

'Gogol Mogol,' Nick told her.

'I don't under –'

'You talked about it when I brought you the honey and lemon,' he said gently, reaching forward to take her hand in his, and then lifting it up so that her fingers curled around the mug. Her eyes lifted from the mug to his as she took it from him and brought it up to her nose, inhaling deeply.

'*Bozhe moy,*'* she breathed, lifting her other hand to wrap around the mug and hold it to her like it was the most precious thing she had ever seen. 'You ... you make for me?' Her whispered words were thick with the Russian accent she normally suppressed. He nodded slowly, becoming a little alarmed by her out-of-character reaction; he could have sworn her eyes were actually wet for a moment. Slowly she placed the mug down on the kitchen counter with as much care as you would take over a priceless piece of china. Once she was free of it she hesitated for a second, still staring at him like she couldn't believe he was real, the vulnerable expression on her face totally at odds with what Nick was used to. Then she moved: launching forward into him, the impact nearly forcing him back on one foot. Her arms clamped around him in a vice-like grip and she buried her face in his chest. Nick stood in shock for a second before he enclosed her in his large arms, dropped his face to the top of her head, closed his eyes and inhaled. Holding her small body to his, he felt relief sweep through him, like having her close but not in his arms had been some sort of unrecognized strain.

'Golly,' Bertie said, breaking the silence, and Nick felt Goodie stiffen in his arms. He had, on occasion, thought that Bertie could do with a good punch in the face, but in that moment he would have quite happily strangled him. 'Much better than old Dicky's reaction, although I doubt you'd have been quite as keen on cuddling him, the state he was in.'

Goodnight

Goodie tried to pull out of Nick's arms and they stiffened around her, his need to keep her close so strong it was almost instinctive. But then Ed laid a hand on Nick's shoulder. Nick turned his face to him and Ed shook his head once. Nick sighed and reluctantly loosened his grip so that she could push herself away.

'Hey, Goodie Two Shoes,' Ed said softly as she moved away until her back hit the counter. 'You look a bit better, love.' Goodie's eyes flicked between the three men and it took a few seconds but then the shutters came down, blocking out any trace of vulnerability from before.

'I am fine,' she rasped, making her way around the kitchen island to put even more space between them. 'I need to ...' She trailed off, looking lost for a moment; then she glanced down at what she was wearing, and to Nick's complete amazement she blushed. '... get dressed.' She turned on her heel and practically ran to her bedroom, slamming the door behind her.

'Don't push her,' Ed said under his breath to Nick. 'Let her come to you. Don't make her feel trapped.'

Nick huffed out a breath and tore his hands through his hair. Having never had to put in the slightest bit of effort for anything he wanted in his life before, especially women, he wasn't sure he had the patience to deal with Goodie. Then he remembered the feel of her in his arms and the clean, citrussy scent of her hair and he knew that he would just have to develop it, and fast.

'I don't know.' He shook his head. 'It feels like one step forward, ten steps back with her. Could be I never break through. I'm not sure that ...' He broke off as the bedroom door opened again. Goodie walked back to the kitchen island, still in his shirt, ignoring all of them. She went straight to the Gogol Mogol, snatched it off the surface and stalked back to her room, clutching it to her chest. Nick watched with astonishment as she slammed the door again.

And then he smiled.

* *Bozhe moy* – Oh my God

Chapter 19

Yukanol Fukov

GOODIE LET HER FINGERS RELAX IN SALEM'S HAIR AS THE lift stopped on the penthouse floor. She could feel Nick watching her and resisted the urge to tell him to stop. Unfortunately the whole nursing-her-back-to-health (although she doubted she would have carked it had Nick not intervened doing his Knight-in-Shining-Honey-and-Lemon routine), and her ridiculous reaction to the Gogol Mogol, meant that now he appeared to feel free to be, in her opinion, over-familiar.

It would help if she didn't actually find his sense of humour, the way he looked out for Bertie and Ed, his commanding presence in the boardroom and his attention (including the way he watched her) irresistible, but she just couldn't help herself. Men, even attractive men, had always been regarded with some form of suspicion and vague dislike by Goodie – either that or total indifference. Sam was one exception to this rule; she respected Sam, God knows he'd earned it; she could count him as a friend. But with Nick ... somehow she felt like she was falling off a cliff, totally out of control, trying to grab on to something to stop herself but never quite managing it. For the first time since Goodie was nine years old she felt fear, and it was terrifying.

As soon as the doors were open she shot out of the lift, forcing herself to walk to her apartment door and not flat-out run like she wanted: that would show weakness, that would show him he affected her.

She felt heat at her back as she wrestled with the lock, and snapped her head around, looking up into his beautiful face, complete with thick five o'clock shadow. He smiled. That was the other thing: that fucking, *fucking* dimple. For some reason it made her stomach hollow out and her heart race. Before she'd met Nick she'd had full control over her autonomic nervous system: she could go without oxygen for up to eight minutes if required, she could slow her heart rate under battle circumstances in order to take the perfect shot – she was a goddamn *machine* for Christ's sake. Why was she so affected by a fucking dimple?

The really perverse thing was that she went out of her way to *provoke* its appearance. Goodie had never tried to please anyone before (unless of course it served her purposes); she certainly never tried to make anyone smile. But with Nick she found herself dropping more and more deadpan little jokes here and there: in response to the HR team's third interrogation about Goodie's full name in the reception area she had stared at them all for a moment as they blocked her and Nick's way, and then told them her full name was: 'Yukanol Fukov.' One of the more dopey ones even made her spell it out for them. By the time Nick and Goodie had made it back to his office he was shaking with laughter and the dimple was out again in full force.

He'd laughed even harder when Bertie had sidled in and said, 'Good grief, not surprised you kept that one up your sleeve for so long. Fukov must be devilishly tricky to pull off as a surname over here. Can't say I've heard a lady called Yukanol before ... um ... not that it isn't ...'

Goodie took pity on him. 'Bertie,' she interrupted; he looked over at her and she winked. 'You can call me Yuko.' Bertie beamed, obviously interpreting this as a high honour indeed, and Nick started laughing again. One of the worst things was that Nick's laughter *and* his fucking dimple both made Goodie smile. She was smiling all the bloody time at the moment, like her face had taken on a life of its own.

'What are you doing?' she asked, turning back to open her door. Nick's large hand reached up above her head and pushed it open with her, and to her exasperation he then followed her inside before she could shut it in his face.

'I thought we could watch something; get a takeaway; hang out.' Nick ambled over to her sofa as he said all this, then flopped down on it, put his massive feet up on the coffee table, and grabbed the remote.

'I have things to do,' Goodie bit out, watching Salem (the traitor) pad over to where Nick was sitting and put his head on his lap.

'Like what?'

Goodie scowled at him. She was planning on doing what she had done every night since she'd been ill: make some Gogol Mogol, curl up on the sofa to reread *The Lion, the Witch and the Wardrobe*, and try to remember her mother. Until Nick had handed her that drink she hadn't realized how much of her childhood before that traumatic day when she was nine she'd blocked out. For some reason forgetting nearly everything about her mother made her feel desolate and guilty now. If Goodie didn't remember her, then it was like she never existed: just another murdered whore in the slums of Cherepovets City. Just a statistic. So she would sit on the sofa and smell the Gogol Mogol, trying to conjure up her image; but everything was cloudy. Goodie could see her mother's blonde hair but not how long it was or how she wore it; see the outline of her face but none of her features. Maybe it wasn't healthy to be dwelling on this, but somehow Goodie felt she *had* to.

'That is none of your business,' she snapped at him. 'I am off the clock: the building's security system is airtight; the far guards are outside. You don't need me.'

'Maybe *you* need *me*,' Nick said softly, and she snorted, turning away from him and stomping to the kitchen. She came back with two bottles of beer in her hands, dumped one in front of Nick's feet and then sat on the other end of the sofa with hers.

'I will have curry,' she told him, curling her feet underneath her and focusing on the television screen, which he had turned onto the news. Out of the corner of her eye she could see he had turned to face her, his arm draping across the back of the sofa, and even though she couldn't see his face she could *feel* his smile.

'What kind of curry do you like?' he asked, digging his phone out of his pocket. Goodie just shrugged, remaining focused on the screen. 'Hey,' he called softly, and she reluctantly turned towards him. 'What kind of curry do you want, honey? This is not a state secret; you can tell me.' His voice was soft but he was still smiling slightly and his eyes were dancing. Everything about his body language was open: the way he sat, his outspread arms, his body facing hers. That was one of the things she had noticed about Nick that she found hopelessly appealing: he was so open, so charming, he could put anyone at ease within seconds of meeting them no matter what. Her total and complete opposite, she thought, as she noted her own body language: arms wrapped around herself, body curled towards the side of the sofa away from him; defensive, closed. She forced her arms to loosen their grip on her sides and turned to

Goodnight

face him, realizing that the way she was sitting showed she was uncomfortable. It showed weakness. She was not afraid of him.

'I like anything with a kick,' she told him.

'Of course you do,' he muttered through a chuckle, putting the phone to his ear.

∽

IT WAS AFTER THEY'D EATEN THE CURRY, AFTER WATCHING *Star Wars* together on the sofa (Nick had been incensed that Goodie had never seen any of the *Star Wars* films – he acted like it was some sort of emergency situation to be rectified), and after Goodie had drunk two bottles of beer. Nick flicked off the television and the room dimmed to just the soft glow from a small lamp on a side table. He had been inching towards her all night. When the curry arrived he'd jumped up to get it and then moved to the middle of the sofa to set it all out. After they'd finished he had insisted on clearing away the plates and containers. Salem, as if in league with Nick, had taken that opportunity to jump up on the sofa and spread his huge furry body out with a loud sigh of contentment, meaning that when Nick returned he ended up sitting even closer to Goodie. So close, in fact, that he had slung his arm up behind her head on the back of the sofa, and eventually he had let it drop to her shoulder and pulled her against him. She pushed up but he just kept her pinned to his chest muttering 'settle' into her hair and kissing the side of her head. And, God help her, with his warm chest under her cheek, his clean, woodsy scent all around her, she couldn't help herself: she settled.

For over an hour the steady beat of his heart and the sound of his breathing surrounded her, and she felt ... peaceful. This was not normal for Goodie; there were very few things in her life that had brought her that kind of peace. So when the room dimmed and his heartbeat was all she could hear she went a little mad. She pushed back from him slightly so that she could look up into his beautiful face. Her hand lifted of its own accord to trace the stubble on his cheek, his eyebrow, and finally to snake its way into his thick, dark hair. She stared at his mouth and could feel his heartbeat pick up under her other hand on his chest. Then she kissed him. It was a light brush of the lips before she pulled back, but only far enough to rest her forehead against his. Their mouths were millimetres apart and their breath mingled as their eyes locked. She could feel his big body tensing under her hand, feel the strain he was exerting to hold himself back.

'Let go,' she whispered into his mouth, and it was like she'd tripped a switch. The arm that was already around her shoulders tightened, pulling her body flush against his, and his other hand plunged into her hair so that he could tilt her head back and kiss her. This kiss was not light; it was out of control, brutal, almost desperate. He pushed her back until she was lying against the arm of the sofa, pressing her into the leather, one of his hands still in her hair and the other sliding under the hem of her T-shirt. Goodie tried to hold onto the feel of this amazing man, tried not to slide from the moment, but her mind had other ideas and her body stiffened as she drifted away from what was happening. Nick stilled on top of her, then drew back. He searched her face, a small frown forming between his brows.

'Baby,' he breathed, and she blinked. Why had he stopped? 'Baby, come back to me.' Slowly she let herself return from automatic pilot until she was really looking at him.

'What is the matter?' she asked as he stroked the side of her head. As his hands moved behind her ear they found the scar tissue she had there which carved down across the back of her neck under her hairline.

Goodnight

'What the ...?' he muttered as he turned her head to the side so that he could see the scar more clearly. 'What happened?'

Goodie shrugged. 'It could have been worse; could have been my carotid he sliced. It was a lesson for me: never turn your back on your enemy.' Nick's eyes darkened and his jaw clenched. His hand continued down her neck to her clavicle and then across to her shoulder, pushing her top to the side. Goodie sighed as he encountered more scar tissue.

'Fucking hell,' he muttered, peering down at the circular scar, his face strangely pale. 'You were shot.'

Goodie rolled her eyes, then reached up and cupped his face with her hand, putting pressure on his cheek so that he looked away from her scar and into her eyes. 'I have many scars, Nick,' she told him, and his jaw clenched even tighter. 'You must understand. For someone like me it is different. It is what I am trained for ... all I am good for. Yes, I have many scars, but for every scar on my body there are many, many more that I have inflicted on others. Don't forget that. Don't forget who I am.'

'You're wrong; Pain and violence are not all you're good for,' Nick said, his voice rising in anger. He pushed away from her abruptly to the other side of the sofa and ran both hands through his hair. Goodie blinked at the ceiling for a minute, then sat herself up and curled her legs beneath her, body language defensive again. Okay, so he didn't like scars; he wouldn't be the first and he certainly would not be the last. Her throat felt tight as she swallowed; she chalked it up to the after-effects of her illness. She heard Nick take a deep breath, and could feel the tension rolling off him even with the distance separating them.

'Right,' he said into the silence, jumping to his feet. Goodie turned away towards Salem and stroked his head absently, expecting to hear the door slam after Nick. A shadow blocked out the light from the lamp and she turned in surprise to see him looming over her. He seemed calmer, but she could still see a muscle ticking in his jaw. He squatted down in front of her and reached out to take both of her hands in his. 'I'm sorry you were hurt,' he said softly, leaning in slowly to kiss the scar behind her ear, and then pulling her shirt back to kiss the one on her shoulder.

'Life is pain,' Goodie muttered, and felt his tension fill the room again. He leaned back to look her in the eyes, his face hovering close to hers.

'It doesn't have to be, baby,' he said, his voice still soft.

'Maybe not for you.' His jaw clenched again and his hands tightened their grip on hers for a moment, before he closed the gap between them and kissed her swiftly on the mouth, then on her nose. It was the kind of casual, sweet affection that Goodie had never really experienced. The vice around her throat tightened and she swallowed.

'I'll just have to convince you otherwise,' he said, his total and utter confidence oozing from every word. He pulled her up to stand with him and led her over to her door. She was frowning when he turned back to her, which for some reason made him smile, dimple and all. He brushed her mouth with his once more before pulling open her door. 'Tomorrow, then, bright and early.'

Goodie stood staring at the door after Nick had closed it. Her hand went to her mouth and her fingers touched her lips almost reverently before she shook her head and turned away.

Chapter 20

He's up to something

GOODIE GLANCED AT HER WATCH AND TUCKED HER PHONE between her ear and her shoulder as she walked to the wardrobe. 'Is there any security around the house?' She grabbed a pair of faded jeans and started pulling them on.

'Well, it's in St John's Wood so there's a patrol anyway in the area,' Sam told her. 'The house itself has an alarm system but I doubt it will be activated.' Goodie frowned.

'We can negotiate that. Once the guests are all there, and they're inside and we're out, they could activate the system. They'd just have to tell everyone not to open any windows or leave the house without deactivating.'

'Nick wants you inside.'

Goodie snorted. 'Tough.'

'He says it's non negotiable. He says he's worried about a threat *in* the house.'

'He's not fucking worried about a threat in the house. He's *never* worried about any threats full stop.'

'Well,' Sam said carefully. '*We* work for *him*, Goodie. We probably should do as he asks for a change.'

'He's up to something.'

Sam sighed. 'I expect so.'

'Well, I'm not changing.'

'He said it's casual anyway. He specifically told me you didn't have to dress up. It was important to him that you knew that.' Goodie rubbed her chest absently against the sudden constriction she was feeling.

Nick noticed things. He knew she didn't like wearing that stuff.

She pushed her hair back with the hand not holding the phone and stared up at the ceiling. It was this kind of thing that was getting to her, that was burrowing underneath her reserve. The small stuff he did to make her that bit more comfortable; that bit ... happier. She knew he phoned ahead about Salem everywhere they went. She wasn't stupid, dogs would not be allowed in most executive buildings in the city; somehow he could tell she needed Salem in the lifts. How he knew about her claustrophobia she wasn't sure, but she suspected he had read her body language. This in itself was impressive; Goodie knew that she didn't give much away.

She pushed open the door of her flat, coming face to face with Sam and shoving her mobile into the pocket of her jeans. Sam watched as she sighed and pulled on her leather jacket, zipping it up to her chin. She swept her blonde fringe out of her eyes before putting her hands on her hips. 'Right then, you coming?' There was annoyance threaded through her voice, but also just a hint of what may have been excitement. Her blue eyes caught his, and she raised her eyebrows. Sam had always known Goodie was beautiful, but over the last few weeks her features had become more animated, her eyes held more sparkle, he had even caught a couple of half smiles. As a result her beauty was more pronounced than he'd ever seen. It was almost blinding. He cared about Goodie; he just hoped

Nick knew what he was doing ... and who he was dealing with.

∼

Goodie stayed two steps behind Nick as they approached the house. There had been some battles about this way of doing things over the last two weeks: she rarely walked at his side; depending on where the far guard was she was either a few steps behind or in front. Nick had gone through a stage of slowing down to try and fall in step with her or power-walking to catch her up. Only the threat of her switching with Sam had made him back off. She scanned the drive and her mouth hitched up at the side when she saw a Porsche parked up next to an Aston Martin and blocked in by a large Range Rover. Rich, entitled and arrogant was not her brand of vodka. When she looked back towards the front door she nearly ran into Nick, who had stopped and was watching her, smiling enough for the dimple to make an appearance.

'I know,' he told her. 'You think the whole house is full of wankers and I don't blame you; but not all my mates are like Clive.'

Since Clive left the house that day he had been keeping a low profile. He never came to the office any more and mainly coordinated the project with Nick via email. Nick, Ed and Bertie had just presumed that he was keeping his distance after the split with Tilly, and, given the way Clive had been treating his sister, Nick seemed to be relieved.

Nick stepped forward and closed the distance between them, shocking her by grabbing her hand. She shook him off but he just grabbed it again.

'You want to lose your arm?' she asked through her teeth as he tugged her forward.

'Now, I thought the idea was to get me inside safe spaces as quickly as possible,' he said, still smiling as he tugged her up the steps to the front door of the large Edwardian house, 'so I'm guessing that fighting with me out in the open over petty stuff like a spot of hand-holding is a bit of a no-no.' When they reached the top step he grinned at her and dropped her hand, only to wrap his arm around her shoulders after ringing the doorbell.

'What are you –?'

'Darlings!' Goodie stopped short as the door was flung open and a small blonde woman flew at them. She kissed Nick on the cheek, practically strangling him in the process, then she threw herself at Goodie, giving her the same treatment. 'We're all so excited that Flopsy brought his new girlfriend.' The blonde was now bouncing up and down on her alarmingly high heels. She was wearing a strange combination of ripped tights, netting skirt and multiple T-shirts, with even more scarves around her neck. To top it off she had a furry headband sitting across her forehead and her blonde hair was piled in a haphazard fashion on top of her head. In Goodie's opinion she looked mentally ill.

'Flopsy!' a large man shouted from behind the blonde, coming forward to slap Nick on the back repeatedly. 'Good to see you, old man.' Goodie recognized this man's standard 'posh bloke' uniform: red trousers, shirt with collar turned up, sheepish grin and messy hair. 'Hi there,' he boomed at Goodie, giving her a slightly gentler back slap. 'I'm Giles, a.k.a. Cottontail. Good to meet you finally. Flopsy's been banging on about you for long enough. Got a glimpse of you at that charity ball last month but you were on the job; sticking to the shadows and all that business.'

'I am on job now,' Goodie told him, and he frowned.

Goodnight

'Not tonight, beautiful,' he said smoothly. 'Tonight's a party.'

Salem barked once and Goodie glanced behind her. 'Can we move inside?' she said.

'Oh of course!' said the blonde, bouncing out of their way and waving them to follow her in. 'I'm such a terrible dunderhead. Please, come in. I *love* your dog.'

'What is a dunderhead?' Goodie asked Nick under her breath as he followed her inside. 'Sounds painful.'

As the door closed behind them Nick started chuckling and pulled Goodie into his side, kissing her temple and giving her shoulders a firm squeeze. Goodie felt the familiar hollowing out in her stomach and tightening in her chest at Nick's laughter. She smiled up at him, and then froze. Turning her head slowly, she took in her surroundings. Usually the first thing she did on entering any space was scan it for its occupants, exits, possible threats; she was allowing Nick to scramble her mind. There were about fifteen people crowding the large hallway, all smiling and all looking ridiculously curious. In amongst them she could see Bertie, Tilly, and Ed. Most of the men were wearing either red or mustard-yellow trousers, Tilly looked like she still had her jodhpurs on, and Ed of course was in his standard garb of ripped jeans and a T-shirt (this one with two test tubes on the front, one telling the other it was 'overreacting').

'What ho!' Bertie boomed, striding forward through the small crowd to do his share of back-slapping for Nick and a brief hug for Goodie. Tilly was next with a far more exuberant-slash-bone-crushing hug for Goodie. As she watched all the beaming, curious faces, Goodie felt a strange sense of hopelessness. She had a feeling that her plan to stick to the outskirts and remain very much in employee mode for the evening was unlikely to happen.

'Do you know if Nick did any sort of Big Brother routine with Clive?' Tilly asked.

They had just finished the meal. The whole evening had been totally bizarre to Goodie. It was obvious that these people were Nick's best friends; apart from the fact they all called him 'Flopsy' (Cottontail, Mopsy and Peter were also in attendance), there was also the easy, casual affection and teasing that came with years, if not decades, of friendship.

You would have thought, considering how long they'd all known each other, that it would have been tricky to include obvious outsiders like Ed and Goodie, but it proved to be quite the opposite. It was as if they all found both Ed and Goodie the most fascinating human beings to walk the earth. They even listened to Ed's cold fusion explanation with rapt attention, and the scant information they were able to extract from Goodie seemed to hold them all completely spellbound.

She fiddled with the stem of her wineglass, then grabbed her water and took a large swallow. Nick might want to deny it but she *was* actually on the job.

'I don't know,' she told Tilly. 'Would it be so bad if he had?'

Tilly grimaced. 'You noticed as well, did you? He turned out to be a nasty piece of work in the end; didn't take my ending things very well at all – to be honest I thought he was going to make a bit of a nuisance of himself. Nick denies warning him off, but even if he did, I guess it was for the best. He, um ...' Tilly's hand went up to her cheek automatically before she realized what she was doing and tucked it back in her lap, '... he wasn't very nice actually. I suppose I could have given him another chance but Arabella ... she ...'

Goodie turned more towards her and caught her eyes.

Goodnight

'People do not change,' she told Tilly firmly. Tilly nodded slowly, and then managed a weak smile.

'I wish I hadn't been so frightfully stupid though,' she whispered. 'It's just that ... well, I've bumbled along since the divorce, no real job, no real direction, kid in tow. I'm not exactly the catch of the century.'

'Don't ever let someone who does not know your value dictate your worth,' Goodie told her. 'You and your daughter are worth ten of him.'

'Oh my goodness,' Tilly said, her voice a little choked. 'I think that's one of the nicest things anyone has ever said to me.'

'I did not say it to be nice,' Goodie told her. 'I am not nice: I only speak the truth.'

'Thank you,' Tilly whispered, and to Goodie's horror her eyes filled with tears.

'Hey, you.' Ed had reached across the table to Tilly, laying his hand over her arm. 'Alright?'

Tilly blinked rapidly as Ed caught Goodie's eye and she shook her head once.

'I'm fine, Ed,' Tilly said, her eyes still wet but a wide smile now dominating her face as she turned to him. 'Must be off in a jiffy though, babysitter and all that.'

'I'll take you,' Ed told her, and Goodie was surprised to hear how firm his voice was. She wouldn't have thought that Ed *did* firm, not really.

'Oh ...' Tilly blushed, her eyes sparkling and tears now very much a thing of the past, 'well, I don't want to put you out or anything. I know what a bore it is to have to leave early from things, Clive was always saying that –'

'Clive,' Ed cut her off, his voice harder than Goodie had ever heard it, 'is a dickhead. No argument: I'm taking you home.' He ran his hand down her forearm to her hand and held it possessively. Tilly looked down at their linked hands and blinked, then nodded with a small, pleased smile on her face.

'No one's going anywhere until we've played the hat game,' the small blonde hostess piped up from her end of the table, bouncing up and down in her seat. 'Boys against girls!'

Goodie was not aware that people still played games like this. She had never, even as a child, had a chance to do anything even remotely like charades, and that strange feeling of helplessness enveloped her as she was squashed onto the 'girls' sofa' in the vast living room opposite the boys, and was instructed to write down famous names to put in a hat.

You had to first describe, then act out, then use one word to describe the names in the hat to your team in three different rounds. At first the game seemed simple but the rules grew more convoluted and seemed to change as the rounds progressed. Also, cheating appeared to be acceptable practice (hiding names behind your back was fine as long as nobody saw – but if you were caught a violent struggle with one of the opposing team would invariably occur to restore the name to the hat).

The girls won by a ridiculous margin. Goodie had a crazily accurate ability to retain information. The boys didn't stand a chance. And it was the strangest thing. She started laughing when she watched Nick act out 'the arse end of nowhere' (apparently places were allowed in the hat also – a rule change which only emerged halfway through the game), and for the rest of the game she just couldn't stop. In her twenty-nine years Goodie could count on one hand the number of times she'd actually laughed; in one evening she'd managed to smash all previous records to pieces. The evening finished off with 'Fungal Bum Candle' – a game which involved having a mushroom dangling from a piece of string attached to the back of your trousers and attempting to put out a candle on the floor with it.

It was the most ridiculous, utterly bonkers endeavour Goodie had ever witnessed. By the end of the evening her cheeks were actually wet with tears of laughter. Nick had done his fair share of laughing too, but she had noticed that more often than not he was happy to watch her, and nearly always had her in his immediate radius: his hand on her back before they sat for dinner, his arm around the back of her chair during dinner, holding her hand on the sofa when he extracted her from the girls' sofa after the hat game had finally concluded. She allowed it. She was coming to realize that when it came to this man she would allow pretty much anything.

No, Goodie hadn't felt fear in a good long while, but when it came to him she was terrified.

Chapter 21

Here with you

Nick was smiling as he walked into his office. He had left Bertie trying to explain the merits of moss to a long-suffering Goodie; who knew how many types of the bloody stuff there were? He opened his laptop and was about to click on the file for the presentation that afternoon when his phone beeped, signalling a text.

I have something.

He blinked at the message. Walker had been on the job for three months now and he had yet to communicate in any sort of positive fashion. The name must have helped. Nick had begun to think of her as Anya since the day he saw her react to it. Even if it wasn't hers it suited her better than Goodie (and certainly better than Yukanol Fukov – which she was now down as officially with HR).

Send it, he texted back. After a few moments his phone rang in his hand and he frowned. Walker was such a tight-arse Nick had never known him to be the one to phone using his own money, especially not when he would be paying a premium to call from Russia.

Goodnight

'What?' Nick snapped down the phone.

'Nick,' Walker started, then was silent.

'Yes?' Nick said slowly, losing patience.

'What we've found … It …' Walker trailed off and Nick leaned back in his chair to stare up at the ceiling in frustration. '… mate, it's a little … fucked up.'

'Just send it,' Nick gritted out through his teeth. 'I'm paying you to obtain information for me. The least you can do after months of bugger all is to send what you finally *do* have.'

'This woman … is she …?' Walker broke off and there was another goddamn pause.

'Is she what?' Nick asked, starting to get angry now.

'Is she okay?' Walker asked softly, and Nick blinked.

'What the hell do you mean?'

'I mean … is she …?' Walker cleared his throat. 'Nick, I've never seen anything like this. What I've got, it's … you need to be careful with this girl.'

Nick frowned. This was the first time he'd ever heard Walker sound remotely unsure of himself. He heard Sam's voice in his head: '*Some things are best left buried.*'

'Just bloody send it,' he clipped, his hand tightening around the phone.

Walker sighed.

'Okay … right, it's done.'

Nick didn't bother saying goodbye, he just hung up and moved to his laptop. The new email was there waiting for him. He hesitated before clicking open the attachment. As the image filled the screen he sucked in a deep breath, and then stopped breathing altogether. He sat completely frozen for at least a minute before he finally breathed out in a rush. He reached forward as if to touch the screen with his finger, but pulled back when he realized what he was doing. His hand instead went to his face and he was shocked when it came away wet from his cheeks. Nick couldn't remember the last time he'd cried.

'Hey, big man,' Bertie's voice sounded through the monitor, and Nick started in his chair, wiping the tears from his face and slamming down the lid of his laptop. 'Anything you need me to get ready?'

Nick cleared his throat and straightened his tie, then pressed the button on the intercom. 'Send Goodie in,' he told Bertie.

'You called, High Commander,' Goodie said as she pushed into the office.

'Shut the door,' Nick told her, his voice still rough from the emotion he was fighting to hold back. Goodie frowned at him, but shut the door behind her, walked to his desk and cocked her head to the side.

'There is problem?' she asked, and he stood abruptly from his chair to stalk around his desk.

'Nick?' she asked as he came towards her, a determined look on his face. When she was within reaching distance he made a grab for her and pulled her into him for a bone-crushing hug. Something eased in his chest as he felt her small body, warm in his arms.

She was alive.

She was here.

She would never be hurt again.

He repeated those three things over and over as he held her. His heart was hammering as if he'd run a marathon, and he was fighting the renewed stinging behind his eyes. It took him a minute but he managed to push it back. When he pulled away a fraction and looked down at her face, he saw the soft expression mixed with confusion in her beautiful ice-blue eyes, and a small, bewildered smile on her lips. He felt a shot of pride go through him. Before the last few weeks she did not give *anyone*

Goodnight

soft expressions, she did not allow physical affection, and she never, never smiled. He had done that. He gave her a short, brief, hard kiss, then pulled back again.

'Are you mentally unstable?' she asked him, and he laughed, breaking the tension.

'Maybe a little.' He kissed the end of her nose and searched her face again before tracing the small crescent scar next to her eye with his fingers. His jaw clenched for a moment before he repeated in his mind the three statements from earlier to calm him.

'You are weird,' she told him, and he nodded.

'You're not exactly the poster child for normal,' he shot back, and then watched the smile fade from her face.

'No, I'm not,' she told him, her voice back to cold and expressionless as she tried to pull away from him.

'I'm teasing,' he said, keeping his arms around her with some difficulty. 'Normal's boring.' She rolled her eyes and he felt the constriction in his chest lighten; eye-rolling was another sign of the new and improved, more human Goodie. 'Listen, once we're done with this next meeting would you come over to mine? I need to talk to you about something.'

Goodie shrugged. 'Okay ... is it about your mental health problems?' He laughed and shook his head. 'Your biscuit addiction?' she asked, eyeing the nearly empty basket of biscuits and muffins he'd received earlier from a client. 'Bertie's red trouser addiction? Your mustard-yellow trouser addiction?'

'Not all of us dress almost exclusively in black, Goodie.' She snorted and he smiled. 'Tell me you'll come over later.'

'Of course I will,' she said, giving him a squeeze and then pushing away from him. 'Now get your shit together or you'll be late.' As she left the room Nick closed his eyes, brought one hand up to the back of his neck and the other to rub his forehead. It was no good. That image was there to stay. It would haunt him until he died.

Thousands of miles away in a brutally cold, unrelentingly depressing part of Cherepovets City, Walker stared at the photograph in his hand and shuddered. The little girl standing in the centre of the photo was looking straight at the camera. The one eye not swollen shut was cold and blank. She was covered in blood, and it was only just possible to make out the white blonde of her hair. Her feet were bare and her torn, dirty, blood-soaked clothes hung off her tiny frame. Her jaw was tight and her mouth was a thin stubborn line. Instead of the fear and pain you would expect to see in her face there was anger, defiance. But that didn't change the fact that she was just a little girl. Walker took a deep breath and stared instead at the other image he was holding. The woman in it had the same white blonde hair as the child, the same defiant expression.

'I hope you've found your peace,' he muttered at the image before shoving them both into the file he had compiled. Nick better know what the fuck he was doing.

∼

Casual affection.

Goodie had had so little of this in her life that it was coming as a bit of a shock to the system. Nick seemed to thrive on it, and slowly – very slowly – Goodie was starting to see why. The Night of the Gogol Mogol had been a turning point for her. Since then she had been allowing Nick to gradually chip away at her defences. And since the night with his friends she was starting to trust him. He cared about her. It didn't help that all day it was her job to watch him. She found very small things about him were ridiculously attractive: his forearms as he pushed his shirt up, his hair ruffled at the end of the day, his five

Goodnight

o'clock shadow, his fucking dimple. So Goodie had made a decision: she wanted Nick; all that was holding her back was fear; and Goodie was no coward. Katie's words from three years ago had been drifting through her brain more frequently now: *'You can feel, just like anyone else. You could live a different life if you wanted.'* Could she? After all this time, could she try for a different life?

'Yo,' she called as she pushed through the door to Nick's flat. He emerged from the kitchen looking harassed.

'Shit,' he said, poking his head around the corner from the kitchen, 'hold on.' He ducked back out of sight and Goodie frowned at the smell of burning as she walked down the corridor.

'What happened here?' she asked. All the kitchen counters were covered with debris, every single pot and pan was dirty, and a stressed-looking Nick was extracting something ominously black from the oven. He scowled down at the offending casserole dish and then heaved a huge sigh.

'I wanted to make you a Coulibiac.' He shrugged as her eyebrows went up. 'I mean, you seemed to like the Gogol Mogol and you said you wanted to remember more about your mother, so I called Mum and this was the only Russian dish she knew to talk me through.'

'My mother may have stretched to Gogol Mogol but I have a feeling that Russian-style home cooking will not remind me of her,' Goodie said, softening her words with a smile. Nick rubbed the back of his neck and grinned sheepishly.

'Sorry, stupid idea.'

'Not stupid ... I just had a different childhood to you.'

For some reason Nick's expression darkened and he clenched both hands into fists at his sides. 'I know, Goodie, that's actually what I wanted to talk to you about. You see, I know this chap ... he's pretty good with finding out about –'

'Shhh,' Goodie whispered; she had come around the kitchen island to stand in front of Nick and put her fingers on his lips. She didn't know what he was banging on about, but it could wait. 'I love that you try to do this for me,' she told him, the fingers on his lips moving to slip into his thick hair and pull his head down to hers. Over the last month kissing had been a regular thing but Nick always put a stop there. Tonight Goodie was determined: she was not going to shut down and go somewhere else in her head, she was not going to just go through the motions with him, for the first time in her life she was going to allow herself to actually *feel* something for someone.

'I want you,' she whispered into his mouth, and his whole body jerked in reaction before he lifted her up and sat her on the island, shoving pots and pans aside and sending them clattering to the floor. One of his hands went under her T-shirt and the other into her hair and he kissed her almost desperately before he leaned back and ripped her T-shirt up and over her head. He swallowed as he looked down at her and she could see his mind working behind his beautiful eyes. He wanted her but he wanted her to stay *here* with him, he wanted her to really feel something. Goodie had never encountered any man who even gave the vaguest of shits where her mind was at, once she was willingly half-naked, and she felt her chest tighten as she looked up at him. Sitting up, she framed his face with both hands and stared into his eyes.

'I'm here with you,' she told him. 'I will stay here, I promise. I want you.' He scanned her face for a moment. Whatever he saw there must have reassured him because he then picked her up with her legs straddling his waist and walked her to his bedroom.

Chapter 22
Fall in soldier

'Hello,' Goodie murmured as Nick blinked slowly awake. Her head was resting on her hands on his chest, and her blue eyes were staring up into his.

'Hey,' Nick said, his voice thick with sleep. 'How long have you been up?'

She smiled.

'Little while,' she told him, turning her head to lay it flat on her hands and then absently tracing patterns on his chest with her fingers. He brought both arms up around her to give her a firm squeeze, and then kissed the top of her head.

'I need to tell you something,' she said into the comfortable silence.

'You can tell me anything, baby,' he said into her hair, breathing in the clean, citrussy smell of her hair.

'I ...' she broke off, then stopped tracing his chest for a moment to push up from him and stare into his eyes, 'I am not whore.'

He frowned. 'Goodie, honey, I know you're not –'

'I am *not*,' she told him, either ignoring or not taking in what he was saying, her face looking almost pained. 'But I have done things ... I have ...' She broke off again and closed her eyes slowly, taking a deep breath in through her nose before she continued. 'I am not whore but I have had to do things that would make you think that maybe –'

'Goodie, you don't have to –'

'I *want* to tell you this,' she said, fierce determination lighting her eyes. 'I need you to know that I may have been with those men but I was never *with* them. You understand? Not like last night. Not like I was with you.'

'I understand,' he told her, all teasing leaving his voice, his expression suddenly serious. 'Thank you for giving me that.' Her blue eyes, so full of apprehension and tension, softened and her face lit with the widest smile he'd ever seen from her.

'Jesus Christ,' he muttered. 'You are so unbelievably beautiful.'

Her smile faded and the delighted look on her face slowly changed to the one he recognized from last night as she moved to fully straddle him and slid her body up his chest. She kissed his neck, his jaw, his cheek, the corner of his eye, until finally she gave his ear a small nip and he laughed, flipped her underneath him and used both hands to push her hair out of her gorgeous, flushed, smiling face.

'I'm glad you've only really been with me,' he told her, kissing her lightly on the nose. 'If you think about it you were actually kind of a virgin.'

Goodie snorted. 'I am *not* virgin. Believe me.'

Nick grinned. 'You are mine though.'

'Yes. *Lyobov moya*,'* she whispered. 'I am yours.'

Goodnight

'But it's ridiculous,' Nick said, the tone of his voice perilously close to a whinge. Goodie was learning that if there was one thing Nick liked it was to get his way.

'Is not ridiculous,' she told him, trying to pull her hand free – but unless she actually wanted to hurt him that would be an impossible task.

'Come on, baby,' he murmured into the side of her head, kissing her below her ear. 'Nothing's going to happen. Let me hold your hand.'

Goodie sighed. Nick might like to get his way but when he was being like this she found that she also liked to let him have it. 'You need new close protection officer,' she grumbled as she allowed him to link his fingers firmly with hers and lead her out of the building.

'I like my close protection officer, thank you,' Nick said through a cheeky grin. 'As close as possible if you don't mind.' Goodie laughed and punched him on his arm.

What she didn't do was scan the street; otherwise she may have seen in time.

Otherwise she might have been able to stop him.

She felt Nick's body jerk and saw his eyes widen as he grabbed his shoulder.

'Nick!' Goodie screamed as he staggered back. She tore his suit jacket open and watched in horror as blood bloomed out across the white shirt below.

'Get him the fuck inside *now!*' bellowed Sam from across the street. Goodie was frozen in shock and fear as she stared at the blood. She felt Sam push past her to Nick and watched as he hauled him back into the foyer. 'Goodie, snap out of it. Give me some goddamn help here for Christ's sake.' She ran inside after them and then covered her mouth to stifle a sob as Sam propped Nick up behind the reception desk and tore off his jacket to put pressure on his shoulder. She could vaguely hear the concierge phoning for an ambulance in the background, and Sam's frantic voice, but all she could register was the blood. Nick's beautiful body was bleeding. Her hands went into her hair and she pulled desperately and painfully at it as she took a step back. She realized she was shaking.

'Goodie.' She heard Nick's voice and managed to focus on him through her panic. 'Baby, come away from the windows.' She shook her head and took another step back. 'Darling, I'm okay, I'm fine. Come away from the window; it's not safe.'

'You're ... you're hurt,' she forced out in an agonized whisper. 'You're bleeding.'

'Stop fucking pandering around me and get her away from the goddamn window,' Nick shouted at Sam, who was putting pressure on his shoulder. Sam let out a whistle and Salem came bounding in from the pavement, padding up to Goodie and pushing into her side.

'The dog's not going to cut it,' Nick growled at Sam, 'go and get her. That's an order.'

'Shut up, you arrogant twat,' Sam spat out. 'What did you think was going to happen? Jesus. I knew I shouldn't have let you anywhere near her.'

All Goodie could make out over the buzzing in her head was the sound of their voices, not the actual words. All she could see was that blood, so much blood.

'Goodnight!' Sam shouted in Russian. Her head snapped up and her hands dropped from her hair. She came back to awareness with a shuddering jolt. 'Fall in, soldier.' Her gaze became focused and she straightened, turning to Sam. 'Come here,' he told her, and she walked across the room. 'Stay down.' She dropped to her knees next to them behind the desk, her eyes still trained on Sam. Nick's hand closed over hers.

'Hey,' he said. 'Hey, honey, come back to me.' As had happened once before in her life, the pain and fear Goodie had

Goodnight

felt had been washed away by white-hot anger and determination. She turned her now cold blue eyes to him and watched as he flinched at the expression on her face.

'I'm here,' she told him, pulling her hand from his to wrap it around his wrist whilst she reached up with the other hand to lay it on the centre of his bloodstained chest. 'You will *not* be hurt again.'

Nick frowned. 'You're not *here* here,' he insisted, ignoring Sam as he rolled his eyes and muttered, 'Crazy bastard,' under his breath. Sirens from outside the building cut off Goodie's reply, and then there was a flurry of activity as paramedics filled the foyer.

As they whisked Nick away to the waiting ambulance Goodie pulled out her phone and put it to her ear.

'I need favour,' she said, noticing Sam watching her out of the corner of her eye. 'Any price.' She shut her eyes briefly at the reply she was expecting but had been hoping not to hear. 'I'll do it,' she said as her eyes opened and Sam frowned.

∼

'Where is she?' Nick asked for what must have been the thousandth time.

Sam sighed. 'I've told you; she's outside in the corridor, guarding the door.'

The bullet had been removed. It had lodged under Nick's collarbone but not pierced his lung. He was lucky.

'Tell her to come in here then.'

'Nick, she won't.'

'Tell her it's an order.'

'Look, mate, I'm sorry but she's a bit ... um ... shook up, okay? Maybe it's best to give her a little while.'

Nick slapped his hand down on the bed in frustration. 'I

know she's shook up, you prick. I was there; I saw the look on her face. What I won't bloody put up with is going back to square fucking one with her again. I won't have it.' Nick was well aware that what he'd achieved with Goodie was nothing short of a miracle. She was not shutting down on him again. Not when he'd got this far. 'You tell her to come in here or I'll get out of this bed and get her myself.'

'What do you want?' She was standing in the doorway of his room, her whole body rigid with tension and her small fists bunched at her sides.

'Goodie, come over here,' Nick said, keeping his voice low and even, and trying not to let his frustration show.

She took a few steps into the room and then stopped, crossing her arms over her chest. Nick had sent his family home an hour ago. With his family here he hadn't been able to make the fuss he needed to get her into the room, and he knew that damage control must start urgently.

'I'm fine,' he told her. 'My arm's in a sling but only so I keep it still for a few days and don't do anything stupid. You don't need to worry, okay?'

'You were shot.' Her words were said in weird, flat tone that instantly made Nick's stomach turn over with panic. 'You are not fine. Not even close.'

'Listen we'll go home tonight; I don't even have to stay in here. We can order a takeaway, talk it out. It was nothing.'

That got a reaction. Her face twisted in anger, a white rim forming around her tight mouth. 'It was *not* nothing,' she said, her voice shaking slightly.

'Baby, come here,' he pleaded.

'You are *not* fine,' she shouted this time, her eyes flashing with fury. 'This,' she pointed between the two of them, then let her arm drop to curl her hand back into a fist, 'this is not okay. You were *hurt*. You could have been *killed*.'

Goodnight

    Nick opened his mouth to speak, then shut it when he saw them: Goodie's eyes had filled with tears and two had escaped to fall down her cheeks. She blinked and touched her face, bringing her hand away to stare at it as though she couldn't quite believe what she was seeing. Her eyes flashed back to his and he almost flinched from the pain and fear he saw in them.

    'You were hurt,' she repeated, this time in a whisper, taking a step back. 'I'm not doing this anymore. I can't protect you, not like this.' With that she turned and left the room, but not before he saw two more tears escape.

* *Lyobov moya* – my love

Chapter 23
Life is pain

'Nick, darling, are you sure about this?' Lila asked. She was leaning against his kitchen island looking perfect in a deep blue gown that reminded him painfully of the one Goodie had worn to his parents' party.

'I'm sure,' he said gruffly, fiddling with his cufflink and swearing under his breath when it slipped his grip and clattered onto the granite counter top. Lila clicked her tongue, slapped her hand down on the cufflink before it could roll onto the floor, and then started to thread it through Nick's sleeve. She sighed.

'Do you really think this is going to make a difference?'

Nick snatched his sleeve away from her once she was done, and moved to the other side of the island to down the shot of brandy he had waiting for him. 'I've tried everything. I'm losing patience. Maybe this will shake her up a bit. God knows nothing else I do seems to make a blind bit of difference.'

It was a month since the shooting. Nick had healed quickly; he'd had to. Even the slightest flinch of discomfort would cause Goodie to visibly wince and that pain in her eyes to intensify.

Goodnight

Security had been stepped up significantly. He now had Sam as an additional close protection officer, and two far guards. But things were about to change. All the deals were nearly done; soon they could get cold fusion off the ground and then the threat to his life would be negligible. Once they weren't needed any more to provide the momentum to the project, he and Ed would be safe.

In truth the idea and the interest had become bigger than anyone had ever anticipated. Even if their opponents did somehow manage to hurt Nick or Ed, the project itself would now be unstoppable; there was too much investment, too much confidence in it for it to fold now. Once the final deal was completed in the next few days, Nick doubted he would even need protection; it would likely just continue as a precaution. He had thought that closing this deal would be the pinnacle of his life so far. He should be ecstatic, but he found he couldn't be. Not without her.

He had thought he could talk Goodie around and break through her cold formality once he came out of hospital; after all, he was adept at getting his own way, he'd been charming and manipulating the women in his life since he was five years old. But he was coming to realize that with Goodie this was not going to be the case. She kept her distance from him, avoided direct eye contact unless it was strictly necessary, and had even changed the locks on her flat by the time he was home from the hospital. She refused to talk to him about the shooting.

After a couple of weeks when he was feeling stronger, he'd cornered her in the office to try and talk some sense into her. She'd stared down at his hands on her arms like they were diseased, then cut off whatever he'd been trying to say with: 'Let me go or I will kick you in the groin so hard you'll be tasting your own balls for breakfast.' The look in her eye told him she would do it, too. When he hadn't immediately released her, she had wrenched so violently away from him that he had been worried she'd dislocate her shoulders.

So yes, Nick thought that this was the only play he had left to make. He wanted to shake things up, and patience was not one of his virtues.

'Look, Nick-Nack, lying is never a great idea,' Lila warned him, 'God knows I'm not this chick's biggest fan, what with her occupying the slightly scary area between normal and cold-blooded psychopath, but she *did* save my life. I feel I owe her something at least. This could hurt her.'

Nick shook off the sinking feeling in the pit of his stomach when he thought about hurting Goodie. This was for her own good. She needed to snap out of it. 'I'm not trying to hurt her. I just want to make her think, that's all. She'll come around.'

Lila shook her head but slipped her arm through his regardless.

'Okay, gorgeous,' she muttered, pasting a wide smile on her face, 'if you're sure. But I'd better get a decent amount of press out of this; you owe me.'

∽

Goodie rapped twice on the dividing glass in the limo and it slid down.

'Keep the partition down,' she told Matt the driver, who nodded in response, not taking his eyes off the road ahead. 'Did you go over the plans of the building last night? You know we're using the back service entrance?'

'Goodie,' Sam said in a low voice as Matt nodded again, 'he knows. You know he knows. We went over it *five* times yesterday. You made him do a drive-by in the early hours of this morning. It's sorted.'

She gave a jerky nod, then sat back in her seat. As her gaze

Goodnight

skittered over the happy couple opposite her she found herself sliding her hand into Salem's fur. Even if he wasn't allowed in the building she was now glad she'd chosen to bring him this far. The feel of his warm body under her hand helped her claw back from the pain to a place of complete focus.

When she'd seen Nick emerge from his flat with the perfect brunette on his arm, Goodie had nearly, *nearly* let herself go. After a month of maintaining complete control around him, the absolute desolation she felt seeing him with another woman was almost overpowering. Before she even knew what she was doing she had taken two steps back from them into a less-than-impressed Salem. It had seemed like Nick was going to break away from the brunette at that stage – his body had swayed towards Goodie and his face had softened. But then she managed to get a hold of herself and blank her expression, greeting them both in the most functional way possible and moving to the lift to press the call button. She'd had to swallow twice in the lift to get rid of the constriction in her throat and the feeling that she might vomit.

The view out of the corner of her eye of Lila's arm through Nick's, combined with the usual claustrophobia, was enough to very nearly bring Goodie to her knees. But she would not be beaten; she was a professional; she was a warrior; she was not weak. So what if the woman was gorgeous in a stunning floor-length gown and Goodie was in her dark security clothes with minimal make-up? She was there to do a job. She was there to keep Nick safe, and that, she told herself, was all she cared about.

Finally he was acknowledging her place as an employee, which was what she wanted. Wasn't it? Then why did her chest feel so tight that each breath seemed like an effort? Why did she have the almost unbearable urge to crawl away and hide?

'Oh dear,' Lila said, shifting closer to Nick on the back seat. 'So, no red carpet for us? What a shame.'

Goodie didn't respond. She didn't even turn her head. Over the last month, unless Nick or whoever he was with spoke directly to her, she hadn't acknowledged them at all. Bertie and Ed had made cautious approaches but she'd shut them down. The memory of her loss of control when Nick was shot was too fresh. She would not fail. Not again.

As they neared the back entrance she made eye contact with Nick and then Lila in turn. 'Keep your head down,' she told them in a low voice, 'keep moving. Stick together. Priority is to get into the building. They're expecting you at the other end. The far guards are in place.'

'You're going straight in too aren't you?' Nick asked. She looked at him and saw he was frowning.

'Sam will stay with you. I am going to check the perimeter.' Nick's jaw tightened and his eyes flashed.

'If you don't go straight into that goddamn building, I'm not moving. I'll stand right out there in the open.'

'This is not a joke,' Goodie hissed, her temper warring with the icy control she was trying desperately to cling onto. 'You *will* do as we advise.'

'I'm not joking,' he told her as he reached forward to grip her shoulder. 'I'll do it, Goodie. I won't let you hang around outside whilst I scuttle in to keep safe.'

'Sam will stay with you, that's the best way we can –'

'*You'll* stay with me.'

'No, Nick, I will no –'

'You're coming with me.'

Goodie felt the last strand of her fraying temper give way. 'Perfect. Yes, good plan. And so when you are hurt, *again*, I will be there to freeze and do absolutely fuck all, *again*. I'll be there to watch you bleed out on the dirty pavement, not even moving you to shelter. Yes, Nick, great plan. *Zhopa.*'

'Don't call me an arsehole.'

Goodie rolled her eyes, regretting teaching him Russian swear words.

'Goodie, look at me.' His voice had softened. Reluctantly she moved her gaze back to his and clenched her jaw so hard it hurt when she saw the concern in his expression. 'It wasn't your fault and I'm fine. You can't keep –'

'We're here.' Sam cut Nick off. 'Goodie, go with them. He means it; he'll stand out there exposed if you don't.'

'Thanks, man,' Nick muttered. Sam gave him and Lila a disgusted look as they pulled up to a stop, and if Nick wasn't mistaken he called him the same as Goodie had under his breath, this time in English.

∼

'May I say, that's a frightfully nice blouse you're wearing this evening, Yuko.'

Despite how she was feeling, Goodie very nearly smiled. 'Bertie, I'm wearing a security uniform.'

'Oh golly, so you are.' Bertie laughed, then gave one of his particularly loud snorts.

Goodie laid her hand gently on his arm. 'Maybe if you get talking to a lady, look at what they are wearing before you compliment them tonight, yes?'

'Yes ... well,' Bertie shifted uncomfortably. 'It's just I always come out looking like a right boob with the ladies, but they're always so dashed pretty and clever and ... I'm afraid I end up buggering it up.' He glanced to the side and his face fell even further. 'Oh balls, that's just what I need.'

'Bertie.' Goodie's head shot up as she heard Clive's voice.

There was a group of people blocking his view of her, so he must have thought it safe to approach his target. 'Still weasling around after Nick I see, hanging on his coattails and all that?'

'I ... well ... I ...'

'And who are you panting after now with your lame-blouse compliments? Don't tell me you've finally found a bird that'll ...' Clive trailed off as the people in front of Goodie moved to the side and she came into view. His face drained of colour and his eyes widened. Goodie took a step towards him and realized he was literally shaking with fear. She looked straight into his eyes, leaned forward and uttered a quiet, 'Boo.' Clive leapt back with his hands out in front of him, his colour so bad now that he actually looked a little green. For the first time in four weeks Goodie smiled.

'Clive, old man,' Bertie said, watching in confusion as Clive leapt away from Goodie. 'Are you quite all right? Eat one of those dodgy prawn numbers earlier, did you? Glad I steered clear if they're giving everyone dicky tummies.'

Clive didn't even glance in Bertie's direction. He kept his gaze locked on Goodie and continued backing away. Goodie mouthed 'Fuck off' to him, and then, when he wasn't moving quite quickly enough, she added: 'Now.' He simply turned on his heel and fled. She watched him until he was safely out of the side exit. Tilly was here tonight and Goodie did not want that prick upsetting her.

'Don't listen to him, Bertie,' she said after she was sure Clive was not coming back. 'He is but dirt on your shoe.'

Bertie chuckled. 'Well, I'm not sure about that but I'll admit he is a tad bit of an unpleasant fellow, all in.' It was the first truly negative thing Goodie had ever heard Bertie say about anyone.

'He *is* as dirt on your shoe. You're a better man than you think you are, Bertram Chambers.'

Goodnight

Bertie flushed bright red and smiled at her. 'Gosh ... well, you're a damn, damn fine lady yourself,' he told her, almost moving in for a hug but losing his nerve at the last minute and going for an awkward shoulder pat instead. As he pulled his hand away she made a last-minute decision. She would be gone soon and Bertie had given her so much, made her smile so many times. She caught his hand as he pulled it back and held it with both of hers before she brought it up to the centre of his chest and laid it flat, saying: 'No strength without heart.' Then she dropped his hand and stepped back.

'I'm sorry, what did you – ?'

Goodie realized that she had spoken in Russian. She looked Bertie in the eye. 'No strength without heart,' she repeated, this time in English. When he frowned in confusion she told him: 'Kindness is everything Bertie. That is where true strength comes from. You are a strong man; don't you forget it.' Bertie blinked a few times and swallowed.

'Thank you,' he said, his voice thick with emotion. 'I think you're a right topper as well.'

Goodie nodded, her eyes caught on a flash of red on the dance floor. She watched as Nick held Lila flush to his body, moving with her in sync to the beat. They were staring into each other's eyes. He said something into her ear and she threw her head back in laughter before moving even closer to him to give him a squeeze. They looked perfect together and as Goodie watched them she realized that the reason they looked so well matched was because they were both creatures of light, both able to be happy, to laugh and smile easily.

Goodie knew that she was not.

She was a creature of the dark; her place was in the shadows. A monster created out of violence and pain. The mystery was not how Nick could forget what they shared so quickly, it was why he even looked her way at all.

'I'm sorry, old girl,' Bertie muttered; he had followed her gaze out to the dance floor. 'I'm sure he doesn't want to upset you. Maybe he –'

Goodie gave a hollow laugh and shifted her gaze to Bertie.

'Upset me? He'd have to do better than that.'

'Well, I mean, I know it must be painful ... after what you two shared and everything – to see –'

'Life is pain,' Goodie said as her gaze returned to the couple on the dance floor. 'Believe me, I'm used to it.'

'Don't say that, please,' Goodie heard a soft voice say in Russian from her other side and glanced across to see Natasha standing next to her. Goodie frowned and quickly scanned the room before focusing back on the beautiful brunette.

'Don't be stupid,' Goodie said under her breath to Tasha, 'what if you're seen.'

'He's busy enough,' Tasha returned, nodding over to the other side of the room where Dmitry was surrounded by at least five women vying for his attention. 'I have to speak to you.'

Bertie cleared his throat from Goodie's other side and both women turned in his direction. 'Hello,' he said, 'jolly good to meet you again. Afraid my Russian's a bit on the rusty side. I didn't realize that you were a friend of Good –'

'No,' both women said in unison. Goodie stepped back and melted into the crowd muttering her goodbye to Bertie as she went, and Natasha stepped forward and leaned into Bertie, her perfect lips smiling and forming the perfect distraction.

'May I say that's an awfully nice bl ... I mean dress you're wearing this evening,' Goodie heard him say as she walked away from them, and shook her head. Bertie needed some new material. As she moved to the very edge of the room, her gaze alternated between Dmitry and Nick and Lila on the dance floor before she did another scan of the room and saw Geoff almost filling the doorway. She closed her eyes for a moment and took a deep breath whilst the relief washed over her. When she opened them again, Geoff was making his way over to her, and she moved to meet him halfway.

'You sure about this?' Geoff asked.

'Of course.'

'Does Sam know?'

'Yes.'

'But not Nick?' As if they had a will of their own, Goodie's eyes strayed back to the dance floor and to the gorgeous couple still locked in a tight embrace.

'*Nyeht,*' she said, slipping unconsciously into Russian. 'I think he'll survive,' she told Geoff dryly. He flicked a dark look at the couple and shook his head. She thought she heard him mutter 'fucking idiot' under his breath before looking back at Goodie.

'Will you ...?' he broke off and rubbed the back of his neck before focusing on her again. 'Where are you going?'

'To finish this,' she told him, then melted back through the crowd and out through the doorway.

Chapter 24

They've heard her screaming

Dmitry was tired and he was pissed off. Who did that stupid bitch Natasha think she was? Not only had she had the audacity to dump him out of the blue, but she'd also waited to do it until he had left the goddamn ballroom with no chance of shagging any of the willing and available pussy there. He had pushed open his bedroom door and started to undo his cufflinks when he felt the cold metal against his throat.

'Call off your dogs, Alexandrov,' he heard muttered into his ear in a low female voice. He sucked in a breath to scream but felt the metal press more firmly against his skin, and a trickle of blood run down his neck. 'Scream and I slit your throat.' He nodded and the knife eased back but still maintained some pressure.

'How did you get in here?' he asked, keeping his voice steady as he felt a droplet of sweat fall from his forehead to collect with the blood on his neck.

'I can access anywhere I want. Nothing can stop me: no security system, no amount of manpower. You'd best remember

Goodnight

that. I know what you're doing, I know what you've set in motion, and I'm telling you that you need to call them off, you need to cancel the order: Chambers and Southern are not to be touched, not if you want to live. The deals are done anyway. Wiping them out now isn't going to make any difference. You can't hold back progress. Haven't you made enough money from your oil already? Give it up.'

Dmitry swallowed. 'Who are you?' he asked, his voice hoarse with fear.

'Your nightmare,' she whispered, this time in his native tongue. 'Don't worry; we'll meet again and next time you'll be sure to see my face. He felt the pressure ease from his throat and a gust of breeze behind him. After a moment he spun around to face an empty room.

∽

'Bertie,' Katie said, her voice rising uncharacteristically in anger. 'You let me in to see him, you *twp** bugger, or I swear I'll break that door down.'

'He said that he wasn't to be disturbed and I –'

Katie rolled her eyes, pushed Bertie out of the way easily despite his size and the fact she was heavily pregnant, and stormed into Nick's office with Salem padding along behind her. There were two large men sitting across from Nick: one had a full, greying beard and a potbelly, and the other was younger with more muscle and blonde hair. Nick looked between her and Salem, then pushed his chair back almost violently to stand up.

'Where is she?' he asked accusingly, and Katie's eyebrows went up into her hairline.

'Don't take that tone with me, Nick Chambers,' Katie said,

glaring at Nick whilst Salem sat next to her, fixing him with a hard stare and letting out a small growl. 'You're the bloody reason she's buggered off to lands unknown, you great big idiot. Ugh!' She flopped down on the leather sofa facing the desk and chairs and let out an exasperated breath. 'As if you give a shit anyway,' she muttered, and Nick stalked around his desk towards her until he was towering over her, literally vibrating with anger. 'I shouldn't have come. Sam *told* me not to come. He *said* there was no point. He'll be furious when he finds out I —'

'What's going on?' Nick snapped, cutting her off. 'Why do you have Salem?' Salem was still sitting, staring at Nick with his lip slightly curled to reveal his sharp teeth.

'Nick, mate,' the older of the two men said whilst half rising from his chair, 'maybe we better …?'

'Sit down,' Nick barked, and the man fell back into the chair, frowning across at him. Nick didn't take his eyes off Katie. 'Where is she?' he asked her. To her surprise it wasn't just annoyance she could hear in his tone; there was a hint of desperation there too.

She sighed. 'I wouldn't have come here but … well, the guys think they can handle it … I just …' She trailed off and then to her shock saw Nick drop to a squat in front of her and take her hands in his, giving them a squeeze.

'Please, Katie,' he begged, and it was then she noticed the haunted look in his eyes, the dark circles under them and the way his cheekbones stood out more in his face, as if he'd lost weight, 'please tell me where she is. Tell me she's okay.'

'You *do* care about her,' Katie said, almost accusingly as she searched his face.

'Of course I care about her, Katie; I'm in love with her.'

Katie's mouth fell open and for a moment she lost the power of speech. After a few shocked seconds she narrowed her

Goodnight

eyes, pulled her small hands out from under his, balled one into a fist and punched him on the arm.

'Hey! What was that for?'

'That's for being a git and shagging other birds when you're in *love* with someone who had to *watch* you doing it. Jeepers, why are men so bloody *twp*.'

'I didn't shag anyone else, Katie,' Nick told her, rubbing his arm, which gave Katie a very satisfying feeling of triumph.

'Well, you –'

'I didn't. I just wanted to shake things up. She'd shut me out for a whole goddamn month. It was getting ridiculous.'

Katie threw her hands up in the air and rolled her eyes. 'You impatient sod. So you thought you'd throw a tantrum and bugger everything up? Great plan, just fabulous. And now, I suppose, now that she's out of the picture you've forgotten all about h –'

'Jesus Christ, just listen to me.' Nick cut her off, pointing at the men in the chairs across from them. 'These guys have been searching for Goodie non-stop since she upped and left. I've been tearing my hair out trying to find her. Didn't your great big bastard of a husband tell you that?'

Katie frowned. 'Oh … I …' She peered around Nick's body to look at the two men sitting on the chairs opposite his desk, looking vaguely uncomfortable, and she gave them a small wave and a sheepish grin. 'Hi there.' They nodded back at her and Nick pushed up to his feet, stalked back to his desk and sat down heavily in his chair.

'Right,' he said, turning his chair towards Katie. 'Start at the beginning: Where the hell is she?'

'About two weeks ago she came to the house with Salem and asked me to keep him for her. She said that she had a job that she couldn't take him on.' Katie started wringing her hands in her lap and bit her lip. 'I feel so bad but I didn't realize that

209

she would normally take Salem with her on all her jobs. I thought maybe she just didn't want to shell out for a doggy hotel or something. It was only when I spoke to Sam and he went nuts over the fact she'd left the dog that I started to worry. He said ... he said it was a bad sign.' Katie watched as Nick's jaw clenched and his body went alert.

'A bad sign of what?' he asked slowly.

'Sam thought that if she didn't take Salem with her then maybe ...' Katie's eyes filled with tears and she dropped her gaze from his, '... maybe she wasn't expecting to come back,' she muttered at her hands still twisting in her lap. She jumped at the sound of Nick's fist crashing down on the desk and looked up to see him pacing in front of his floor-to-ceiling window, staring out of his office.

'Is she alive?' He paused in his pacing to face Katie, and she almost flinched at the pain she could hear in his voice.

'We think yes,' she rushed to tell him. 'One of the guys she went into the cartel with escaped. He said she took out almost half of the complex before she was taken down. He ... couldn't get to her. She took too many risks; she even *told* him before they went in that he was to run when he could, she told him she wouldn't be leaving unless she'd killed them all. He said it was like ...' A tear escaped to fall down Katie's cheek and she wiped it away. '... he said it was like she had a death wish.'

'How do you know that she's not dead?' Nick's voice was hollow; his eyes when she looked up at him were haunted.

'They planted surveillance stuff before they attacked. Very high tech; totally undetectable. They've heard her ...' Katie swallowed and looked away, more tears falling down her face. 'Oh God, they've heard her screaming.'

At this Nick just simply crumpled; he fell to his knees on the floor, both his hands going up behind his head as he curled up and let out a roar like some sort of animal in pain. Katie

Goodnight

leapt up off the sofa and rushed to him, dropping down to her own knees at his side and putting her arms around his big shaking shoulders. They stayed like that for a moment before suddenly Nick's head came up, he wiped away the wet from his cheeks and he pushed to his feet.

'Where is she?' he barked, loosening his tie and going for his mobile phone.

'Colombia,' Katie told him. 'Sam has the coordinates and everything.'

'Right, I'm going to get her out.'

'Nick, it's not as simple as that. She wasn't on a sanctioned mission. She didn't have permission to be there. Sam tried going to the people who sent her but they don't want to know. It would take a massive amount of firepower, manpower and all sorts of political manoeuvring to get her out.'

'She's right, mate,' the larger gentleman on the chairs cut in. 'If it was a below-the-table job, then –'

'I'm not leaving her there, Harry,' Nick said, his voice laced with steel and his hands bunching into fists. He swiped at his phone and put it to his ear. 'Sam? Right ... no, you listen to me. I want to know what you need to get her out. I want to know which fucking politician I need to intimidate to get us in there and I want to know how soon you can get a team together.' There was a pause for a moment as Nick's face flushed red and his eyes flashed at whatever Sam was saying.

'No,' he shouted. 'You listen to me, you prick. *I'm* going to see that *my woman* gets out of there alive. You have *no idea* the resources I have to hand: I'm richer than God and I'm on first name terms with every member of the cabinet *and* the head of MI6. You should have come to me first.' He listened for another minute before cutting Sam off again. 'Jesus, I'll buy you five fucking helicopters if you need them, you idiot. You source it and I'll buy it.'

For the first time in two weeks Katie felt something bordering on hope. If anyone could get Goodie out, this man could, she just prayed that when they found her there was something left to save.

* *TWP* — STUPID, SIMPLE-MINDED

Chapter 25

Scared stiff

Goodie stared at the concrete ceiling with the one eye that would still open, and ran on repeat the only thing that had kept her amused over the last week since she'd been shoved in this room. She saw in her mind the storage shed explode and the look on those bastards' faces as it did, and despite the split in her lip, she smiled. Goodie knew she was dying. One side of her chest wasn't moving properly, the ribs had been broken and something had happened to the lung. Her left leg was a mess, they'd smashed in her knee with a baseball bat and she could no longer stand on it. Her shoulder was dislocated. Normally she would be able to throw it back in herself, but without the use of her legs, and without being able to move properly with her chest, it was impossible.

She could separate from the pain but not from her memories. That fucking dimple had invaded her consciousness more times than she would have thought possible. His smell, the feel of his hair, the gentle way he touched her: however hard she tried she couldn't repress those thoughts. When it came to feeling pain she was in complete control, but with

Nick ... She let her eye drift shut again and her good arm moved so that she could touch her dry, cracked lips; the memory of his mouth on hers was impossible to shake. Her eye flew open as she heard what could only have been an explosion from out in the complex; she frowned and thought about sitting up, but, looking down at her misshapen arm and leg, decided against it. Whatever was going on out there was unlikely to affect her. She'd be gone by the time anyone broke into this room.

She felt herself drifting again when there was another loud explosion, this time seeming to be in the room itself. Turning her head with some difficulty, she blinked through the smoke that had now filled the small space to see a large figure standing in the doorway. She watched as he scanned the room, saw her lying on the mattress and swore violently before running over to her and putting his hands under her back and knees to lift her.

'You're okay,' she heard Sam's voice say as he pulled her up against his chest.

'Don't ... lie,' Goodie managed to croak out, concentrating on pushing the pain away as she was jostled.

'Fine, you're not okay. But you fucking well will be.'

He turned them, and then they were running. The movement was so violent that she could no longer block out the pain, and the black closed in around her.

∼

'SHE'S SO COLD. WHY IS SHE SO COLD?'

Goodie frowned. It was Nick's voice but not as she'd ever heard it in the past. Never before had she heard real fear there, or any real desperation.

'Get in the sodding seat, Nick,' she heard Sam shout above

Goodnight

the sound of helicopter rotor blades. 'I said you could come in the chopper if you did what you were told.'

'She's fucking ice cold!' Nick shouted, his voice laced with so much panic it was almost painful to hear. She could feel his hands now, cupping her cheeks and resting on her forehead.

'I know!' Sam shouted back. 'She's lost a lot of blood. That's why we need to go right fucking now. So sit down in your *goddamn* seat.' Goodie frowned as she felt Nick's hands leave her face and she slid back into the darkness.

When she woke again it was to bright lights above her head and activity around her. She could feel needles going into her arm, hands cutting away her clothes and people discussing her airway. She blinked open her eye and saw a dark-haired woman in scrubs staring down at her.

'*Hola, señora,*' the woman said, then continued on in Spanish. 'You are safe now but we must put you back to sleep. You understand?' Goodie nodded.

'Hey,' Goodie heard Nick shout, and looked past the nurse to see him standing just behind her, his eyes wide with fear. 'Don't speak to her in Spanish, she doesn't understand –'

'She speaks fluent Spanish, Nick,' Goodie heard Sam's much calmer voice explain from the end of her bed.

'Well, *I* don't understand Spanish, you prick. What are they doing to her?'

The woman in scrubs ignored both of them and Goodie felt cold creep up her arm, something being injected into her veins. The pain receded and she welcomed the darkness again.

The next time Goodie opened her eyes she could see out of both. The lights above her head were still bright, but there was less activity around her now. She looked down to see her body dressed in a hospital gown and a cannula in her arm with blood coming in from a bag above her head. There was a tube coming out of her chest and draining what looked like bloody fluid. Her arm was in a sling and her left leg was in a cast to her thigh. She looked across at the bed opposite her and saw that the patient had a tube in their mouth and a ventilator breathing for them. She was in an intensive care unit. That much was obvious. She looked to the other side and saw a pair of large shoes next to her bed. Frowning, she scanned up the long legs and to the unshaven man asleep in the chair next to her bed. His hair was longer than she remembered, his cheeks more hollow, and there were dark shadows under his eyes, almost like bruises they were so pronounced. As if he could sense her return to consciousness his beautiful eyes flickered open and locked with hers.

'You're awake,' he told her, relief sweeping over his features as he stood from the chair and came to her side. Then, to her shock, he leaned in and touched his forehead to hers, gripping her good hand with his and closing his eyes. Goodie's IQ was well over genius level. She could process situations rapidly. Even with all her injuries and having been sedated for days, she knew.

'You came for me.' She frowned in frustration as her lips moved but no sound came out.

'What, baby?' Nick asked, pulling back and stroking her hair at her temples. 'What are you trying to say?'

'You came for me,' Goodie managed to get out in a hoarse whisper as she blinked up at him in confusion.

'Of course I did, honey. You're mine.'

Goodie shook her head until Nick's hands closed in on either side of her face, holding it still. 'You're stubborn. You're a nutcase. But you're mine, and I'm keeping you.'

∼

'I DON'T KNOW HOW NICK DOES THIS ALL DAY; IT'S SO boring.' Goodie could hear Sam's low rumble cutting through

Goodnight

her dream, and clawed her way back to consciousness with some effort.

'Well, what would you do if it was Katie lying there?' Goodie heard another low voice reply, and blinked her eyes open to see Sam and Geoff facing each other at the side of her bed.

'Fair point,' Sam conceded. Goodie shifted slightly on the bed and sucked in a sharp breath as pain shot through her chest and into her shoulder. Both men turned to face her instead of each other.

'Hey, Sleeping Beauty,' Sam said, stepping close to the bed and laying both hands on the railing. 'How're you feeling?'

'Like ...' Goodie cleared her throat but, frustratingly, was still only able to force out a hoarse whisper, '... shit.'

Sam's face softened for a moment, and then he hardened his expression. 'Yeah? Well, you deserve to feel like shit. Do you know how many risks we had to take to get you out? How worried we've been? Do you even care?'

'Didn't ... ask you to come,' Goodie rasped past her painful throat. Sam looked up at the ceiling as if seeking patience, then focused back on her.

'Did you think we'd leave you there? Did you think we'd leave you to die?'

Goodie closed her eyes to block him out and slowly nodded. When she opened them again Sam was scowling down at her.

'Damn it, Goodie,' he snapped. 'You've got people who care about you now. That carries responsibility. It means that you don't go off on suicide missions on your own. You're not alone anymore, *myshka*.* You have to learn to think about other people.'

'Never asked ...' Goodie cleared her throat again, trying to make her words stronger, '... never asked for that. Never asked for people to care.'

'Well, that's life, isn't it? That's what it's all about.'

'Not my life.'

Sam scowled again and ran both his hands through his hair. 'I owe you *my* life, Goodie – have you forgotten that?' She looked away from him and then felt his finger under her chin to turn her head back again. 'Even if I didn't owe you I would still have wanted to get you out. I care about you. Katie cares about you. Even bloody Geoff cares about you.' Geoff gave a grunt of agreement from Sam's side (which by Geoff's standards was actually quite a display of emotion). 'And that bloke of yours ...' Sam shook his head, a slow grin spreading over his face, '... you know he bought up half the artillery, light aircraft and helicopters in the southern hemisphere to help us get you out. Even insisted on coming with us – was a job to make him stay with the chopper. Had to tell him in the end that some city nancy-boy who's never even held a bebe gun before, leave alone a submachine gun, was only going to hold us back and put you in more danger. We had to wrestle him out of the ward today – he was starting to smell, he'd been sitting here with you so long.'

'Not ... mine,' Goodie rasped, frowning up at Sam, who just chuckled and rolled his eyes.

'You two make a right pair of stubborn nutters, don't you?'

'I told Sam what you said when you left that night, Goodie,' Geoff put in, and Goodie looked at him. 'We need to know what you meant. What was there to finish?' Goodie's mind flashed to the tremble of fear in Dmitry's voice as she'd held the knife to his throat, and she smiled for the first time in days. Coming to Colombia for this job was a small price to pay to the agency that shut down Dmitry's security to allow her access.

Dmitry Alexandrov had been under surveillance for a while, and when Natasha had begged to do something to help,

Goodie foolishly gave her his details. It was only after Goodie found out who was responsible for the knife attack in the alley and then the shooting, that she realized how dangerous Dmitry was. He would do anything to protect his overpriced flow of oil. How he thought he could buy a bloody great mansion practically next door to the Chamberses and still escape Goodie's notice only showed just how incredibly arrogant he was. Goodie had called Natasha off, but not before Tasha had managed to make sure Dmitry was going home alone the night of the ball. The rest was taken care of by people with far more influence than Tasha and only after Goodie had agreed to go to Colombia to finish what she started nine years ago.

'You don't need to know,' she rasped. 'Is finished.'

'Whatever you did, you didn't need to do, Goodie,' Sam told her, his face now serious. 'The danger had passed for Nick and Ed. All the deals were done.'

'Make ...' Goodie swallowed; her throat was beginning to hurt now, '... sure. Make them ... pay.'

Sam rolled his eyes. 'So why did you take *this* job?'

Goodie turned away from him again and heard him sigh loudly. 'We agreed when they approached us last year that it was too high-risk, Goodie. I didn't think you would ever come back here.'

Goodie shrugged, then winced as the movement sent another bolt of pain through her ribs. Sam narrowed his eyes at her.

'I used to believe you were so brave, so resilient; but really, when it comes down to it, really you're not brave at all are you? You're scared stiff.'

Goodie grumbled some particularly unpleasant Russian under her breath and Sam smiled. 'Give life a try, *myshka*,' he said softly as he laid his hand over her good arm on the bed. 'Just let yourself give it a try. You trained to adapt to any environment, to be anything you needed to be. Can't you let yourself be happy? Can't you be who you need to be to be with him?'

Goodie blinked rapidly against the stinging at the back of her eyes and turned her head away again, muttering about the dry air from the air conditioning.

* *MYSHKA* – LITTLE MOUSE

Chapter 26

Time and patience

'We're here,' Goodie's eyes fluttered open and for a moment she was completely disorientated. She looked across at Bertie on the leather seats opposite her, who was giving her a big smile and a thumbs up, and then to Sam, who was looking at Bertie and shaking his head. She felt the leather underneath her good hand, and then looked up at the temperature controls and light switches above her head.

'Hey.' She focused on Nick's face as she felt his large hand cover hers; he was crouching in front of her now, a frown creasing his forehead. 'Are you okay, baby?'

Goodie swallowed; her throat was less painful, but she had yet to regain full use of her voice. 'Private jet,' she croaked out.

'Yes,' Nick smiled, '*My* private jet.'

'Flashy bastard,' she mumbled, and he laughed as he undid her seatbelt and gently drew it to the side.

'Not ... child,' she told him, trying to push his hands away from her lap, which was a tricky business with her right arm still in a sling.

Nick held up his hands in surrender but grinned despite

her annoyance. 'We're at Heathrow. We have to go through customs, then we can head off back home.' Goodie frowned and looked out of the small window onto the runway whilst Nick went about gathering all their stuff together.

She allowed herself to be carried down the steps of the plane in Nick's arms. She'd long since given up fighting with him over this: he'd been doing it with alarming regularity since she left ICU a week ago. A wheelchair awaited her at the bottom of the steps and she scowled at it.

'Crutches,' she croaked out as loud as she could.

'Goodie,' Nick said in a warning tone, 'it's too far; you can't make it on crutches. Please, sweetheart, for me.'

He readjusted her in his arms at that point, and she felt a jolt of pain through her leg, arm and chest. The chest drain had been removed last week but her ribs were still very painful. Goodie didn't wince, she was not a stranger to pain, but she did nod reluctantly and then heard Nick's sigh of relief. He lowered her into the chair and started wheeling her to the terminal building followed by Sam and Bertie. Goodie looked round and gave Sam a significant look and he nodded abruptly – obviously still unhappy with the decision she'd made, but prepared to see it through if it was what she wanted.

They made it through customs and into the arrivals area. To her surprise, Goodie saw Nick's parents' faces in the crowd, and once they made it through she was very gently hugged and kissed by both of them. Goodie allowed this. She even managed a small smile for their benefit whilst Nick's dad clapped him on the back and his mum gave him a more powerful hug than she had bestowed on the still-delicate Goodie.

'*Myshka.*'

Goodie's head snapped up as she heard Natasha's voice, and relief flooded her. The tall brunette strode through the throng of people until she was squatting in front of Goodie.

Goodnight

'I told you not to call me "little mouse",' Goodie said to her in Russian. Natasha reached up and touched the bruising on Goodie's face softly, her eyes taking in the split in her lip, the sling on her arm and the cast on her leg.

'Oh, *little mouse*,' Natasha said in Russian still, her eyes filling with tears, one of which spilled down her perfectly made-up cheek. 'What did you do?'

'I'm fine. I will heal.'

Natasha's eyes slowly widened and a look of horror filled her face. 'Did Dmitry ...?'

Goodie let out a short humourless laugh. 'I'm not stupid. He would never have been able to touch me. I had already sorted out that problem before this happened. The deal I made meant that even if I had died he would be kept in line.'

Natasha's face had paled at the mention of Goodie dying. 'I'm not dead,' Goodie reassured her. 'Not even close.'

'No thanks to *that* arsehole,' Natasha muttered, nodding towards a bemused Nick and giving him her best fake smile. Fortunately only Sam could understand them, and even he was probably struggling given the dialect they were using and speed at which they were talking.

'It was my choice, Tasha,' Goodie said firmly. 'He was not mine to claim. He did nothing wrong.' Natasha narrowed her eyes at Goodie; it would be a while before she forgot the look on her sister's face when she had seen Nick dancing with Lila. 'I just need time to rest. That's why I asked you to come for me.'

'Of course you do,' Natasha said, standing to her full height to look Nick in the eye. 'Hello, Mr Chambers,' she addressed him, extending her hand for him to shake and switching to her perfect English. 'I'll be taking Goodie home with me now.'

'Well ...' Nick said, frowning across at her, 'that's a surprise.

When we last spoke I believe you denied even knowing my girlfriend as a passing acquaintance.'

'I am not your girl –'

'Hello again, Miss Alkaev,' Bertie cut in, and made a grab for Natasha's hand. Pumping it up and down with vigour. 'May I say, that's a terribly nice blouse you're wearing this afternoon.' The force of the handshake was jolting Natasha's body; she glanced down at the form-fitting jumper she had on and her lips tipped up in amusement.

'That's very kind, Mr Chambers.'

'Oh, do please call me Bertie, everyone does,' he said, his hand shaking slowing but still not showing any signs of releasing her any time soon.

'Okay, Bertie, I think you can let her go now,' Claire said gently from his side, and Bertie's face flushed red as he dropped Tasha's hand and stepped back.

'I'm so sorry for any confusion,' Nick put in smoothly, moving behind Goodie's chair and gripping the handles tightly. 'But Goodie is coming with me. We've got everything set up for her at the house. I've built a therapy room, there's an indoor swimming pool, a private physio is coming daily, a nurse will be there to help her get settled, and until she's stronger a private GP is coming to sort out her pain meds. It's all sorted.'

Goodie watched as Natasha frowned across at Nick in confusion, then down at Goodie in the chair.

'I'm *not* going with him,' Goodie said firmly. Nick's jaw tensed for moment before he moved around Goodie's chair to Natasha and pulled her away from the group.

∼

'Please,' Nick said once they were out of hearing distance, 'I don't know what connection you have with Goodie, but I *do* know that you don't trust me. That's my fault, I made a poor judgment in an attempt to make Goodie jealous and get her back. It was stupid of me but I never stopped loving her. I promise you I can look after her better than anyone.' When Natasha crossed her arms over her chest and narrowed her eyes at him in suspicion, he ran both his hands through his hair before saying. 'I was getting through to her. She was changing. I could make her happy. I know I could. Give me that chance. Please.'

'Not much can hurt her,' Natasha said, her voice still cold but her expression slightly softer. 'But you ... you managed it.' Nick winced and she uncrossed her arms to lay her hand on his shoulder. 'Don't do it again.'

Nick's expression cleared and he smiled at her, ruthlessly deploying the dimple. 'Excellent,' he said, his smug tone now back in place, and Natasha sighed.

'Even with my backing it's not going to be that easy to persuade her to –'

'Don't worry about the persuading bit,' Nick said, winking as he skirted around her to go back to Goodie. On his way over he signalled to someone across the crowd, before dropping back down to a crouch in front of Goodie's wheelchair.

'What's going on?' Goodie said through gritted teeth. He tried to take her hand in his but she snatched it away, the sudden movement causing her to flinch in pain and Nick to bite back a curse.

'It's all decided,' he told her, 'you're coming home with us. Natasha's not really set up for you anyway. You need to be sensible about this.' Goodie looked round him at Natasha and scowled.

'Listen, *myshka*,' Natasha said carefully, 'maybe he's right. I mean, it would be tricky at my place and –'

'Fine,' Goodie bit out, bracing both hands on the sides of

her wheelchair to try and stand. 'I've recovered from worse on my own. I'll do it again. I don't need either of –'

'Goodie?' Nick watched as Goodie froze in her misguided attempt to stand and slowly sank back into the chair, her eyes moving to see Arabella in front of her, next to an over-excited Salem. As two sets of eyes locked with hers, both dog and nine-year-old girl moved together. Arabella threw her arms around Goodie's neck and Salem pushed Goodie's good hand up so that she was stroking his head. 'Why would you be on your own?' Arabella asked, her voice displaying just the right amount of hurt and betrayal. 'You've got us to look after you? Why don't you want to come home with us to get better?' Goodie rubbed Salem's neck and then closed her good arm around the little girl.

'Of course I'll come home with you, *lapochka*,'* she muttered into Arabella's hair, glaring at both Nick and Natasha in turn from behind Bella's head.

∼

GOODIE WATCHED ARABELLA PLAY WITH SALEM FROM THE window of the library, then scowled down at her leg and her crutches before throwing the book she was holding onto the coffee table in front of her. It was two days since she'd arrived at the house. Nick, it seemed, could conduct business from the middle of Sussex now. He'd had a conference room set up in the West Wing, and a huge office with a disturbing number of computer screens contained within it. Also in the West Wing was the gym he'd had installed, *and* an endless pool was in a newly constructed building just to the side of the house. Goodie was not sure what to make of all that. She knew that if Nick wanted something he was extremely single-minded in his pursuit of it. And she knew that, for the moment, he wanted her. But to move his entire operation down to Sussex and build a veritable rehabilitation centre for her was a bit much, even for him.

Their first stand-off had been when they arrived back from the airport. It was late; Nick deemed it too late for Goodie to be up and about and told her he would take her to her room. She had point-blank refused to be picked up by him again. When he'd reached for her she flinched away so violently that she'd actually let out a small moan of pain at the movement. Nick had backed away after that, a muscle ticking in his jaw and his fists clenched at his side. Goodie had eyed the stairs and reached for her crutches. She wasn't going to let the fact that propping the crutches under her arms caused almost unbearable tearing pain to ricochet through her ribs and her bad shoulder stop her. She'd been through worse after all. But by the second step sweat was starting to bead on her forehead, and she had to bite her lip to stop herself screaming in agony. It was then she felt a light touch on her arm and turned to look at Nick's mum. Goodie wobbled for a moment and thought she would go down, but then felt the heat at her back as Nick's large body steadied her own.

'Sometimes,' Claire said softly as she moved her hand down to grasp Goodie's where it was gripping the crutch, 'there is strength in accepting help.'

Goodie closed her eyes slowly and loosened her grip on her crutches to lean back into Nick's body. After passing her crutches over to his mum, he lifted Goodie very carefully into his arms like she was made of crystal. The movement was painful, but nothing compared to standing on her bad leg with the crutches. She looked up to the tanned column of his throat, and a wave of exhaustion overcame her so powerfully that she found herself tucking her face into his neck and taking in a deep breath of his clean scent.

Her eyes had closed by the time they made it to the bedroom, so she didn't notice Nick bypassing the spare one she had been in before (when she wasn't sleeping in the boot room that is) and carrying her to his bed. All she knew as she snuggled under the covers was that she was surrounded by everything Nick, and she fell into the deepest sleep she'd had since lying in his arms weeks ago. When she woke up in his bed, however, she was less at peace with the situation. Once she realized which room she was in she'd sat up and swung her legs over the side of the bed, suppressing a wince of pain and looking around for her crutches. Just as she was considering making a lunge for them where they were propped up against the side table out of her reach, the bedroom door opened and Nick's infuriatingly beautiful face, complete with smile *and* dimple, emerged from behind it. Once he saw she was fully awake he walked in and approached the bed.

'Why am I in your bed?' Goodie asked through gritted teeth, trying to resist the urge to punch him in his smug face – something she knew that for the moment would hurt her far more than him.

Nick rubbed the back of his neck (still smiling, the bastard), and then spread his hands. 'Look, it's bigger than the others; it has a bath in the en suite and a plasma screen on the wall. It makes sense that you stay here.'

'I can't stay in the same room as you,' she told him, her goddamn weak-as-shit voice breaking again as she tried to make her words sound as firm as possible. Her throat was sore and her head was starting to pound. She stared down at her hands and thought about that lunge for the crutches again.

'I'm sorry,' she heard Nick say as she felt the bed depress next to her. Those two words succeeded in getting her attention: Nick rarely apologized for anything. 'Look, I won't stay in here with you. I just want you to be here ... in my room. I can't really explain why, but after you left and all that searching ... then not knowing if we could get you out, hearing you ...' He broke off and his shoulders slumped as he shook his head slowly. 'Here,' he said, handing the mug he was carrying to Goodie without raising his head to look at her.

She hesitated for a moment, but after another dry swallow past her aching throat she accepted it. Looking down, she saw that the white liquid was gently steaming. The familiar scent filled her nostrils and she felt her chest tighten. She took a long sip and let her eyes close as the Gogol Mogol soothed her throat. Once finished, she placed the cup on the side table and shuffled back into the bed, settling onto the pillows. Nick's head came up and his shoulders straightened as he looked over at her. She reached over to lay her hand on his on the bed.

'Thank you,' she told him. 'I'll stay here ... if it's what you want.'

He smiled. The dimple came out. Gogol Mogol, dimple, rabid concern, humour, a face almost too beautiful to be real: she was screwed. But Goodie was tired. She needed to heal. She decided she would allow herself this, allow herself for once in her life to be looked after. When she was well again, when she could at least *walk* properly, she would find the strength to leave him.

The fear she had felt when she saw his blood still haunted her dreams. The pain of seeing him in another woman's arms was still fresh. She couldn't risk coming apart again; and anyway, now that he no longer needed protection, he was safer without her. He might think she was what he wanted for now but eventually he would realize how damaged she actually was. Bright, beautiful, larger than life, well-adjusted men did not stay with women who were not only scarred physically, but who had so many marks on their souls they would never be redeemed. She reached for the

Gogol Mogol again and let the warmth of it seep right down to her bones.

Yes, she would allow herself to give in, for now.

After that day it was established that Nick would carry her up and down stairs. As a consequence she and Salem had barely left his room in the last forty-eight hours, choosing to eat all her meals in there rather than brave the rest of the house and Nick's family. Nick had sat with her when he wasn't working – the three of them lying on his huge bed watching films together (Nick was horrified that as a 'lady of a military persuasion' she had never watched *Commando* or *Predator* before, and succeeded in actually making her laugh with his Arnie impressions throughout both).

Arabella had sneaked in once when Nick wasn't there and forced Goodie to watch something called *Frozen*. This involved a large amount of out-of-tune singing from the nine-year-old so that Goodie and Salem would get the 'full experience'. After the first three rewinds of 'Let It Go', Salem had actually buried his head under one of Goodie's pillows with a low whine. For Goodie's part no amount of aggressive, tuneless sing-shouting could take away from having Arabella snuggled into her good side, her animated little face full of enthusiasm. She asked what Goodie's favourite Disney film was when it was finished, and Goodie had smiled, tilted her head to the side and told her: *Frozen*. Arabella frowned. 'What? Even more than the ones you watched as a kid?'

Goodie ran her hand through the girl's soft, dark hair. She never lied to children. 'I have nothing to compare it to, *lapochka*,' she told her softly. 'I have never seen a film like this before.' Arabella's mouth had hung open in shock, her eyes widening as she tried to comprehend a childhood with no Disney.

'Well, at least you've got plenty of time to catch up now,'

she declared rather ominously, and Goodie smiled a slightly strained smile at the prospect of Arabella force-feeding her thousands more animated musicals.

She heard the door click open and a relatively soft 'What ho!' before she turned to see Nick's dad pushing into the room. She jerked her chin in his direction in greeting, then went back to watching the girl and dog rolling about on the lawn. 'Tricky business, this being-injured lark,' Monty continued, as usual unfazed by Goodie's lack of verbal response to him. 'Frustrating and all that.' Goodie sighed as he sat down on the chair opposite; it looked like he was settling in for a while. She flicked another glance over at him, noticing that he was pulling the chessboard out from under the table. 'All it takes is time and patience,' he said as he started to set up the pieces. 'That's all anything ever takes to heal though, isn't it? A jolly good bit of time and patience.'

'Some wounds don't heal,' Goodie muttered, unconsciously lifting her hand up to the small scar next to her eye.

'They might leave scars. You might never forget, but with time pain fades. With time you can learn to remember, but not to let the scars control who you are.' Goodie had turned away from the wrestling pair outside and was now staring at Monty. She held his gaze for a long moment before looking down at the chessboard.

'You want to play or what?' she asked, and was so busy helping to set up the pieces that she didn't catch Monty's smile.

* *LAPOCHKA* – SWEETIE-PIE

Chapter 27

Make me better

'Hello, boys,' Goodie said, and she pushed her way into the conference room. Bertie, ever the gentleman, shot from his seat to pull out a chair for her as she hobbled over to them. She had been at the house for four weeks and was down to one crutch. The discomfort in her chest was now something she could ignore and her shoulder was much stronger; all that was letting her down was her leg. The plaster was finally off but it remained weak and, without the hated crutch, would give way.

However, Goodie was stronger, she was independent again; she no longer needed looking after. What she needed to do was to leave, to get back to her old life. Staying in this house was dangerous.

She spent most of her mornings playing chess with Monty in the library, or reading. She had then started going down to the kitchen, as this was where she would invariably find Salem (he was a big fan of the Aga), and she'd help Claire, Mrs B. and sometimes Tilly (when she wasn't out with the horses) with the day's cooking (basically doing all the chopping – Mrs B. was constantly amazed by the way Goodie handled a knife, she

Goodnight

reckoned Goodie was better than any KitchenAid you could buy). Then when Arabella came home from school Goodie would go out with her and Salem; she couldn't run and muck about with them, but she could walk out to the woods and at least *be* with them.

Then there was her physiotherapist: a tall, strapping Australian man called Bruce, who cycled everywhere, then proceeded to wear his lycra in his sessions with Goodie. Goodie had always had a dry sense of humour. She knew she could make people laugh if she wanted, but the urge to do it had been rare in times past. Now she found that she practically lived for making the Chambers family laugh, since she had said to Tilly, Mrs B. and Nick's mum that she felt 'a terrifying mixture of reluctant arousal and abject horror' at the amount of time she had to spend close to his lycra-outlined, obnoxiously large manhood.

Now whenever he came into the kitchen to fetch her for her sessions, all the ladies had to stop themselves looking down at his crotch, and couldn't even speak to him through their suppressed laughter. Luckily he seemed happy to put it down to posh eccentricity rather than an obsession with his meat and two veg.

So she'd fallen into this comfortable routine and so far had managed to push aside her fear. But now that she was stronger the fear was growing. She wouldn't need rehab forever. She couldn't afford to get closer to these people. Even if she wanted to stay, she doubted that her past would let her.

'Congratulations,' she told Ed. 'I hear your little idea actually works.'

Ed smiled and nodded his head enthusiastically.

'My poor grandad would be turning over in his grave,' he said happily. 'He was a miner, see; not all that into alternative energy.'

'He would be proud,' Goodie told him. 'You – you will change the world now.'

Ed blushed and smoothed down the front of his 'Kiss a Geek' T-shirt. 'Don't be daft,' he muttered.

'Not daft,' Goodie told him firmly, and when he shook his head she let Nick take her crutch and guide her down onto one of the chairs. 'When I was a child in Russia I was cold ... all the time. So cold. There is no happiness when you are that cold. You cannot take joy from anything. Being cold turns *you* cold, in here,' Goodie said as she pressed a hand to her chest. 'Makes you a different person. You ... *you* will bring warmth to these people, I think. Energy without limits – without harm to the environment. That is why you will change lives.'

'Jolly well said,' Bertie put in, clapping Ed on the back a few times for good measure. Goodie smiled. She was pleased Ed was happy. The success of the project meant more to her than she had ever let on before. In the beginning, before she had started to care for Nick, it was the only reason she'd agreed to protect them. Their lives were important. They would make a difference. That was still true now and that was part of the reason she had to leave.

'I came here to speak to you all,' she said as she felt Nick's arm drape across the back of her chair and his body move closer to hers. 'I cannot stay here any longer. I am recovered. Natasha is picking me up today.' The atmosphere in the room changed from happy to alert in an instant. She felt Nick's body next to hers go tight and her chair move as he gripped the back of it.

'But Goodie, old girl ... don't you think –'

∾

Goodnight

'Bert, Ed could you leave us a moment? Get a cup of tea or something?' Nick was trying to keep his voice level and light, but the words came out as somewhat of a growl.

'Of course, mate,' Ed said, jumping up and nearly tripping over his chair in his efforts to get out of the room and away from the thick atmosphere. 'Come on, Bertie,' Ed said as he pushed the door open. Bertie had got to his feet but was standing his ground.

'I ... well, that's to say, I ...' Bertie took a deep breath and squared his shoulders. 'I think it would be a blasted shame if you were to just ... well ... vanish into thin bloody air again. I think you're a damn fine girl and a good sport and, well ...'

'Thank you, Bertie,' Goodie said. He gave her a quick nod, gave Nick a significant look as if to say 'sort this out, you moron', and stalked out of the room.

'I think I want to adopt your cousin,' Goodie told Nick through a chuckle as the door slammed after him.

'Not sure you can adopt a thirty-seven-year-old man, Goodie,' Nick said, relaxing as he saw her smile. 'But I guess if the authorities were going to arrange it for anyone, Bertie would be the most likely to qualify.'

He turned his chair towards Goodie's and pulled hers into him so that her legs were between his, with both his hands resting on her armrests and him leaning into her. Goodie had noticed this about Nick, he used his proximity to his advantage. If he wanted to convince her of something he would always find a way to occupy her personal space. He knew the impact being close to him had on her; she rather thought that with the right training he would have made a fairly lethal operative in the field. He was certainly manipulative enough.

'Now, what's all this about leaving?' he asked.

Goodie leaned back into her chair but she could still smell him, still make out every detail of his beautiful face, focused intensely on hers. 'I can't stay here, Nick. You don't –' she took a deep breath and tried to push her chair away from his, but his hands gripped her arm rests more firmly '– you don't know me,' she finished on a whisper. He slowly leaned in further until she could feel his breath on her cheek, and his hand came up to push her now shoulder-length blonde hair behind her ear.

'I know you, baby,' he said, his voice low, and Goodie fought back a shiver, remembering just how well he *did* know her, at least in that sense.

'Nick, I –' She was cut off as his mouth closed over hers. She froze for a moment but the feel of him and her need for him drowned out the voice of reason in her head, and when both his warm, large, strong hands wound into her hair she lost control. Pushing him backwards with her hands to his chest and her mouth still fastened to his, they both moved until she had left her chair and was straddling him on his. The kiss became desperate and her hands slid down to pull his shirt out of his trousers so that she could touch the skin of his stomach and move up to the hard planes of his chest. She pulled her mouth from his and moaned low in her throat at the feel of him, resting her forehead on his.

And that was when it happened.

His arms slid around her back, under her T-shirt, and his breath left him in a loud exhale before he whispered: 'Anya,' into her ear.

Goodie froze.

'What did you say?' she asked slowly, jerking her head away from his.

Nick's eyes widened and his body went rigid with tension. 'Goodie, I ...' Acting on impulse, she wrenched away from him and stumbled to her feet, wincing as her leg almost gave way with the sudden weight through it, and grabbing onto the table for support.

Goodnight

'Goodie, listen to me ...' Nick had risen from the chair and lifted his hand to support her elbow, but she pulled away from him violently, causing another tearing pain through her leg, but at this point she was beyond caring. The room actually felt like it was spinning as she backed away from him, using the chairs for support because her crutch was on Nick's other side. She hadn't been called that name for twenty years.

Nick held his hands up, palm down. 'Goodie,' he said, low and even, as if approaching a wounded animal, 'baby, you're going to hurt yourself. Please calm down and let me explain.'

'How do you know that name?' she asked, moving to the other side of the conference table and ignoring the throbbing ache in her leg.

'You'll take this the wrong way, honey, but I had to know more about you. It was driving me nuts and I ... I'm not good with being in the dark.'

'Who told you that name?' Her voice was now cold, completely devoid of expression, as were her eyes. Her quick mind was processing everything at lightning speed. She had thought her past was buried, but if anyone had the resources to dig it up it was of course Nick. The deception and betrayal cut deep, but what really chilled her was that this knowledge was *dangerous*. This stupid, stubborn mule of a man had put himself in danger to satisfy his insatiable curiosity about her.

Nick sighed. 'I found out the bloody name by myself. *You* told me that much.' Goodie frowned at him and he continued. 'You reacted. You flinched when her name was called. It was small, nobody else but me would have ever noticed but ... God, Goodie, I watch you all the time. You're the most beautiful thing I've ever seen. I just wanted to know more about you ... to *have* something –'

'You have everything,' she said. To her horror her voice broke and the shame of that weakness made her anger grow

237

even more. '*Everything.* Why would you go digging when I had already given you all I had.'

'I'm sorry, Goodie, I just –'

'Look,' Goodie cut him off, her gaze shearing away from him as she considered her options. It was obvious that he was not going to tell her his source. She had no way of extracting the information she needed like this. 'Natasha will be here soon. I can't talk about this now. I need to lie down, get the weight off my leg and take something for the pain.'

'Listen, I –'

'I'm in *pain*, Nick.' Goodie watched as he ran his hands through his hair and let out a long sigh.

'Okay,' he said, reaching back for her crutch and then moving to her. He followed after as she hobbled to the stairs, and as was normal for them now she allowed him to lift her to climb them, but instead of breathing him in and clutching around his neck as she normally would, she let her arms settle loosely in her lap and turned her head away. He laid her down in his bed; she rolled onto her side, facing the window, and closed her eyes.

A good few minutes passed, but once she heard the door softly close behind him her eyes popped open. He would be going back to his office but his laptop was in the bedroom. Observation was one of Goodie's particular skills. As well as a photographic memory when it came to written pages, she had almost perfect recall of the layout of a room and the items inside it. She'd noticed Nick leave his laptop in the room this morning when he came to bring her a cup of tea. The bank of computers in his office meant he rarely had to use it during the day and he often left it lying around. Goodie had had no need to hack it before. She had studied Nick well before she started working for him. This, however, was different. This was about *her*.

Goodnight

She sat up and swung her legs over the bed, grabbed her crutch and pushed to her feet. Once she was sitting at the small desk near the window she opened the lid of the laptop and then entered the password. She knew all of Nick's passwords, just like she knew everything else about him: from his shoe size, to his GCSE results, to the names of every woman he'd ever slept with (that knowledge had proved painful on occasion, especially when she was forced to watch him dance with one of the women he'd shagged on a semi-regular basis over the years).

It took a few minutes to hack every corner of his hard drive until she found what she was looking for. Before she opened the file, she paused to look at the private investigator's name and contact details, then took a deep breath. Something was stopping her from making the last few key-strokes she needed, and she found herself just staring at the screen as the seconds ticked by. The hair on the back of her neck stood on end, and a cold feeling of foreboding swept over her as she forced her fingers to move.

The screen changed as a scanned document filled it: she took in her name, her mother's name, her date of birth (something she hadn't acknowledged in over twenty years). A few more key-strokes, and instead of more documents an image filled the screen. Goodie wasn't shocked by the blood or the hollow emptiness in the blue eyes staring back at her, but she was surprised by how young she looked: even younger than Arabella. An image of Arabella going through what Goodie had at the same age went through her mind, and she was swamped by a sick feeling of horror.

I was just a child, she thought as she dragged her consciousness away from that image. She frowned. Had she ever been a child in the true sense of the word? Closing her eyes for a moment, she drew in a breath and her fingers flew back to the keys. At the next image she froze. The image of a blonde woman with a small, equally blonde child in her lap appeared, another dark-haired child standing at their sides and leaning into them both. Their arms were around each other, the blonde child was smiling a wide smile into the camera, and the dark-haired child's head was thrown back in laughter. But the woman's eyes were on the blonde child's face; her smile was smaller than her children's and her blue eyes were soft. Goodie reached out a finger and traced the woman's beautiful face on the screen as the memories started invading.

'Mama,' Anya said into her mother's soft hair in Russian, 'throat sore. Make me better.'

'Ugh, you've got a cold, Anya,' groaned Tasha from her position on the ratty sofa, rolling her eyes.

'Don't worry, *myshka*, I can make better,' Anya heard her mother murmur, and felt the arms around her give her a squeeze as she was carried through to the tiny kitchen. She was sat at the small table as her mother moved to the stove, pouring the white mixture into Anya's mug. She then placed the mug in front of Anya and stroked her hair as Anya drank the warm liquid, easing the pain in her throat and lessening the shivers that wracked her body. She took Anya's hand when she had finished, and guided her to the bedroom they shared. They lay down together and Anya's eyes closed as her mother stroked her hair. She heard the bedroom door open but was buried so far into her mother's chest that she couldn't make out Tasha's words.

'She's fine, *kotyonok*,'* Anya heard her mother say. Then she felt heat at her back as Tasha came in behind her to wrap her arms around both of them. Anya had drifted off to sleep, warm and surrounded by love.

Goodie blinked at the screen but was unable to tear her eyes away. She was wrong when she thought she'd never been looked after before. She'd been loved, totally and unconditionally. After the horror of what happened to her mother and the nightmare of everything that happened after that night, she'd blocked out those memories. That way she could deal with being separated from Tasha. She could deal with anything because she no longer felt pain or loss; but in turn she no longer really ever felt happiness or joy.

 Not until him.
 Not until Nick.

* *KOTYONOK* – KITTEN

Chapter 28

You promise?

'You've had plenty of time, but she still called for *me*.' Goodie froze outside the library as she heard Tasha's voice float through the door. 'I'm not leaving without her. Not if she wants to go. I won't let her down. God knows she's never, ever failed *me* before.'

'She's running away because she's scared; she –'

'Goodie is not scared of anything. You don't know what she's faced ... what she's done ...'

'I know.' Nick's firm declaration hung in the air, silencing Tasha.

'What did you say?' Goodie could only just make out Tasha's whisper through the crack in the door, and felt her chest constrict at the fear she could hear in her sister's voice. It was Goodie who had put that fear there – her need for secrecy at all costs that made Tasha so terrified of the truth.

'I know who you are.' Nick's voice had softened and she heard him take a step towards Tasha. 'I know what happened; how you were separated.'

'Then you know what she sacrificed for me,' Tasha said, her

Goodnight

voice choked with tears. 'How she went with them willingly so long as *I*, the older sister, the one who should have been doing the protecting, was adopted into a good family. I had every opportunity, every chance at happiness whilst she was trained to be ...' Tasha trailed off, her sobs filling the library, and Goodie was done. She hobbled forward as fast as she could and both Nick and Natasha turned as they heard the door push open. Goodie paused at the doorway for a moment, her eyes on Tasha's tear-streaked face.

'*Kotyonok*,' Goodie called softly across the room. Tasha's shoulder stopped shaking and her mouth fell open in shock.

'*Myshka?*' she asked slowly. 'What did you call me?'

'I remember,' Goodie said simply. Tasha closed her eyes, took a deep breath in and then shot across the room to engulf Goodie in a hug.

'You remember?' she asked, pulling back and searching Goodie's face. 'Do you ... can you remember *her?*'

'Everything.' Tasha's body sagged into Goodie's, which with her bad leg nearly caused them to go down. But just as they were about to stumble Tasha was extracted from Goodie's arms and Nick was there for Goodie to lean into heavily. To her surprise when she looked up from the floor she saw that a red-faced, clearly furious Bertie had stormed into the room and was holding Tasha, staring daggers at Nick and Goodie.

'What the bloody hell is going on here?' he snapped. 'Why is Tash crying? You lot and your confounded drama that follows you around. I'll thank you to leave Tasha out of it.'

'Bertie, you numpty; I'm happy,' Tasha said through her sobs.

'You're ... what in the blazes?' Bertie sighed and held her closer, letting her cry into his shoulder. 'I will never understand ladies,' he admitted helplessly.

Goodie looked up at Nick's concerned face, then stood on

her one functioning tiptoe to give him a kiss on the cheek. He frowned in confusion but gave her a small squeeze in response. Her leg had started throbbing again and as if he could read her mind he moved her to the sofa, sitting her down next to him.

Tasha eventually lifted her head from Bertie's chest and gave him a watery smile, which he returned. 'Look, I'm sorry but you lot are going to have to explain what's going on.'

Tasha looked across at Goodie who nodded her head in agreement.

'Goodie and I are sisters, Bertie,' Tasha told him as she took his hand and led him to the opposite sofa.

'Uh ... sisters? ... But?'

Goodie laughed. 'I know we look nothing alike ... different fathers. But we lived with my mother until I was nine and Tasha was twelve. There were difficulties but ...' Goodie paused and looked at Natasha. 'Mama was a wonderful woman. She loved us, she cared about us and she did what she had to do to look after us.'

Tasha's eyes again filled with tears and Goodie felt a shard of guilt for all the cold things she had said about their mama in the past. She realized that it had hurt Tasha to think Goodie couldn't remember any of the good in their childhood, any of the love the three of them shared. Goodie had shut her down every time Tasha brought it up, not allowing either of them to relive any of the happy memories together. Goodie knew why her mind had shut off that part of her childhood. To know how she was loved and what she had lost would have made her weak. For the last twenty years weakness was not something Goodie could allow. But now ...

'What happened?' Bertie asked, his eyes darting between Goodie and Tasha. Goodie felt Nick stiffen beside her and she laid her hand on his.

'Mama died,' Goodie told him, her voice steady. 'And we

Goodnight

were separated. Tasha went to a family and I ... I went somewhere else.'

'Not just any family,' Tasha said, her voice breaking with small sobs again. 'Goodie made it so that I was with the best family available. I had everything whilst she –'

'We are different, Tasha,' Goodie told her. 'I was fine. I've always been fine.'

'How did you find each other again?' Bertie asked. Goodie noticed that Nick did not ask any questions of his own. No doubt his private detective had rooted all this out as well. Goodie thought that maybe she should have been angry, but how could she really complain when *she* knew every single detail about *him* before they even met?

'Tasha had a stalker. She needed protection. I have always known where she was and how she was, but avoided contact. When I found out about the stalker I manoeuvred myself into her protection.'

'Jeepers! A stalker!' Bertie looked shocked and concerned. A flash of an image Goodie kept locked away and brought out from time to time when she needed cheering up came to mind. It was how Tasha's stalker had looked after Goodie had finished with him. She smiled at the memory.

'Don't worry, Bertie. I don't think he'll surface again.'

'No,' Nick said, a small smile tugging at his lips. 'I don't expect he will.'

Tasha gave Nick a sharp look. Goodie thought that he probably knew better than she did what had happened to that piece of shit.

'Anyway, after all the stalker business Goodie kept an eye on me, and of course I run the –'

'Enough,' Goodie snapped in Russian, cutting Tasha off.

Tasha rolled her eyes. 'What's wrong with talking about it? How can anyone use *that* information against you?' she said back, also in Russian. Goodie looked away from her to the window and shifted uncomfortably on the sofa. Tasha didn't understand, but it *did* make a difference to how people perceived her. She needed them to believe how ruthless she was. Glancing down at her leg, she sighed as she thought that maybe that wouldn't be such an issue anymore.

'I know about the foundation,' Nick said quietly, in only slightly broken Russian. Goodie's head snapped around and she looked at him with wide eyes.

'Since when do you speak my language?' she asked. 'And how do you know about the foundation? There are no links back to me.'

Nick shrugged. 'I started learning months ago after that charity dinner when I couldn't understand you. It ... annoyed me. It seemed like another way for you to keep things from me.' (This was again spoken in Russian. He was actually pretty good, although instead of actually saying 'charity dinner' he'd called it a 'free meal', and Goodie was sure he didn't mean to say 'she was keeping frogs from him').

'Can you all bally well speak in the Queen's,' Bertie huffed. 'Russian's not really one of my strengths. Now, get me onto French and we'd be away. I mean –'

'Ah!' Goodie cried, unable to resist. '*Vous parlez couramment Francais! Ou avez-vous appris?*'*

'Er ... *la gare est la prochaine a gauche?*'*

Goodie pressed her lips together as she heard a muffled snort from Tasha, who leaned across to give Bertie a kiss on the cheek. Bertie's frown disappeared and he blushed bright red, but managed to return the hand-squeeze.

'Bertie, I run a foundation called *No Strength without Heart*. It helps people in cold climates with no money for energy. Funds projects to provide communities with energy, and links those that can't afford it to the mains. I fundraise and

Goodnight

I contribute from my modelling career, but ...' She looked across at Goodie who frowned at her and shook her head.

'Most of the money comes from Goodie,' Nick said, ignoring her warning glance.

'Gosh, how did you come by all that cash?' sweet, wonderful, naïve Bertie asked, and Goodie smiled.

'The business I'm in can be quite lucrative.' Her smile dropped and she frowned down at her leg. 'Although ... not recently.' She looked up as she heard Tasha laugh.

'I wouldn't worry about funding, *myshka*,' she said through her laughter, winking at Nick. 'We've got more in the pot than ever.'

Goodie sucked in a sharp breath and looked up at Nick. He nodded once and she looked away, tucking her hair behind her ears. 'Thank you,' she said under her breath, and felt him squeeze her shoulders. The foundation meant everything to her.

'Bertie?' Nick asked, staring down at Goodie. Could you take Tasha to the kitchen, maybe get a cup of tea for her or something?'

'Goodness, yes, of course, old boy!' Bertie blustered, puffing his chest out like he'd just been asked to engage in mortal combat for Tasha rather than just make her a cup of tea. 'Mrs B.'s got some ginger nuts in too,' Bertie told Tasha, the genuine excitement in his voice (one of Bertie's great passions, just like his cousin, was biscuits) making Tasha chuckle as he led her out of the room. Once they'd shut the door after them, Nick turned back to Goodie.

'Are you angry?' he asked.

Goodie cocked her head to the side and frowned. 'Why would I be angry? You used the resources at your disposal to get the result you wanted; I do that all the time.'

'Oh ... I thought –'

'I'm not angry but ... no more. It's dangerous what you have done. The past needs to stay in the past. The man you sent over there, the questions he asked; you put him in danger.'

'Shit.' Nick's face paled. 'I didn't think of that.'

'But I want to say thank you.'

'What? Why?'

'You've given me my mama back. Seeing her face, her eyes, her smile. Now I can remember. But you've been bringing her back to me for months, even without the photos you had found.'

'What do you mean?'

'You look after me. Nobody since Mama has ever done that.' Salem bumped her hand with his head as if he could actually understand her words, and she laughed. 'Okay, big guy – nobody of the human variety, that is.'

'Goodie, I've looked after you since we got you back, but before that I think we can all say you were fairly self-sufficient.'

She shook her head and Nick's eyes widened with shock as hers filled with tears. 'You don't get it, do you?' she said as one tear escaped down her cheek. 'Asking Sam about me, wanting me to be safe, noticing my fear of confined spaces and making it so I had Salem; your patience, your kindness, coaxing me out of my self-imposed shell; the –' she gave a small sob and he reached for her, engulfing her in his arms and pressing her face into his chest '– the Gogol Mogol ...' Her breath hitched again but she fought down the tears and pushed slightly away from him so she could look up at his face; she had to get everything out. 'I don't know why you want me. I'm not saying I understand it but ... you've got me. You've brought me to life and I'm yours. I won't leave you again unless you send me away, *lyubov moya*.'*

Nick was silent for a long moment. 'Goodie?'

'Yes?'

'Do you know what you just called me?'

Goodnight

Goodie smiled. 'Nick, I am Russian. I think I know my own language.'

He swallowed, his own eyes feeling suspiciously wet (which as far as Nick was concerned was down to the excessive furniture polish employed by an over-exuberant Mrs B.). 'You know I love you too, right?'

'I think I figured that out by now. It's either that or you really are clinically insane.' He smiled (and if Goodie hadn't been totally sure of her decision, that dimple would have sealed the deal), then he took her face in his hands, running his nose along hers and kissing her briefly before muttering, 'You'll stay with me? You promise.' She nodded, then kissed him again, laughing as he pushed her back into the sofa. Unfortunately by the time they heard the soft knock at the door things had heated up sufficiently for neither of them to notice or care.

'Ah!' a red-faced, horrified Bertie said from the doorway. 'Er … Tasha sent me to check … well … um … looks like everything's chugging along nicely here, I'll just …' and he backed out hurriedly through the door. Goodie face-planted into Nick's neck, and then, to his shocked pleasure, she burst out laughing.

---

* Vous parlez couramment Francais! Ou avez-vous appris? – You speak fluent French! Where did you learn?

   * Er ... la Gare est la prochaine a gauche? – Er ... The station is the next left?

Chapter 29

Heat from thin air

'THE BLADE YOU ARE THROWING IS DOUBLE-EDGED, BENJI,' Goodie said from her position sitting on a tree stump, 'it needs a hammer grip: four fingers wrapped around and thumb over the top.' She watched as Benji readjusted his hand and then smiled. 'Great. Okay, weight on dominant leg.'

'Which one's my dominant leg?'

Goodie sighed and stood up slowly, giving a very patient Salem a quick stroke before she picked up her crutch and hobbled over to Benji.

'Give me the knife a sec,' she said, holding out her hand. After she'd put the knife back in its holster, she turned to Benji. 'Now, look at the target again.' He stood with his back to her and she gave him a firm shove, making him go forward on his right leg.

'Oi!' he said as he righted himself. 'What was that for?'

Goodie laughed. 'Now we know which is your dominant foot, *ebanashka*.'*

'I am not crazy,' replied Benji, and Goodie laughed again.

'You are little bit –' she held her thumb and forefinger

millimeters apart, still smiling '– crazy. But luckily for you I like crazy, so this is okay.' Benji rolled his eyes as she handed him back the knife, and then stared at her as she hobbled back to her log. He saw her wince as she sat down, and he scuffed his shoe on the ground, looking down at his feet.

'I'm sorry you were hurt, Goodie,' he mumbled at his shoes.

'This was not your fault,' Goodie told him, and he shrugged.

'Still, it must make you bloody cross. Especially you. I mean, you were like a Russian Lara Croft or something.' Goodie laughed again.

'I don't mind this,' she said, lifting the crutch slightly and looking down at her leg.

Benji frowned at her in confusion. The Goodie he knew didn't laugh and definitely wouldn't accept an incapacitating injury so easily. 'But you're ...' he trailed off, shifting uncomfortably in front of her.

'Weak?' Goodie finished for him, and he flushed red with embarrassment.

'I didn't mean –'

'There are other ways to be strong Benji,' she said. 'And besides, weakness can be an advantage, it can give you power.' Benji tilted his head and narrowed his eyes.

'What do you mean?' he asked.

Goodie smiled and waved her hand through the air dismissively. 'Enough sharing and touchy-feely nonsense,' she said. 'You want to learn to throw knife with skill or not?' Benji looked at her for a moment longer, his sharp mind ticking over at an alarming rate. Goodie waited patiently and held his gaze until he sighed and turned back to the target.

'Raise your hand higher. Straight wrist this time. The tree is further than before; you don't want the blade to spin as fast.

Breath in, out, and throw.' The knife flew out of his hand and hit the tree, dead centre.

∽

'Hey,' Nick called as he strode over the field at the back of Katie's house towards Benji and Goodie. 'Where did you two get to?' His gaze fell to where her knife holster sat on her lower leg, hidden inside her boot, but as he frowned Goodie stumbled slightly on the uneven ground, her crutch slipping on the mud, and Nick ran to her side to hold her arm, all his suspicions wiped away with concern.

'Benji was just pointing out the local wildlife,' Goodie told him.

'Really?' Nick asked slowly.

'Yep, I'm quite the ornithologist actually,' Benji said, not skipping a beat. He was, just like Goodie, an accomplished liar. Nick's eyes narrowed as he looked over at the lanky boy.

'Right, what's that then?' he asked, pointing at a small brown bird hopping onto a molehill in front of them.

'A dunnock,' Benji said confidently; he'd read a book on birds last year, and, like Goodie, he had a photographic memory.

Nick sighed. 'I don't know if you two together is a good combination.'

'Yeah, Mum and Dad reckon that too,' Benji said, grinning at Goodie, then catching sight of his brothers playing football in Katie's garden and sprinting off towards them.

'What is it about you and that kid?' Nick asked, smiling at Goodie as he half lifted her over a molehill.

She shrugged. 'I first met Benji when he was eighteen months old and I was doing freelance work for his father. Benji could already speak in full sentences. After being around him

Goodnight

in Rob's office for all of half an hour he came up to me, pulled me down to his level, put his hand against my cheek and asked me: "Why are you sad? What happened to make you sad?" Just like that he asked me something nobody else would have dreamed of asking: cut through the bullshit to what he perceived to be the heart of the matter. He is exceptional.'

'What did you tell him?'

'I told him the truth. I told him that I wasn't sad, that I didn't feel much of anything at all. He asked what would make me happy and I told him I didn't know.'

Nick opened the gate into Katie's garden, then took Goodie's hand now that they were on more even ground. Past the boys playing football on the lawn, Goodie could see Katie, Sam with Anya on his hip, and the boys' parents Sarah (who was cuddling Katie and Sam's new baby girl) and Rob laughing in the kitchen at what Katie was pulling out of the oven. Goodie waved to Geoff who was acting as far guard outside the house and he nodded back. After another month at Nick's parents' Goodie wanted to see Katie and thank her for going to Nick after she was taken; and she wanted to thank Rob for becoming part of her rescue team (since his wife, Sarah, had her fifth boy he had largely been UK-based, but had made an exception for Goodie). Goodie hated that she had put them in danger, and knew that there was never anything that would be enough to repay them. When she apologized to Sarah and Katie though, they both hugged her and told her not to be daft. There was, however, steel in Sarah's eyes after she released Goodie and said: 'Don't do it again.'

Nick, it seemed, was not a fan of physical distance separating him from Goodie, so he'd come with her to Wales. Goodie stifled a laugh as she watched Sarah tip whatever sludge Katie had cooked into the bin. Last night Goodie had realized just how much Nick loved her as she watched him valiantly clear his plate of Katie's attempt at lasagna. She was glad there wouldn't be a repeat performance today: she could see Sam rifling through the takeaway menus.

Goodie tugged Nick to a stop before they started up the steps to the back door, and he turned to her. 'You know I'm happy now, don't you?' He nodded and dropped her hand so that he could slip his arms around her waist and pull her to him.

'I know, honey,' he said into her hair.

'You know it's you, don't you?' she whispered, pushing her hands under his arms to move in closer. 'You've made me happy. You've brought me back.'

∽

NICK NEARLY CHOKED ON HIS BEER WHEN SHE EMERGED from the bedroom of the penthouse. She was wearing a short silver dress with wide straps to hide the bullet wound to her shoulder. Her hair was clipped up on one side with a silver hair comb, her eyes were smoky and her lips pale. Before Goodie had really let him in he had thought she was stunning, but now with her smiling and happy, despite the limp and the cane she had to use, her beauty was almost otherworldly. He knew he wasn't the only one to notice this. She'd attracted attention before, but now when she walked into a room all eyes were drawn to her immediately.

The press had gone wild for her since she'd moved back to London with him. He'd taken her out with Ed, Tilly, Bertie and Natasha for one meal in Soho and they'd been swamped with attention. Goodie was surprised the next week when all the photos were of her on Nick's arm: she was used to seeing Natasha in print but not herself. She was initially 'Mystery Blonde', but to prevent anyone digging too deep Nick had allowed his new PR manager (Clive had long since slunk away) to play up her connection with Natasha and the NSWH Foundation. Her injuries were explained by a story about a car accident, but her name was trickier. She had no less than seven aliases to choose from, all of which had birth certificates, passports, the works. She chose the one with the longest, most unpronounceable surname, as this would be repeated and printed the least. But just when Nick was about to email the information across, she grabbed his hand and stopped him hitting send.

'Change it,' she'd said, 'make it Anya – Anya Myshka.' Nick had sat up in shock and frowned at her.

'Is that safe?'

She shrugged. 'There's no harm. Obviously my surname was never really "little mouse". My first name was lost in the system decades ago. I haven't used it once since childhood.'

'Does this mean I can call you Anya?' he asked tentatively; he didn't want to spark a reaction like the last time.

'Of all people, I want you to call me that.'

He smiled at her, showing his dimple.

She was still a sucker for his dimple.

So it was a long time, and not before Nick had very thoroughly road-tested the reinstatement of her old name, before he actually sent that email.

'You look amazing,' he told her as she slipped on the flat, silver ballet pumps (her leg still wouldn't allow her to wear high heels). She gave him a small smile as she straightened and leaned heavily on her stick, but he couldn't miss the shadow that passed over her face. His own smile dipped as his mind was filled with the image of Goodie sitting with Arabella months ago:

'*I hate this,*' *Goodie said, grabbing a handful of blue material,* '*and this,*' *she indicated to her face and hair, which was swept up off her neck in an elegant style,* 'with such intensity that sometimes I feel like they are actually burning my skin.'

'Hey,' Goodie called as she made her way across the room, 'you okay? You look like you've seen a ghost.'

'I ... I'm fine,' he said, blanking his expression and shaking off the dark thoughts. 'Let's go.'

∼

GOODIE COCKED HER HEAD TO THE SIDE AS SHE STARED AT the Indian minister for energy. She wanted to punch him, preferably in his testicles. But she suspected that a black-tie state dinner would not be the most appropriate venue for that, so she held back ... just. He had been asking Ed about the possibilities for cold fusion, about how easily it could be implemented, and above all how much it would cost. Halfway through this conversation he'd turned to the Indian ambassador beside him and muttered in Hindi: 'This guy is nuts; making heat from thin air? Why am I listening to this stupid bastard? These English banging on about the bloody environment all the time, trying to get us to stop burning coal whilst sitting in their warm houses.'

'Maybe *you* are the stupid bastard,' Goodie said in perfect Hindi. The minister, who had previously only glanced at Goodie's breasts rather than her face, turned sharply towards her, his eyes widening in shock. She smiled at him as if she had paid him a great compliment rather than an insult. 'Maybe you should listen more carefully. They *are* making energy from thin air. It's already happened. Do your research. *Your* people need low-cost energy more than most. They won't thank you for passing this up. The solution is staring you in the face. Do you want to be remembered as the man who turned his back on the biggest revolution in energy in the

Goodnight

21st century, or do you want to be remembered as the man who led India out of developing-country status and into world-leader status?' The minister's face was red and he was scowling. Goodie took a step closer to him and lowered her voice. 'Now, you can either take offence and storm away, or you can listen to what this man has to say. You're used to having the power but in this situation you do not. You need what he has and you need it badly. I suggest you take option two.'

The minister opened his mouth, and then shut it again. His heightened colour gradually receded and he smoothed over his furious expression, before turning back to a mystified Ed. Goodie smiled.

'Good decision,' she muttered under her breath as she passed him, and he sent her once last furious look as she limped away.

'Golly,' Bertie said as he caught up with her in her traverse across the large room towards Nick. 'Did I overhear you speaking Indian?'

Goodie laughed so hard that she had to lean on her stick for support. When she looked up, her eyes met Nick's as he moved towards her and Bertie. Once he made it to her he discreetly took her stick and placed her arm on his, so that she could lean on him instead. She managed to get herself under control with some effort. Nick raised his eyebrows in question.

'Bertie overheard me "speaking Indian".'

'Ah, Bertie.'

Goodie looked up as Natasha emerged from the crowd and linked her arm through Bertie's, kissing his cheek.

As Tasha started to explain to Bertie exactly what was so funny, Nick leaned down to Goodie's ear. 'Are you okay?' he asked.

'I'm fine,' she said, frowning up at him. 'Why?'

He shrugged. 'It's just that was the first time I've seen you laugh all night.'

Goodie looked around the room. Most people had polite smiles on their faces the same as she had been wearing all night. Hardly anyone was laughing. 'What's this really about?'

Nick shifted uncomfortably. 'I know you don't like to have to dress up, play a part. You've done so much of it before. I hate that being with me means you have to keep doing it.' He rubbed the back of his neck. 'I want you to be living a different life. To be happy.'

Goodie rolled her eyes. 'You think I am so sensitive that I can't wear formal clothes and act for a while? Have you *met* me?'

'I'm not saying you can't do it. I'm saying you don't enjoy it. I know how you feel wearing this stuff.'

'Okay.' She sighed. 'I'll admit I'm not a fan of them. Before, when I had to wear clothes like this it meant ...' She paused as she noticed Nick's body stiffen. 'Look, it's not the same now, and I wouldn't want to come somewhere like this without ... armour, without power.'

He threw his hands up, then ran them both through his hair in frustration. 'You wouldn't *have* to come somewhere like this if it wasn't for me. Look, I don't have to do this. We don't even have to be in London. We could go anywhere we wanted.'

'And leave Ed and Bertie to handle everything?'

He shrugged. 'I have got other executives, you know: capable chaps, too. It wouldn't matter if –'

She stepped closer to him and reached up to put her fingers over his mouth, stopping him midsentence.

'What you and Ed are doing is important to me too, okay? I wasn't just trained in violence; I was trained to manipulate any situation I needed to. I can help you; I've *been* helping you. That makes me happy, understand?'

Goodnight

He searched her face for a long moment before his frown smoothed out and he finally smiled.

'Exactly how many languages do you speak anyway?' Nick asked out of the corner of his mouth as they approached the Chinese ambassador. Goodie smiled and when they were welcomed into the group she bowed to the ambassador, greeting him in perfect Mandarin.

* *EBANASHKA* — CRAZY PERSON

Chapter 30

Created from darkness

As they emerged from the hall to a bank of paparazzi, Nick wasn't even with it enough to feel the usual annoyance. If he was honest he was feeling a little shell-shocked. Goodie had systematically charmed every foreign diplomat they had yet to get on board with cold fusion. She was incredible. He frowned as he noticed her leaning more heavily on him, her limp more pronounced now; it had been a long evening.

'You're not going to be happy if I pick you up in front of the cameras are you?' he whispered into his ear.

'Try it, Posh Boy, and I will cut your balls off with a spoon,' she said out of the side of her mouth, which was stretched into a forced smile. Just as Nick had started to laugh a shot rang out across the street.

'Goodie!' he shouted as she was torn away from him and he was swamped by his security team. He looked on in horror as she was shuffled to the side of the concourse, nearly going down without the support of her stick. His team began pushing him towards his waiting limousine. 'What the fuck are you *doing?*'

Goodnight

he shouted as they tried to push him inside. 'Don't leave her behind, you pricks.'

Nick was strong and he was big; even the three large men grappling with him couldn't force him into the car. Just as he was about to break free and go to her he saw a look of determination cross Geoff's face. The bastard drew his fist back, then let it fly to deliver a forceful blow into Nick's abdomen, causing him to double over and enabling the other men to shove him onto the backseat and slam the door in his face. Geoff jumped into the other side of the limo as Nick was still gasping for breath. Nick heard another of the men bang on the roof twice and the car shot forward onto the road.

'What the ... ugh ...' Nick forced himself upright. 'What the fuck are you doing?' he roared once he could breath again.

'This is all protocol, sir,' Geoff said calmly. Nick's control snapped and he punched Geoff in the face. Geoff's head snapped back with the force of the blow, which Nick found intensely satisfying until Geoff straightened, rubbed his jaw for a moment and gave a long-suffering sigh.

'Protocol my arse!' Nick shouted, banging on the divider between them and his driver. 'Go back and get her for Christ's sake.' Geoff's phone rang and he answered it, nodding a couple of times.

'Right, yes. No worries. See you back at base.' He ended the call and turned to Nick. 'She's safe.' Nick closed his eyes in relief. 'It was a false alarm: a kid letting off a banger on the pavement. Nothing to worry about. Goodie's in a taxi behind us.'

'Okay,' Nick said slowly, his relief being overtaken with fury. 'I'm glad she's safe. Now would you mind explaining to me why *my girlfriend* is in a *goddamn taxi*, on her own? Why no fucker went to protect her when what sounded like a gunshot went off on a public street? And why nobody who works for me listened to a bloody word I said back there?'

'Like I said, it was all in the proto –'

'Who's sodding protocol are you on about?' Nick shouted. 'Who would create a protocol where we ditch the most important fucking person?'

Geoff let out another long sigh and rubbed his hand down his face. 'She did, you idiot.'

'Geoff, I'm warning you: you're coming close to getting punched again and this time I'll go for a far more painful area than your face. What are you talking about?'

Geoff rolled his eyes. 'You never actually fired her you know. She's still technically head of security. The protocols are *her* protocols.'

Nick frowned. 'What do you mean?'

'I mean that in the event of an emergency or any kind of attack she wanted us to not only make you the priority, but to make sure that she was separated from you and left behind. She called herself …' Geoff looked down at his feet and his voice dropped lower. 'She called herself "dead wood", mate.'

Nick sucked in a sharp angry breath and balled his hands into fists. 'Right,' he said in a tight voice through gritted teeth. 'As of tomorrow she's fucking fired and the protocols are going to change. You listen to *me* now. You can double up the security if it makes her feel better but I want the priority to be her. You're not saving my arse without making sure she's safe as well. Jesus Christ. Stubborn, stupid, bloody ridiculous woman.'

Geoff sat back in his seat, looked out of the tinted window and smiled.

∼

Goodnight

Goodie watched him pacing their bedroom from where she sat on the large bed and pressed her lips together to suppress a smile; she had a feeling that with the mood he was in he wouldn't appreciate it. For her part the only emotion she was feeling was overwhelming relief and gratitude that he was okay. He could be as angry as he wanted so long as he was still walking, talking, beautiful, vibrant and *alive*. Nick stopped midway across the room and pointed at her.

'You're fired,' he bit out before spinning on his heel and striding across the room again.

'Very Alan Sugar,' Goodie said, and he threw her a dirty look.

'Don't try to be cute, Goodie. I'm fucking furious right now. I want to know why you told the guys to ditch you if we were attacked? He said you called yourself "dead wood". What in God's name was going through your head?'

'Nick, I'm sorry but in that situation I *am* dead wood. I wouldn't be able to protect you; I wouldn't even be able to keep up.'

'You're being ridiculous. You –'

'And if somebody comes for *me* ... I ... I wanted them to be able to extract me without having to go through you. Do you understand?'

Nick stopped mid-stride and turned to her, his face draining of colour. 'What do you mean "if somebody comes for you"? Who's going to come?'

'Probably nobody,' Goodie said quickly. 'But Nick ... I ...'

Nick walked over to her and dropped down on his knees in front of her, gathering both of her hands in his. 'Why is anybody going to come for you? Please, Goodie, no more secrets.'

Goodie gave his hands a squeeze. 'It is unlikely, but I am exposed now. My picture has been in the press.'

'Christ,' Nick swore, ripping his hands away from hers and standing abruptly so he could resume his pacing. 'I didn't even think about that. It didn't even cross my mind. I'm such a selfish ba –'

Goodie smacked both her hands down on the bed in frustration. 'It is *not* you who has a past where you've made enemies. This is not your fault. Anyway I am not stupid; I went through all the possibilities before the first night we went out in public. There is little chance that anyone would connect who I was with the person in the public eye now. My jobs involved mostly sticking to the shadows, very few of my targets would recognize me and quite honestly those that could have done are ... um ...' Goodie took a deep breath. She knew Nick had seen most of the files on her, about her life before, but he hadn't seen them all. '... neutralized.' Nick stopped pacing; his eyes widened and he swallowed.

'Right, that's ... good.'

'Yes, it is. Also, if anyone did recognize me they would be unlikely to view me as a credible threat. Not now.'

'But it *could* happen. I mean, you've thought about it.'

'There is a remote chance it could happen. That is why I wanted to be separated from you, Nick. If they want to take me they will take me. No amount of security will stop them, and I would rather you were not in their way.'

'Now you listen to me. I don't care what you would rather. You've shown yourself to have extremely poor judgment when it comes to your own personal safety and I am not going to tolerate it. You're mine. Nobody gets to you; nobody takes you away from me. That part of your life is *over* now. The life you've chosen, a life with *me*, involves safety, it involves security, and it's going to be as bloody boring as I can make it, okay? And you're going to love it.'

'Okay, *lyubov moya*, okay,' Goodie said quietly, resisting the urge to smile.

'Okay,' Nick replied grumpily, then strode over to her again, took her face in his hands, bent down to give her a hard, possessive kiss, and then rested his forehead on hers. 'I might not be some fancy, multilingual, highly trained secret agent type, and I might have to employ the help of countless security people, but I can protect my own goddamn woman.

'Bossy,' she muttered, slipping her hands around his neck.

'Stubborn,' he said back, smiling before he pushed her back into the bed.

∼

'Are you sure about this?' Sam asked, and Goodie rolled her eyes.

'I'm here now. It's a bit too late for second thoughts.'

'Do you really know what you're getting yourself into? There's no going back, no escape,' he muttered darkly.

Goodie narrowed her eyes at him. 'You make it sound worse than the Sabaneta Prison in Venezuela.' Sam shrugged and pressed his lips together.

'You better be careful – the walls have ears, you know.' Sam glanced around the alcove furtively and Goodie suppressed a laugh.

'Don't worry, she's in no fit state for eavesdropping.' Goodie took a step back and looked out to the entryway of the church where Tilly, Katie, Natasha and Arabella were waiting. Katie was sitting on a bench, her head in her hands. Natasha was leaning up against a pillar, her face green. One of Tilly's hands was holding an overexcited Arabella back from storming into the church, and the other was pressed to her temple.

'What did you do to them?' Sam asked, a smile breaking

through his previously serious expression.

'It's their own fault,' Goodie defended. 'If they hadn't been threatening all sorts of beauty bollocks for this morning I wouldn't have had to incapacitate them.'

'I've never seen Katie so hungover.'

'How was I to know she couldn't hold her vodka?' Goodie said innocently.

The girls had insisted on a proper hen party. They'd wanted to take Goodie into London but the furthest they managed to make her go was to the village pub. Once there they had told her all the manicures, pedicures, makeovers and hair appointments that they'd booked in before the ceremony. Goodie had nodded along, but she had never suffered a pedicure in her life (not that she even had a full complement of toes), and she was not going to start now. So she bought a bottle of vodka from the bar. Got some shot glasses, and told the girls that this was how they did hen parties in Russia; that it would mean a lot to her if they would follow the same traditions. So they matched her shot for shot.

None of them had emerged from bed until at least midday, and when they did, two out of three had done it vomiting. The most they had been able to manage before they had to leave the main house was drag on their dresses and spend a painful few minutes on their hair and make-up. They all left Goodie blessedly alone to get ready in peace. She'd pulled on her simple, pale ivory silk dress, left her hair down (as she knew that was how Nick preferred it) with just an ornate comb borrowed from Natasha securing it at the side, and spent her usual five minutes on her make-up.

Sam smiled and then slowly he reached forward, his hand going under her hair, which she'd now grown out to below her shoulders. He wrapped his fingers around the back of her neck and gave her a gentle squeeze before pulling her in for a hug.

Goodnight

'I'm glad you got your happy too, honey,' he muttered into her hair. 'Hold on to it. Fight for it.' He pulled back and searched her face. Her expression was hard, determined.

'I intend to,' she said. The absolute conviction in her voice made Sam pause for a moment.

'Goodie, is there something I should kn –?'

'Are you lot coming or what?' Goodie and Sam turned to see Benji standing outside the alcove, his hands on his hips and an annoyed expression on his face. 'It's bloody boring sitting about in church, you know.' He was wearing the same morning suit and green tie as Sam, which in turn matched the dresses (and in fact the complexions) of the three women in the entryway. 'Come on, I've been ushering the crap out of this thing for an hour already. Let's get the show on the road so we can get to the food.' Goodie laughed and Sam smiled. Seeing her now he could almost believe he had imagined that look of grim resolution on her face from a moment ago.

~

CLAIRE CHAMBERS WATCHED AS THE BEAUTIFUL BLONDE woman made her way down the aisle to her son. From the moment he could speak Nick had been charming his way through life with absolute ease. Everything he touched turned to gold. She'd been worried that when he did settle down he wouldn't properly appreciate his other half, as Claire had assumed that would fall into his lap with as little effort as everything else. She couldn't have been further from the truth, and her son couldn't have chosen a more difficult woman to love.

Claire was proud of Nick for so many things; he was exceptional. But if she was honest, the way he'd restored this broken woman back to herself was, in her opinion, his greatest achievement. Anya might not be full of the light and optimism her son was, but over the last few months her smiles were more frequent and her humour had shone through.

Yes, she was not of the light like her son, she was created from darkness, but in Claire's opinion that made her the perfect counterpoint to him. She had the edge that Nick needed in his life, and a fierce loyalty to him and the family that Claire appreciated. Claire wasn't stupid. She knew who had got rid of that abusive bastard who had threatened her daughter and granddaughter's happiness. Anya was good at what she did but on that occasion her research had been a little lacking: Claire never went fishing with the family. She saw the state Clive was in when he limped out of the house with his tail between his legs, and she saw the fear in his eyes when he'd seen Anya at that charity event. Anya had saved her son's life, she'd saved her daughter and granddaughter who knows how much unhappiness, she'd given Claire's nephew more confidence than he'd had in years; and she'd beaten her husband at chess ... repeatedly.

Yes, Claire knew she had a lot to be grateful for when it came to her future daughter-in-law, but there were two reasons she was truly happy with Nick's choice. The first was how much Anya loved him: Claire could see it in the way she tracked his movements, the contentment in her eyes when he was close and the way her face changed when he touched her with affection; like she was part bemused, part amazed, but mostly radiantly happy. The second reason was that darkness, that edge Anya had; there was no way she would let any harm come to Nick. She would do what needed to be done to keep him safe, and although Nick insisted the danger had passed, Claire wasn't that naïve. There would always be threats to powerful men like him. To have Anya on his team with her brand of loyalty and devotion was more than Claire could ever have hoped for.

Chapter 31

Messy

GOODIE LIMPED TOWARDS THE TREE SLOWLY, THEN PAUSED about five feet away. Her chest constricted painfully as she looked up at the lights twinkling over the entire massive eight-foot monster erected in the Chambers' living room. For over twenty years she had successfully avoided all reminders of Christmas. One of the memories she hadn't been able to leave behind was the reflection of the Christmas lights in her mother's lifeless eyes that night. She looked down at the floor for a moment and took a deep breath in as she felt someone take the hand that wasn't leaning on her stick. She looked over at her sister and saw that she not only had tears in her eyes, but some were streaming down her face. Tasha squeezed her hand and Goodie nodded, closing her eyes for a brief moment and shifting her hand so that it was gripping Tasha's wrist. The steady pulse under her fingers helped to calm her.

They were here; they were alive; that was what mattered.

It was the first time the sisters had been together at Christmas since that night. Tasha had of course tried to make it happen after they were back in contact, but Goodie absolutely refused. Back then she simply couldn't risk the emotion it was likely to provoke. But now ... now she had a family for herself and that she could give Tasha. Now she needed to bury the past. She needed to be strong. Her hand went down to her stomach and her mouth set in a determined line. By next year avoiding Christmas would definitely not be an option.

'Anya, darling,' Goodie's gaze snapped to Claire and the box of baubles she was holding out to her. 'Do you mind helping out? We've got a lot of tree to cover by dinner.' Goodie's hand actually shook as she took the box from Claire, whose concerned eyes flashed to Tasha's tear-stained face. Tash gave a quick shake of her head as Goodie moved to the tree.

'What ho!' The living room door crashed open as Bertie barrelled in, closely followed by the rest of them. This included Nick, Monty, Uncle Giles, Auntie Rose, Tilly, Arabella and Ed.

'The tree!' shouted Arabella, shoving her way through the adults and skidding to a halt next to Goodie. 'What are you doing just standing there, slow-Jo?' she said, tugging Goodie's hand out of Tasha's and dragging her forward. 'Let's get baubling!' Bels let her hand go when they were next to the tree and started rifling through the box of decorations. 'Hurrah!' she shouted, holding a lump of dry clay encrusted with glitter and other festive detritus. 'This is one of *my* creations. Can you believe I made it when I was only three?' Goodie looked at the misshapen lump, then at Arabella's face, shining with excitement. She wasn't sure that the creation of this object was much of an achievement at any age and she didn't like to lie to children, so she smiled instead.

'Mummy says I've always been extremely talented artistically.' She shoved the lump into Goodie's hand. 'I'll let you put it on the tree,' she said, her voice very serious to communicate the gravity of this honour.

Goodnight

'Tasha?' Bertie's worried voice caught Goodie's attention. She looked back to see that Bertie had curled her sister into his side and was wiping away her tears.

'What's up with Auntie Tasha?' Arabella asked, peering around Goodie to look at the couple.

'Your Aunt Tasha is allergic to Christmas trees, squirt,' Nick said, ruffling her hair and then wrapping his big hand around the back of Goodie's neck. 'You okay?' he whispered in her ear, stroking the side of her neck with his thumb. She nodded, reaching up with an unsteady hand to hang the sad-looking lump off one of the branches. When she was done Nick pulled her back into him, wrapped both his arms around her chest and rested his head on top of hers. She closed her eyes slowly, the beating of his heart reassuring against her back, and reached up to curl her hand around his wrist.

'Gosh, how awful for you,' Arabella said to Tash with real feeling. 'Christmas trees, of all things. Do you swell up like a puffer fish?' She tilted her head to the side and eyed Tasha expectantly.

Tasha laughed. 'No, honey.'

Arabella's shoulders slumped with disappointment. 'Ed swells up around the horses,' she said. 'It makes him look super-weird. But he says he's accli ... acclimatose ... acclimat –'

'Acclimatizing,' Ed put in, smiling down at Arabella with lips that were still slightly swollen. Ed's attempts to spend time with, and win, Tilly and Arabella would either succeed, or result in some sort of horse-induced anaphylaxis by the time he was through. Goodie had caught Tilly watching Ed when she thought nobody was looking. The fact Arabella adored him was also a big plus point in his favour, but Clive had done enough damage to Tilly's self-esteem and her ability to trust that it was looking like she'd never give Ed a chance. 'Right, chaps,' Ed said, clapping his hands together. 'It's brass monkeys out there,

I'd best be off if I'm to make it to Essex without the old girl freezing up on me.'

Despite the success of cold fusion, Ed was still at a loss when it came to material possessions. He would not upgrade his ancient beat-up Ford Focus until it literally spluttered its last. The fact that his security team travelled in an infinitely better car than him was seemingly irrelevant. He bent down to give Arabella a hug. After she had squeezed him tightly, she pulled back to peer into his bloodshot eyes and lift his swollen eyelids.

'I think the acclimit ... acclimitoesing is working,' she told him, giving him a huge smile and kissing his red cheek.

He chuckled. 'Sure it is, love.'

'You're leaving?' Tilly's voice cut through the relaxed atmosphere, a pitch higher than normal.

'Yes, Tils,' Ed said softly.

'But ...'

Goodie turned to see that Tilly was frowning as she swallowed and took a step towards Ed. 'But I thought ...' She trailed off and glanced at the rest of the family, obviously concerned by how much she was giving away. 'I mean, is it safe? You driving this late in that heap? Can't you just ...' She took another step forward and reached out to touch his arm. 'Can't you just stay?'

Ed smiled, a new light of determination firing in his eyes before he pulled Tilly in for a hug. 'I've got to spend it with my family, love,' he said as he pulled away to study her disappointed face.

'Right, yes, of course. Jolly good. Bloody silly of me,' she bumbled on, pushing against his chest to move away.

'I'll come back,' he told her, his arms staying tight around her body.

'You will?' she breathed, stopping her struggles.

'I promise,' he said, and in front of everyone he gave her a brief kiss on the lips before moving away.

'Gross!' yelled Arabella, but Goodie noticed she was smiling and her cheeks were pink with pleasure.

Goodie watched the ten-year-old and sighed. Warm, happy, loved, secure; no worries other than school and homework and maybe keeping her room clean. This was how life should be; this was how Goodie would make life for *her* child; how she would keep life for the Chambers family. Nothing would touch them; she would make sure of it.

∼

'Have you ever met her?' Bill asked Martin as they walked up to the huge front door of the Chambers mansion. 'I mean when she was active.' Bill was ten years younger and had only been with the service for the last three, having been recruited straight after his finals at Cambridge where he'd come top in the year, his exam scores setting actual records and putting him on MI6's radar.

'I was on clean-up after her once,' Martin said, wincing and rubbing the back of his neck as he strode forward. 'Messy.' He shuddered and shoved both hands into his pockets.

'Yeah, I've read the reports.' One of Bill's strengths was research and one of his obsessions was Goodnight. He'd read everything he could lay his hands on about her; it was part of the reason he was here with Martin for this assignment.

'Jesus,' Martin whispered as he looked up at the imposing stone building, 'she's landed on her feet at least.'

'Goodnight has enough money of her own,' Bill mumbled as he started up the stone steps. 'There must be something else holding her here.'

'Or someone.'

Bill frowned. 'That just doesn't fit her profile. She doesn't do ... attachments.' By the time they had reached the top step the door had swung open. A slender, breathtakingly beautiful blonde woman, leaning heavily on a walking stick, was framed in the doorway.

'Hello, boys,' she said, her voice low and even, not betraying a shred of surprise.

'Uh ... hi,' Bill stammered, feeling weirdly intimidated, despite her obvious physical weakness.

Martin sighed and stepped forward, holding out his hand for her to shake. 'Mrs Chambers, we are so sorry for the intrusion. My name is –'

'I know who you are and where you are from,' she cut him off, her cold expression making him drop his hand back to his side.

'Darling, what are you ...?' A tall, well-built, dark-haired man came up behind Goodnight and wrapped an arm around her shoulder, pulling her into his side. 'Oh.' He frowned as he looked down at Bill and Martin. 'Er ... hi there.' Bill almost let out a nervous laugh as the man he recognized from his pictures in the press pulled Goodnight back and slightly behind him as if he was protecting her: totally bizarre.

'Mr Chambers,' Martin addressed him and extended his hand for a second time. This time it wasn't left hanging, but the force behind Nick Chambers' grip almost made Martin wish it had been. 'I'm Martin Lacey and this is my colleague William Shepton. So sorry to intrude on your evening but we were wondering if we could talk to your wife briefly.'

'Well, that would depend,' Nick said, pushing Goodnight even further behind him before planting his feet wide and crossing his arms over his chest, 'on who you are and what exactly you're doing on my doorstep at nine o'clock at night.'

'We're civil servants, Mr Chambers,' Bill put in smoothly.

Goodnight

'Oh, right then,' Nick said, 'thanks *so* much for clearing that up for me. Not at all vague.'

'There were some government contracts that your wife was involved in, and we're here to discuss them.'

'Is my wife still involved in any contracts?' Nick asked, both his eyebrows rising.

'Well ...' Martin shifted uncomfortably on the step, flicking a glance over to Bill who was staring at Goodnight with his mouth slightly open: no help there. 'Not that I know of.'

'Okay,' Nick lifted a hand to the door, 'so there seems to be precious little to talk about then.'

'Mr Chambers,' Martin said again, putting his hand out to block the door that was rapidly closing on his face. 'I really must –'

'Let them in, Nick.' The door opened fully again and all men turned to look at Goodnight. She had one hand wrapped around Nick's wrist and was looking up at him with a determined look on her face. 'If they wish to talk to me they will do it. Putting them off tonight won't make a difference.' Nick's jaw clenched for a moment as he searched his wife's face, and his grip tightened on the door. Just as Martin thought he would slam the door in their faces anyway, he saw Nick's grip relax and he stepped back, giving both Martin and Bill a curt nod to enter.

'Follow us,' Nick said, starting down the corridor. Instead of striding ahead, as you would expect, given the type of man he was, he shortened his stride, checking that his wife, who had a pronounced limp and was still leaning heavily on her stick, was keeping up. He pushed open another huge oak door leading them inside a vast living room. There was an old man sitting by the fireplace, his hand poised over a chessboard.

'Dad,' Nick said, 'these chaps need a quick chat with Anya. Do you mind ...?'

'I see,' the man said, rubbing his beard and eyeing Martin and Bill with curiousity. 'I'll leave you to it then.' He stood and walked past them, pausing at Goodnight to kiss her cheek and squeeze her hand. 'Let me know when it's safe to come back and finish the game, sweetheart,' he muttered, giving her a brief smile and narrowing his eyes at the two imposters before he slipped out of the room.

The message that both Nick Chambers and his father were both trying to send was obvious: she is ours, she is protected, she is family. Martin rubbed his hands down his face. It looked as though Bill's research for once had fallen short. If the last ten minutes was anything to go by, Goodnight had formed attachments left, right and centre: strong ones, and with powerful people.

Chapter 32

Finished

As the door closed behind the older Mr Chambers, Nick indicated for Martin and Bill to sit in two armchairs across the room. Goodnight and Nick sat on a small sofa opposite, with Nick's arm flung across the back of it behind Goodie's shoulders. Martin noticed Goodie's hands move to her stomach. He was a fairly hardened agent. Not much surprised him, but the shock of seeing Goodnight cradling a small but very distinct bump in her abdomen caused him to suck in a sharp breath. All eyes flashed to him and he cleared his throat to cover his reaction.

'Mr Chambers, would it be possible to have a brief word with your wife alone?' Nick stiffened and moved closer to Goodnight, scowling across at Martin.

'We have no secrets between us,' he said, his anger making his words sharp. 'Anything you have to say to Anya can be said to me.'

'There may not be secrets between the two of you, Mr Chambers,' Martin said carefully, 'but I can assure you there are things that I am not permitted to share with anyone other than those directly involved or those with appropriate security clearance.'

'If you muppets think you can come into my house in the middle of the night and demand to speak to my pregnant wife without me here, you're insane. I'll not have –'

'Nick-Nack, *lyubov moya*,' Goodnight said softly, laying her hand over his leg and smiling up at him. Neither Martin nor Bill had seen Goodnight smile in any of the few research photographs they had of her. They'd known she was beautiful, but until she'd smiled they hadn't realized quite how dazzling she could truly be. 'They will not hurt me and they must speak to me.' Nick gave a quick shake of his head and opened his mouth to speak but Goodnight reached up to put a finger over it to stop him. 'It will not take long; then they can leave and it will be over. All of it. Finished.' Nick stared at her for a long moment, then clenched his jaw.

'Okay,' he said, giving her hand at his mouth a squeeze and then standing between the sofa and the chairs. 'I won't be far though,' he told the men pointedly. 'Shout if you need me,' he said more softly to Goodnight, and then turned on his heel and stalked out of the room. Both men watched him leave. When they turned back to Goodnight she still seemed perfectly relaxed, but somehow her face had lost all the softness from before, her eyes were cold, expressionless.

'So, gentlemen,' she started, her Russian accent filtering a little more thickly through her words. 'You want to talk ... talk.'

Martin cleared his throat again. 'Right ... well ...' He lost concentration for a moment as she stared at him, her head cocked to the side. For some reason he felt a shiver of fear creep down his spine. 'The last contract you had with the agency was terminated eighteen months ago.'

Goodnight nodded. 'The protection of Mr Chambers. Although this was *not* government funded.'

'No ... I ...'

'In fact I have not performed paid work for the British government in many years. Quite frankly your rates are not high enough.'

Martin ran his hands through his hair. 'No, you haven't. But, as I understand it, you do have information which could be of a sensitive nature should it be allowed to –'

'I have never broken confidentiality and I am not about to start now. How would that benefit me?'

'Well, no. I'm sure it wouldn't benefit you *now*, but if in the future there came a time ...'

'Are you asking if I would use the information I have if I needed to? If so then I'm afraid I don't have an answer for you. All I can say is I am not so easy to silence, no? I am no longer in the shadows. I have an identity now – a high-profile one; it is this and not my anonymity that gives me power this time.' She leaned forward and dropped her voice to a whisper. 'You think if I disappeared he would not find me? You think nobody would ask questions?'

'Mrs Chambers, I'm not suggesting –'

'My point is,' she cut him off, her voice back to normal volume, 'that as far as Legoland is concerned they need to pray that *they* can keep *me* happy and reassured, not the other way around.'

The familiar use of the nickname for MI6 headquarters, combined with the implied threat, was enough to make Martin's face flush red with angry heat. 'Look,' he said, further annoyed when she didn't so much as flinch at his sharp tone, 'we need to know you're not active any more. Someone with your skills and contacts could still be a threat to –'

He was cut off by Goodnight's laughter. The angry colour drained out of his face and he sat back into the sofa as he watched her.

'A threat?' she eventually managed to get out when she'd calmed down. 'You *do* realize that without this stick I am virtually immobile? That even with it I cannot get up stairs on my own? I have to be carried up them like a baby. Do you know what it is like to have to ask the man you love to carry you up the stairs so you can get to bed? To have to limp down the aisle to marry him? To know that you won't be able to run with the children he gives you? To know that once you are heavy with his child you may be rendered nearly totally immobile? I am no threat.' There were tears in her eyes, partly from her laughter but, Martin guessed, not entirely.

'You've recovered from injuries before,' Bill put in. 'Eight years ago you had a gunshot wound to your abdomen and shoulder, six years ago you dislocated both shoulders; you broke your right leg ten years ago. I mean, even as a teenager you –'

'I have no desire to go through my sordid medical history with you.' Goodnight transferred her icy expression to Bill, who also shrank back into the sofa. 'Yes, I have recovered before, but the likelihood I will this time is very small. Have you read my hospital reports? My weekly physiotherapy reports?'

'Yes, yes, we met with Bruce. He said you told him we'd come and to answer all our questions. Chap's not averse to a bit of lycra is he?'

For the first time since they had been left alone, Goodnight's lips tipped up slightly. 'I'm glad you too experienced that particular delight.' Martin shuddered. Interviewing a bloke in full lycra, with his cock and balls basically on display, in a smelly gym whilst this guy, for reasons known only to himself, was doing lunges was not Martin's idea of fun. 'He told you, then,' Goodnight continued, her smile now dropping and sadness sweeping her features. 'He won't say it to my face. He believes in the "power of positive thinking", so he won't be

Goodnight

honest. But I know he doesn't think my leg will improve much more.'

Martin looked down at his hands and sighed. The Australian had actually been more pessimistic than even that. He'd said that Goodnight's improvement had plateaued for now, but that he wouldn't be surprised if she deteriorated further. 'So you see, I am not active. I will *never* be active again.'

'I'm sorry,' Martin muttered. Goodnight shrugged.

'My life is about something different now,' she said, again cradling the small bump in her abdomen. 'I have other priorities.'

'But I don't think that –'

'Right,' Martin said sharply, cutting Bill off and giving him a pointed look. 'We have taken up enough of your time, Mrs Chambers. Come on Bill.' Martin gestured to Goodie as he stood. 'Don't get up, we can find our own way out.'

'But Martin,' Bill hissed, 'we should –'

'Bill, it's time to leave,' Martin told him through clenched teeth. He didn't want to hammer any more questions at this woman whose physicality, which had been such an important part of her life, was now stripped away. She was broken. There was no threat here: not any more.

'Out with it,' Martin said into the uncomfortable silence as they trudged back to their car from the house after the heavy door had been slammed in their wake. 'Come on. You're pissed off. You may as well just tell me.'

'Why wouldn't you let me ask any more questions?' Bill said, his voice low but threaded with anger. 'I'm the one who did all the research. I *know* her.'

Martin threw up his hands. 'What more could we have asked? She's visibly pregnant, hobbling around at a snail's pace. Let's just let her get on with her life.'

Bill stopped by the car and looked back up at the house, narrowing his eyes. 'I don't know. Something feels off. Did you see her IQ tests? Her resilience tests? Off the fucking scale.'

'Let it go for Christ's sake,' Martin said. 'What could she possibly do now?'

~

GOODIE LISTENED TO THE SLOW BEATING OF HIS HEART under her ear and his breathing evening out, then lifted her head to prop it up on her hand and watch his face in the moonlight. She traced from his eyebrow down to his strong, stubble-covered jaw with her finger, and smiled. He was so beautiful and he was hers. She leaned forward and kissed his mouth lightly and he didn't move. He was out. Goodie was not surprised; he'd certainly expended a fair bit of energy before falling into a deep sleep. She smiled again and was tempted to snuggle back into his chest but managed to resist. Turning away from him, she slid off the bed naked, and stood beside it on both feet before padding silently to the bathroom: no limp, no stick.

Once in the vast en suite she shut the door and turned on the light. She looked at herself in the full-length mirror and smiled again. Cheeks flushed pink with desire, rounded stomach with his child, long blonde hair falling past her shoulders; she looked content, she looked happy. He'd given her that; he and his family, and Goodie knew how to protect family. After all, she'd been doing it since she was a child. With one last look in the mirror she turned to the laundry basket and pulled out underwear; not the lacy, flimsy kind she tended to wear for Nick, but the kind of industrial sports bra and cotton knickers that could stand up to anything. Next she extracted some tight black trousers, and a black polo-neck jumper, which she pulled down over her bump. Once dressed, she pulled on her hard-wearing leather boots and secured her long hair in a bun before covering it completely with a black beanie hat. She opened her make up bag and started to cover her face in black camo paint. Soon the clear blue and white of her eyes was the only thing breaking up the unrelenting darkness. She smiled and her teeth stood out stark white against the dark background. She moved her hands to her stomach again.

'Time to learn how Mummy protects her family, little one,' she whispered in Russian, before grabbing her black leather gloves and pulling them on. She opened the door silently and moved to the window, where she stood looking down at her watch. The minute it hit two a.m. she slid up the pane and then threw a leg over into the night.

She perched on the stone windowsill, took one last look back at Nick, then turned and dropped gracefully until she was holding on to the sill with only her fingers supporting her weight. Swinging her body like a pendulum, she managed to gain enough momentum to reach the drainpipe at the side of the building. She flew through the air, caught hold of it, and slid down it. Once on the ground she flexed her neck to the side and shook out her arms. Salem was sitting waiting for her on the grass. She tousled the fur on his head briefly, then silently, gracefully, and with no hint of an uneven gait, she ran, Salem running beside her.

Goodie herself may have come out of the shadows, her life may be out in the open, but the image she presented was what she wanted it to be: weak, defenceless, and, above all, not a threat. It had made leaving behind the life she'd lived easier; even those idiots from Legoland didn't question her for long. They saw a washed-up, broken woman; they felt pity. To some that would have been annoying, frustrating even – but not to Goodie. She had never cared about what people thought of her; to her, the only thing that mattered was having the power to protect what was important to you. That streak of fierce loyalty had always been one of the most prominent traits of her personality; and now, with the safety of her family in question, she was not going to fuck around.

The tears she had had in her eyes for the agents when she talked about limping down the aisle at her wedding, about being carried up the stairs, had been genuine. The pretence *did* make her sad, but it was necessary, and Goodie was patient. Really fucking patient. Keeping things from Nick was difficult, but he would not understand what she was doing and he would stop her. Also she sensed that, for a while at least, he *needed* to take care of her; he wanted to carry her up the stairs. Yes, he would be pleased when in a few years she slowly recovered her function, but for now he was happy with her depending on him to some extent, and she was happy to give him that.

How had she done it? Bruce the physio had not always been a physio. When Goodie was out in Iraq on a private contract she'd been deployed with his unit of the marines; and she saved his life. He owed her and she called in that debt as soon as she flew into the UK. They worked together in the gym and the pool Nick had built for her. They were both underground and there was a lock on the gym and pool door. Nick had once asked why he couldn't watch and help her train. She'd told him she didn't want him to see her like that: weak and struggling. When he pressed the issue she'd only had to let her face fall once and give a half sniff before he gave in. He never asked again.

Her other partner in crime was Arabella. People always underestimate children. Goodie did not. She went to the woods with Arabella and Salem everyday. Under the cover of the trees she carried on training, running, lifting logs and branches. Even lifting Arabella, much to her amusement. Goodie had told Bels that she needed to be strong to protect the family, that there was one more thing she needed to do and that nobody could know she was better. Arabella didn't breathe a word; she loved her family, she wanted them protected, and she trusted Goodie.

After two miles in the woods Goodie and Salem came out into a field, then continued with care so as not to be visible from the road. As the house they were aiming for came into view they crouched in the undergrowth and waited. It took twenty minutes but eventually a guard walked past. Goodie lifted a hand, palm down then lowered it, and Salem dropped to lie on the ground. Then she moved out into the open, padded over behind the guard. When she was close enough she uncapped the needle at the end of the syringe she had between her teeth and stabbed it into the side of the guard's thick neck. He grunted, clutched at his neck and whipped around, but she was too quick, staying out of his line of vision. After a moment he stumbled, and then with a long groan he fell to the floor.

Goodie watched him for a few seconds until she heard him give out a loud snore. She turned to Salem who had raised his head with his ears pricked forward. Lifting both hands palm down this time, she lowered them and Salem's head dropped back to his paws. Goodie nodded towards the man lying in the grass and Salem turned his head to watch him. She looked up at the large, imposing mansion and the scaffolding erected along the side wall, and she smiled.

∽

DMITRY FELT THE WEIGHT SETTLE ON HIS STOMACH AND smiled in his sleep. He loved the frisky ones. He blinked open his eyes and tried to focus on the dark figure looming over him, but the room was pitch black. As he swam up to full consciousness he frowned: he couldn't remember bringing a woman home with him last night, and anyway he wasn't in London. He hardly ever took women back to the country house. It was then that he felt something cover his mouth which sealed his lips together with implacable force. Panicking now, he grunted and reached up to pull the tape off, but felt the cold metal against his neck.

'You should have done as I asked, Alexandrov,' a woman's voice whispered into his ear, and he froze in terror. 'You notice I speak to you in English. This is because we, both of us, live *here* now. When you live somewhere you abide to their laws, their customs.' She paused for a moment, then continued in Russian. 'But you didn't do that, did you, Dmitry? You stuck to the old ways, and you hired someone from the old country to do your dirty work. I made the exception for him and I will make it for you too. I'm happy to revert back to how things were if that's how you want it: happy to do things in the old way. Do you know how I earned my name?' The Russian nodded carefully against the knife. She leaned forward over him until he could feel her breath on his cheek before she whispered in his ear: '*Spokoynoy nochi zhopa.*'*

* Spokoynoy nochi zhopa – Goodnight, asshole

Epilogue

Call me Goodie

'Look, I'm sorry. I know it's not exactly fair but Mum is *nuts* about Christmas,' Mikhail said as they pulled up in front of the massive house.

Emma smoothed down her dress, avoiding eye contact with him, and stared out of the window at the stone steps and the huge entryway. 'My family are also quite keen on Christmas, Mikey,' she muttered, pushing her red hair behind her ears and then letting her shoulders slump. She'd been with Mikhail Chambers for nine months now. They met on the wards over a patient and had had an immediate flaming row. She was a surgical trainee, he was medical; she thought her patient should go to ICU, he thought they should be referred to palliative care. Annoyingly it turned out he was right, and what made her even more furious was when he'd looked down his nose at her and muttered: 'Surgeons: bloody muppets,' as he left the ward. She had been sorely tempted to fling the over-full and loosely capped pot of urine in her hand right at his blonde, handsome, arrogant head.

The next day when he brought her a Cadbury's Creme Egg

to apologize, she *had* flung that back at him, lying about being lactose intolerant (which was annoying because she sodding loved a good creme egg). She started softening when he brought her a soymilk latte the next day (not something they dished out in the canteen, so she knew he would have had to walk the half a mile to the nearest Costa to get it). By the end of the week he'd caught her eating a full box of Malteasers in the mess, and told her she had to go out with him that night to apologize for lying or he would report her to the General Medical Council for probity issues.

Since then the relationship had moved at warp speed. When August came and it was time to leave the hospital accommodation, they had moved in together. Emma had been shocked that Mikey had managed to find a flat so central, with an actual view of Hyde Park, for such an amazingly cheap rate, but she worked so hard she didn't have the time or the wherewithal to question it. He'd met her parents, charmed them and the rest of her family to bits, then a month ago he'd asked her dad if he could marry her, and the next day he got down on one knee outside the patient bay where they'd had their first argument and asked her.

So you'd think everything was perfect, and it was. Only she hadn't met his family, and up until now he hadn't even offered to take her. She knew they were important to him; he talked loads on the phone to them, often speaking in quiet, affectionate Russian with his mum or his Auntie Tasha, teasing his dad, shouting 'What ho!' down the phone to his 'Mad Uncle Bertie', bantering with his two sisters and many cousins, making funny voices for his nephews and nieces, talking weird science stuff with his Uncle Ed or horses with his Auntie Tilly and his cousin Arabella. But he never offered Emma the phone, never even mentioned her to any of them.

She'd begun to feel like a dirty secret, and then out of the

Goodnight

blue last week he'd asked if she would come and spend Christmas with them. Time off was precious as a junior doctor. Emma had been working last Christmas and had been looking forward to spending it with her family this year, especially with all the recent trouble her mum and dad had been having. She didn't want to spend it with people she'd never met before, and now that she was outside this bloody great mansion she was feeling even more homesick. Why hadn't he said his family lived in a massive stately home? Thinking of how proud she'd been to take him along to see her parents' small terraced house made her feel a little ill now. She paled further when she remembered all the problems they'd had at home over the last few months. She'd been too embarrassed to tell Mikey about it, and now that she knew how loaded he and his family was she was glad she'd kept her mouth shut. There was no way she was taking him back there any time soon.

'I know, and I'm really sorry, but I wouldn't have asked if it wasn't really important. Next year your family could come here if they wanted. That's how my big sister does it; her bloke's family thought it was a bit weird at first but they're used to it now.'

'Wow, your mum must be *really* crazy about Christmas.'

'Ever since I can remember she's been the most obsessively festive person I know, bar maybe Auntie Tasha.' He shrugged. 'Dad took us aside one year, it was about the time we'd all figured out Father Christmas wasn't real and had started wanting to play on our iPads and be grumpy teenage twats rather than join in properly with the family. He'd told us that Mum wasn't as lucky as us, and at our age there was nobody around for her who gave a shit if she had a good Christmas or even if she was warm enough or had enough food. It's the most angry I've ever seen Dad get.' He grinned. 'I still pretend I believe in Father Christmas now.'

Emma let out a nervous giggle. 'I'm not sharing a room with you if your crazy mum is coming in in the middle of the night with your stocking, you weirdo.'

Mikey laughed with her. 'Maybe she'll make an exception this year since you're new; but I warn you, she still does it for my sister and her husband, and they've been married for five years.' As their laughter faded he turned towards her and took her hand, pulling it into his lap.

'Ems.' He looked down at their linked hands and shifted uncomfortably in his seat for a moment. 'Have you heard of Nick and Anya Chambers, and Ed Southern?'

'Of course I have I –' Emma froze before her wide eyes flashed to his. She'd never linked Mikey to *that* Chambers. Never would have even considered he could be related to the men behind the worldwide energy revolution. 'Oh my God.'

'I'm sorry I didn't tell you,' he said quickly, squeezing her hand more tightly. 'It's just security is so tight, secrecy is drummed into us. Dad got shot once, see, years ago, and then this Russian bloke who lives a few miles away was killed in the night in his own bloody bed. This guy was into oil pipelines and they reckoned it was all somehow linked, so it scared everyone enough that Mum and Dad went security crazy when we were little. Things are better now but it still feels weird talking about what they do.' He rubbed the back of his neck, frowning up at the house. 'And look, I know this is going to sound bad but sometimes when people know you have money it can change what they think of you.' Emma tried to pull her hand away and he gripped it more firmly. 'Hey,' he said, leaning across the gearstick to give her a brief kiss. 'I know that doesn't matter to you, okay? I'm sorry I wasn't more honest.'

Emma looked up at the steps again. 'You didn't get that flat for the same rent we were paying in hospital accommodation, did you?' She looked back at him and he grinned sheepishly.

Goodnight

'Okay – no. It's Uncle Ed's old place. He bought a house down here so Auntie Tilly could be with the horses full time. I paid all your rent back into your account pretty much as soon as you paid it in so –'

'You did *what?*'

He grinned. 'It's not my fault you and online banking have a weird existential relationship.'

Emma huffed and punched his arm. 'I've got better things to do than check my balance every five minutes, Mr Moneybags.' Mikey laughed, then they sat in silence, Emma still looking up at the door and Mikey keeping a firm grip on her hand. She jumped in her seat when she saw the door open and a large dog come hurtling down the steps followed by two smaller ones. The biggest dog jumped up on Emma's side of the car, barked in through the window, and then just stared at them, its tongue hanging out and its tail going bananas. Mikey laughed and turned from Emma to fling open his door. The dog barked again and then charged around the car to jump up on Mikey and start licking his face with a vengeance.

'Alright, Alright, Myska,' Mikey said through his laughter, rubbing the dog's neck. 'You coming?' he asked Emma as he pushed the dog down and planted his feet outside the car. Emma took a deep breath and opened her door.

As they walked up the stone steps Mikey took her hand and gave it a squeeze; Myska bumped her other hand with her nose and started licking it, causing her to let out a nervous giggle. She looked up to the doorway and saw a blonde, middle-aged, stunning woman standing there, her eyes fixed on their joined hands. Next to her was a tall, dark-haired, middle-aged man with his arm wrapped around the blonde's shoulders. Of course Emma recognized them, there wasn't a human being on the planet who wouldn't. As they arrived at the top step Anya Chambers reached out and caught hold of Mikey's free wrist, wrapping her hand around it. She laid her other hand over his heart and then closed her eyes for a moment and smiled. When she opened them she lurched forward and wrapped her arms around him.

'Mum,' he muttered into her hair, dropping Emma's hand to hug his mother back. 'Mum, this is Emma,' he went on softly as she pulled back and looked over to where Emma was standing. Myshka barked again, nudging Emma's hand so that she was stroking his head, but Mikhail's mum made a hand gesture and the dog trotted to her side, then dropped to the floor.

As the dark-haired man started hugging Mikey and slapping him on the back, Emma opened her mouth to say something coherent, but closed it again. The beautiful blonde was studying her silently, her head cocked to the side. When their eyes met, however, the blonde stepped forward, smiled such a beautiful smile it almost took Emma's breath away, and then pulled Emma in for a hug herself.

'I am so pleased to meet you finally, Emma,' the blonde said, pulling back slightly and framing Emma's face with her hands. 'And I'm sorry about Myshka; he has been thoroughly spoilt by my offspring I'm afraid. Dog training is not one of their strong suits.'

'Thanks, Mrs Chambers, I'm happy to be here,' Emma said. 'And ... and I love dogs.'

'Please call me Anya.'

'Uh ... okay.' Emma smiled to mask her confusion. She had been sure Mikey had not told his family about her yet. What was this 'finally' business about?

'Emma,' Mikey's dad's deep voice broke through her thoughts. 'I'm Nick. Thank you for giving up your Christmas with your family; it means so much to us.' He pulled her into another brief hug, muttering, 'My wife suffers from a little Christmas psychosis I'm afraid. You'll get used to it.'

Goodnight

'What ho, chaps!' boomed a loud, posh voice from down the hall. 'You lot going to stand out there forever or do we all get to meet the new lady?' Nick rolled his eyes as he was shuffled to the side to accommodate a red-faced but attractive middle-aged man, who by his greeting could only be Uncle Bertie.

Uncle Bertie took Emma's hand and said, 'May I say that's a frightfully nice blouse you're wearing.' Emma looked down at her jumper, then back up at Uncle Bertie's earnest expression, before she burst out laughing along with everyone else.

∽

'UH ... HI.' EMMA WAS STANDING ON THE FRONT STEP OF her family home looking down in shock at an immaculate Anya. Anya's head was turned to the side, her narrow-eyed gaze on next-door's terrace. Emma's heart sank. Some of the windows next door were boarded up, there was a broken down car in the driveway and the front lawn was strewn with rubbish, including, if you looked hard enough, condoms and used needles. The contrast with Emma's parents' small front garden was stark; the chaos on the other side of the fence made her dad's manicured lawn and painstakingly weeded tulips look faintly ridiculous.

'Hello, Emma,' Anya said, dragging her eyes from next door to smile up at Emma. Anya was wearing killer high-heeled leather boots over skinny jeans and Emma was in flats, but at five foot eleven Emma was still a couple of inches taller. 'I'm sorry to arrive unannounced but I was in London with Nick and I wanted to meet your family.'

'Oh, right.' Emma managed to recover from her shock and paste a fake smile on her face. 'Mikey's not here though ... I haven't ... um ...' Emma hadn't told Mikhail she was coming home today. She'd been making excuses for weeks to stop him coming to see her family again.

It wasn't just that the crappy area they lived in embarrassed her, because before the squatters next door had moved in she'd been happy for him to visit. It was that she knew if he found out what was happening he would want to fix it somehow, and she just couldn't bear his pity. Her parents' pride would have been hurt and she couldn't bear that either. 'Right, please, come in. Mum and Dad are just in the kitchen. They'll be really um ... they'll be really pleased to meet you.' Emma's hands fluttered nervously before she got it together and moved back from the door to let Anya through.

'Guys, this is Anya Chambers, Mikey's mum,' Emma said as she walked into the cramped kitchen. Emma's dad froze with his cup of tea halfway to his lips; her mum slowly retracted her hand from the chicken's arse she was stuffing, and her brother choked on his 7-Up.

'Oh ... goodness me,' her mum muttered as she withdrew her hands from the chicken. 'Well, it's lovely to meet you, Mrs _'

'Call me Anya, please.' Anya smiled and the full force of her beauty and glamour was like a physical presence in the kitchen.

'Crikey,' muttered Aaron, his mouth falling open in shock.

'I'm Judy,' Emma's mum said, moving to the sink to wash off her hands, then skirting the table to shake Anya's. During all this, Emma's brother and dad remained open-mouthed, her dad's tea still suspended in midair.

'Malcolm, Aaron,' her mum said through gritted teeth, her foot kicking back to smack her husband in the shin. 'Say hello to Mikey's mum.'

'Hello,' Malcolm managed to say, his cup staying where it

Goodnight

was. Aaron for his part just stared. Emma's mum rolled her eyes.

'You have to forgive my son, he's ... well ... he's a teenager. My husband I have no excuses for.'

Anya laughed and placed a hand on Emma's mum's arm reassuringly.

'Please, I'm the one who should apologize. Barging in here on a Sunday. You must think me incredibly pushy. I know I also need to say sorry for taking your daughter away from you on Christmas day. I'm afraid I can be selfish when it comes to the holidays. But I hope next year you might consider all coming to stay with us.'

'Sweet.' Emma rolled her eyes at Aaron's awed whisper. Since she'd told him who Mikhail's parents were he'd been bugging her constantly to meet them.

It took about an hour for her family to relax in Anya's company. Emma had liked her when she'd stayed with the Chambers family over Christmas. She had a dry sense of humour, and when you spoke to her she listened so intently it seemed as if she was hanging on every word, absorbing every gesture. It was weird but also strangely endearing, and it certainly helped her family to warm to her quickly. But just as Emma's mum was about to start serving lunch, it started again. The walls between the two houses weren't exactly thin, but with the volume those pricks next door put their heavy metal noise up to, you'd think the band was performing live in their kitchen. After ten minutes of strained attempts at conversation over the noise, Emma's dad swore under his breath and banged on the connecting wall. A few minutes after that, a loud crash sounded from the living room.

'Jesus Christ,' Emma's dad muttered, pushing up from his chair and stalking out of the kitchen, the others following at a slower pace. A brick was lying in the middle of the carpet surrounded by glass.

'Oh,' Emma's mum said in a broken little whisper, her hand going to her mouth and her tears pooling in her eyes as they all followed her dad into the room. 'When are they going to stop? And with company here and ...'

'It's not actually that bad an area, Anya,' Emma's dad tried to explain, turning towards Anya after having taken his wife into his arms. 'These bloody hooligans moved in a few months ago and since then ...' He trailed off, his eyes now suspiciously wet. Seeing her strong father near tears actually caused Emma physical pain.

'The police just seem to give out ASBOs. They can't put a stop to it,' Emma added, putting her arm around her brother who for once allowed a show of affection. 'Squatters' rights are difficult to get around.'

'Stupid ASBOs,' Aaron spat. 'Those wankers wear that shit like a badge of honour.'

Anya was staring at the brick with her head cocked to the side. After a moment she turned to the family and gave them all a cool smile.

'If you'll excuse me,' she said quietly, her voice somehow colder and her face expressionless. 'I do believe I left something in the car. I won't be a moment.'

They all watched, speechless, as she swept out of the house. Emma turned to her mum and shrugged. 'Guess she got spooked.' Judy's mouth tightened but she held in anything she might have said about Emma's future mother-in law.

'Stuck-up bitch,' Aaron muttered, not being quite as diplomatic.

'Right, come on, love,' her dad said, steering her and her mum away from the mess. 'I'll call the police and the window blokes, and we'll start lunch.

Goodnight

Just after they entered the kitchen, the music shut off and they heard muffled raised voices through the wall instead. Relieved to have some brief respite from the heavy metal, they started eating, but after a minute or two there was a loud crash against the interconnecting wall.

'What the bloody hell?' Emma's dad muttered as they all lowered their utensils and turned towards the noise. Next came the screaming: piercing, fear-filled and blood-curdling. Then silence.

'Malcolm, I think you'd better make those phone calls now,' Judy said in high-pitched voice, and Malcolm nodded, leaving the remains of his lunch to speak to the police. Five minutes later there was a knock on the door and they all froze.

'Probably the police,' Emma muttered.

'Stay here,' Malcolm said, a rare tone of authority in his voice as he addressed his family. He stalked to the door, but when he returned he didn't have the beleaguered policemen they so often had to call to the house with him, it was Anya.

'Here it is,' she said, holding up a bottle of red wine with a huge smile on her face. Her cheeks were flushed and her eyes sparkling. 'Sorry, Judy; if I'd known we were having chicken I would have brought white.'

'Uh ...' Judy glanced at the adjoining wall, then back at Anya. 'That's okay. Look, I hope you don't –'

'I haven't had this much fun in years,' Anya said, practically skipping across the kitchen to take her place at the table. Something on Anya's sleeve caught Emma's eye as Anya lifted her hand to her wineglass. Her pristine white shirt had a smear of red on the cuff. Anya followed the direction of her gaze, then quickly jerked her sand-coloured jumper down to cover the offending stain.

'Damn lipstick gets everywhere,' she said, and when she caught Emma's eye with hers she gave her a wink.

The next knock on the door was the police. They were far more upbeat than Emma had ever seen them.

'Don't know what's gone on over there,' one of the officers said, shaking his head. 'Must have had some sort of barney. They've all been beaten up good and proper; bloody noses, black eyes, one of them can barely stand.' He shrugged. 'Anyway, the good thing is they're all moving on.'

'They're leaving?' Judy breathed. After months of aggravation, fear, and attempts to get them evicted she didn't seem to be able to process the fact that they would just up and leave of their own accord.

'Shocked us too,' the officer said. 'Never come across more stubborn squatters, but you should see them scrambling around to pack up their stuff. They can't get out of there quick enough.'

Anya stayed out of sight in the kitchen during the police visit, claiming that she wouldn't want to get in the way of 'family business', but she emerged just as they were driving away. After she'd said goodbye and managed to hug all the members of Emma's family, even an embarrassed Aaron, Emma showed her to the door.

Anya pulled Emma in for a hug, then moved to the doorstep. Once there, something caught Anya's eye and she turned her head to the side. Emma frowned and leaned out to see what Mikey's mum was looking at. To her surprise the four big, tattooed men and two scantily clad women who had made her parents' lives hell for the last six months were streaming out of the house. They were never exactly dressed for business meetings, but they definitely looked more dishevelled than their normal heroin chic. There were rips in their clothes, which were stained with not only dirt but also obvious splatters of blood. One man was holding a wad of blood-soaked toilet roll up to his nose, another was squinting to try and see through the one eye that wasn't swollen completely shut, and two were limping badly. They were all dragging bin liners full of their stuff. To Emma's confusion, when two of the men caught sight of Anya they froze in their tracks and their bodies stiffened with what appeared to be fear. Anya turned towards them more fully and raised her hand to give them a small finger wave. The movement caused them to flinch in terror before they turned and jogged away from the house.

'Um ... what ...?'

Anya turned back to Emma and smiled, reaching to wrap her hand around Emma's wrist and then place her other hand over Emma's heart. 'I'm glad you're joining my family, Emma. My son loves you very much. You make him happy. Thank you.'

'Uh ... okay, Anya, I –'

Anya withdrew her hands and stepped back. 'Call me Goodie,' she threw over her shoulder with a grin and another wink.

The End

Acknowledgments

A huge thank you to all the readers; I am honoured that you take time out of your lives for my books – it is quite honestly beyond my wildest dreams that people would read my stories and enjoy them. To all the reviewers and bloggers that have helped to spread the word about my books – please know that you have changed my life; I am eternally grateful.

Martin, yet again you've saved my bacon with your editing skills; I resist the urge to send you everything I ever type in my normal life for your perusal – I realize that would be weird. The cover was designed by the fantastic Steve Molloy, who is a genius and a saint for putting up with me.

A special thank you Jane for your eagle eye and vital encouragement from across the Atlantic. Thanks as well to Ruth, Susie, Jess, Curly and Alexa for your fabulous beta reading skills.

Last but not least thank you to my very own romantic hero / husband for his endless support and kid wrangling abilities.

About the Author

Susie Tate is a contemporary romance author and doctor living in beautiful Dorset with her lovely husband, equally lovely (most of the time) three boys and properly lovely dog.

Please use any of the links below to connect with Susie. She really appreciates any feedback on her writing and would love to hear from anyone who has taken the time to read her books.

Official website:
http://www.susietate.com/

Join Facebook reader group:
Susie's Book Badgers

Find Susie on TikTok:
Susie Tate Author

Facebook Page:
https://www.facebook.com/susietateauthor

Printed in Great Britain
by Amazon